THE
ORACLE
OF
STONE STREET

by

THOMAS QUEALY

iUniverse, Inc.
New York   Bloomington

The ORACLE of Stone Street

iUniverse books may be ordered through booksellers or by contacting:

iUniverse
1663 Liberty Drive
Bloomington, IN 47403
www.iuniverse.com
1-800-Authors (1-800-288-4677)

ISBN: 978-1-4401-2239-2 (sc)
ISBN: 978-1-4401-2240-8 (ebook)

Printed in the United States of America

iUniverse rev. date: 4/2/2009

The ORACLE looked out the window at the cobblestone street below and noticed that a large crowd of young Wall Street types was beginning to occupy the rows of outdoor tables. Soon they would be hitting on each other and exchanging phone numbers and e-mail addresses in between sneaking glances at their BlackBerrys. This section of the Stone Street Historical District of Lower Manhattan was lined on both sides with bars, cafes and restaurants and it was also closed off to vehicular traffic. Servers scurried about carrying buckets of beer, burgers with fries, and deep-fried Buffalo wings in hot sauce with chunky blue cheese dressing, his all-time favorite finger-lickin'-good snack.

He glanced at the grandfather's clock in the living room and saw that it was 6:00 P.M. The stock and commodities markets in the United States had closed for the day. Trading in Asia wouldn't commence for another two hours. It was time for him to go to work and make some money.

The ORACLE squeezed under the slightly opened window and tiptoed across the narrow ledge that led to the building's fire escape. After descending three floors he leapt to the top of a lamppost near the open front door of the Ulysses Bar and then shimmied down a rope that was holding aloft a banner advertising Budweiser Beer, another favorite of his. Once on the ground he quickly darted into the bar to check out the clientele. Although it was a lovely evening to dine alfresco, he knew that Wall Street's heavy hitters always did their eating and drinking in the air-conditioned indoors.

He had 600 facial expressions in his repertoire and he was trying to decide which one to wear tonight. Much would depend on the mix of the group he ended up freeloading on. Women seemed to prefer the klutzy, honest look whereas guys wanted him to be pushy and devious. He was a regular at the bar and people smiled at him as he strutted by. Even the people he didn't recognize seemed to know who he was; probably because of that article about him that had appeared in *The Wall Street Journal* last year. It was amazing what a little publicity could do for your reputation.

To an outsider, the crowd dispersed around the oval bar would look like the typical after-work crowd to be found at any other upscale white-collar watering hole in Manhattan. The ORACLE knew, however, that different groups staked out different areas of the bar as their own turf.

The front of Ulysses, where about fifty photographs of James Joyce, the author of the famous Irish novel of the same name, adorned the wall, was tacitly the preserve of investment bankers, the self-proclaimed buccaneers of Wall Street. This group of well-groomed, ivy-league educated men and women wore expensive business suits from *Armani* and *Paul Stuart* and usually drank chocolate martinis and cosmos. They lived on the Upper Eastside, especially on Park Avenue, and had their food delivered by *Fresh Direct*. When he wanted to learn the inside scoop on mergers & acquisitions or hostile takeovers the ORACLE hung around with this crowd.

The left side of the middle of the bar was the domain of the money managers and stock analysts who worked for mutual funds and the investment divisions of money center banks. These people wore suits from *Brooks Brothers* and *J.Press* and tended to be nerdish and have a more sophisticated worldview than the higher paid investment bankers. They generally drank scotch on the rocks and banana daiquiris and excelled at doing *The New York Times* crossword puzzle in ink. Most lived on the Upper Westside and did their grocery shopping at *Zabar's*. When he wanted to learn the latest 'hot stock' picks the ORACLE permitted this group buy him beers.

The right side of the middle of the bar was where the bond people downed their gimlets, whisky sours and gin fizzes with great frequency. They talked incessantly about slicing and dicing collateralized debt obligations, junk bonds, and structured financing. This contingent lived in the New Jersey suburbs or in Westchester and spent their weekends at Little League baseball games or sitting on pricey tractors while mowing the large lawns of their expensive colonial homes. The ORACLE understood a great many things in this world but he didn't understand bonds so he never associated with these people unless, of course, there was no one else around to buy him beers.

The rear of the bar, where a solitary portrait of another famous Ulysses, General Ulysses S. Grant, hung in a recessed corner, was noisier than the other bar areas and it was here that the traders, the gunslingers of Wall Street, made their home away from home. They traded metals, grains, foreign exchange, derivatives, oil, lumber, wool, rubber and a host of other things. These people liked to play games of one-upmanship and were a rough-and-ready lot; they never wore suits or spoke softly. Most of them never went to college and they lived in Staten Island or Brooklyn in new, gigantic houses located in the same neighborhoods they grew up in, near their parents' older, smaller homes. They liked to drink boilermakers and do Jager bombs while kibitzing with the bartenders and servers. The other bar patrons gave this rambunctious group a wide berth. Tonight the ORACLE was worried that there was a bubble in the oil market. He needed to know if he should sell his oil positions at a price of $60 because the market might tank or whether he should buy more because oil was headed to $150 a barrel.

The ORACLE jumped up onto the bar as Kellin, a slender Eurasian bartender and notorious heart-breaker, who was also a full-time veterinary school student during the day, filled a line of shot glasses for the next toast. Traders loved to make toasts.

"Lookie-here," said a whisky-tanned man with a distended belly that hung precariously over his belt, "it's the black and white fur ball trying to score a free brewski."

A wizened older gold trader who looked like a truck driver tickled the cat under the chin. "Kellin, honey, give my little buddy here a Bud Light and then bring us an order of wings."

"Sure, I'll tell the kitchen to put on extra blue cheese dressing for our little friend."

The ORACLE disliked being called a fur ball but he purred a thank-you because he was hungry and thirsty.

A bleached blonde with surgically enhanced breasts picked him up and cradled him like she would a baby. "You're so loveable; I wish my boyfriend was as handsome as you. Are you a good mouser, pussycat?"

The ORACLE meowed that he was even though mice actually scared him.

"I'm tempted to steal you from this bar and take you home with me, you cutie-pie."

"The cat don't belong to the bar," the older man said, "he lives upstairs in this building in the top floor apartment. He only comes down here in the evening when he wants to tie one on."

"What's his name?"

"As far as I know, he hasn't got a name."

The ORACLE stared up at her and blinked three times.

A name suddenly popped into her mind. "I'm going to call him the ORACLE, that's what I'm going to do."

"The ORACLE?   What's an oracle for God's sake?"

"Someone who is very wise and who knows all the answers to life's deep mysteries."

"Is that right?"

"Yes, in ancient Greece the priests believed that the Gods spoke to them through oracles. The high priestess was a woman, her name was Pythia; she was the famous Oracle of Delphi who communicated with Apollo."

"Never heard of her."

"I'm not surprised, you never read a book in your life."

"You got me worried, Estelle, where did you learn all that crap?"

She seemed perplexed. "How the hell *did* I know that? I can't think why but it just came to me. I mean, I'm a parochial school girl from Rego Park. I know as much about ancient Greece as I know about Mars; which is zilch."

"Your mind is screwing with you, hon."

"It must be."

"Maybe you ought to see a doctor."

"Maybe I should."

"Either that, Estelle, or you could use another Jack & Coke."

The blonde put the cat back down on the bar when Kellin began to empty a bottle of Bud Light into a bowl for him. "This must be the only cat in the world that drinks beer. When I told my professor in animal anatomy class about him he didn't believe me. He thought I was making the whole thing up."

"Ah, those professors don't know shit," the older man said, "that's why I quit college in my first semester. They're all blowhards who like to hear themselves pontificate on things they know diddly-squat about."

"Yeah, they're a bunch of bonehead bozos," Estelle agreed, "they'd end up digging ditches if they had to do honest work for a living."

The ORACLE dipped his nose into the bowl and began to lick the amber liquid.

"I read somewhere about a dog in Russia who drank vodka tonics," Estelle said, "he was a Siberian Husky and he loved his *Grey Goose*."

"Yeah, I think I remember seeing that story too."

The plate of wings arrived; Kellin took one aside and placed it on a napkin next to the cat. The others each helped themselves.

The ORACLE bit into the wing, neatly chewing a piece of chicken, and then washed it down with the cold beer.

The blonde looked at the older man. "This cat's got better eating etiquette than you do."

"Eating etiquette, what's that mean?"

"It means you got red sauce all over your fat face. You may know how to make tons of money, my friend, but you still eat like a slob from Hoboken."

"Stop busting my balls, Estelle, you're confusing me again with your unemployed, worthless boyfriend."

The ORACLE finished the beer and shambled farther down the bar while the bartender went to fetch him a re-fill. He paused before two men and then sat down between their half-empty pints of black Guinness.

"This cat's got a wooden leg," the dome-headed oil trader with a craggy face said, "I saw him scoff down four bottles of beer in a little more than an hour one night."

His drinking companion, a tall man with bloodshot eyes and a shaggy beard, scratched his chin like he had fleas. "The little bugger can't weigh more than fifteen pounds, Harry, was he able to walk a straight line after drinking all that alcohol?"

The ORACLE purred even though he didn't like being called a bugger.

"Oh, yeah, he was as sober as a Supreme Court judge."

"I wonder if it's against the law to serve alcohol to cats. Look at him, Pete, he can't be more than five or six years old."

"Yeah, but they say that cats age seven years for every human year so that makes him almost middle-aged by now."

"You got a point." Pete patted the cat on his head.

The ORACLE stared up into his eyes and blinked three times.

"You know, Harry, I've been meaning to ask you about the oil market. You're the go-to-guy on oil, should I go long in the futures market or have I already missed the boat because the price is going to drop like a stone?"

Harry finished off his pint and then snorted as he tapped the bar with the bottom of his empty pint glass to signal Kellin for a fresh one. "Since when are you interested in oil? Every time I raised the subject in the past you told me you were afraid of crude's volatility."

"I ... I dunno ... I just suddenly thought that I need to consider oil for my portfolio. I got no energy exposure now."

Kellin brought another Guinness and a fresh bowl of Bud Light for the cat.

"Do you want the big macroeconomic picture answer with all the fancy bells and whistles about deflation, the debasing of the dollar, the precipitous decline in home prices, the growing budget deficits, and the likelihood of terrorist attacks on oil pipelines in Nigeria? Or do you want the short, no-bullshit, answer?"

"Gimme the short answer, Harry, I got a damn train to catch."

Harry took a deep swig of the stout and smacked his lips. "In my humble opinion, as the most astute oil trader on Wall Street, if I do say so myself, I think that oil prices will drop sharply in the short term because of the global recession, however, by this time next year you'll be paying $10 a gallon for gasoline to fill up that freaking Hummer of yours."

Pete paled noticeably despite having already consumed three boilermakers and two pints. "The country is gonna go down the tubes if that happens, we can't afford ten bucks for gas."

"Get used to it, my friend, life as you know it is going to be history."

"So, Harry, I should short oil now and then go long the middle of next year; is that what you're telling me?"

"Yeah, dump oil tomorrow and buy as much as you can beg, borrow or steal next year. And while you're at it, sell those gas-guzzlers you got parked in your four-car garage, and sell them now. Soon you won't be able to give them away. That goes for that monstrosity of a house you live in too; put it on the market and downsize because real estate is going deeper into the crapper."

The ORACLE finished his beer and then went over and nudged Harry's arm as a thank-you for his investing advice.

"The kitty really likes you," Pete said.

"Ah, the little cutester probably wants another beer. Kellin, honey, bring the three musketeers here another round."

It was after 10 P.M. when Stanley Kane, 44, an ascetic looking tall man with sallow eyes, a shaved head, long sideburns and dressed like an outlaw motorcycle biker from the 1960's -- black T-shirt, black jeans, black garrison belt, black boots, black bandana -- made his way down Stone Street to the front door of his building. Underneath that gruff, irritable exterior, however, beat the heart of a true social conservative. He flared his teeth in disapproval at the large numbers of people still eating and drinking outdoors there at such a late hour during the workweek. As a vegan teetotaler, he hated living above one of the largest bar-restaurants on the street. The smell of stale beer and fried food permeated his apartment seven days a week. And the noise was horrendous even when he wore earplugs, sometimes lasting until last call at 4:00 A.M. in the morning.

Stanley was already in a bad mood even before seeing the crowd in front of his building. He had stopped at Starbuck's on the way home and fumed as he had been forced to wait while the five people ahead of him in line paid for their lattes with credit cards. He hated people who did that; they were symptomatic of everything that was wrong with this country. Americans lived on credit, spending way more than they made, saving nothing for a rainy day.

Thank God he wasn't like them, he paid cash for everything. And if he didn't have the cash, he didn't buy, it was as simple as that. Why couldn't more people be sensible like him? He had no answer to that question. All he knew was that some day the chickens would come home to roost in this country. America was in for a rude awakening.

The black and white cat was waiting for him patiently by the entrance.

"So you went out again, I see, after I specifically asked you not to this morning."

The ORACLE yawned and didn't acknowledge him, gazing wistfully instead at a shapely girl who was paying her check at a nearby table.

"Have you been carousing in that dreadful bar again?"

The cat meowed his innocence.

Stanley bent down and smelled the cat's breath. "You've been drinking beer tonight, you smell like a brewery. I'm outraged!"

The ORACLE burped.

"I should storm into that bar and read them the riot act for serving alcohol to animals. Who do they think they are? It's a disgrace!"

The ORACLE selected a disinterested look for his face because he knew that Stanley would do no such thing. The man talked a good game but, at heart, he was a muckraker without a burning fire in his belly; an activist without an action plan; an idealist out of touch with how the real world worked.

"And who pays for your beers, I'd like to know? *You* certainly don't have any money of your own."

The ORACLE remembered his bank balance to the penny; exclusive of his real estate holdings, he had $2,335,062.51 in his brokerage account at Goldman Sachs in their branch office in Singapore. He was also aware that Stanley hadn't balanced his own checkbook in two years.

"I suppose people buy you beers because they think you're some kind of a hot-shot celebrity."

The caw meowed that it was true; indeed he was a celebrity.

"Well, let me tell you something, buster, I don't care that *The Wall Street Journal* named you the mascot of the Financial District. As far as I'm concerned you're just another boozer like all the rest of those egomaniacs who patronize Ulysses and brag about how much money they make."

The cat yawned again; he had heard all this before.

"And I'll tell you something else too; those fat cats should be put up against a wall and shot for destroying the U.S. economy and making it almost impossible for decent, hard-working, creative people like myself to scratch out a living today. "

The ORACLE was a fat cat himself, at least in the figurative sense, so he pawed at the vestibule door to show that he wanted to go up to the apartment and not listen to any more of this nonsense. As one of the few non-gay male choreographers in New York, Stanley was ignorant of many things outside his area of expertise, and that was especially true of financial matters.

"Ordinary people can't afford to buy apartments in the Financial District anymore because the bankers and traders have driven up the prices sky high. They're trying to make the area into another fancy neighborhood like SOHO or Tribeca. The realtors have even given the area a new name; they call it FiDi. Well, I call it disgraceful, a ploy to drive real estate prices even higher."

The cat meowed impatiently and scratched at the door.

Stanley used his key to open the door and the ORACLE raced up the stairs to the third floor landing so he wouldn't be subjected to any more harangues.

"You're a bad example to felines everywhere," Stanley's staccato voice echoed loudly up the stairwell, "and I'm going to call that reporter and tell him so. I'll get you de-mascoted, Mister Celebrity, then we'll see how popular you are with that Wall Street crowd you hang around with."

The ORACLE sighed and took consolation in the fact that Stanley would be sound asleep within the hour; that left him plenty of time to access the Asian markets.

===

Sure enough, an hour later the ORACLE pushed Stanley's bedroom door fully closed with the butt of his head.

"Is our master finally in Dreamland?" the parrot asked from inside his large cage that was suspended from a hook in a corner of the loft apartment.

The cat nodded and jumped up on the chair facing the PC. His right paw hit the ON button and the computer's screen brightened. He entered the URL for the investment bank and then navigated on its site to Asia.

The parrot hopped out of the cage onto a wooden stand. He was a large multi-colored Macaw with a curved beak, a white face and a white upper chest, a deep red feathered body with powerful green wings, strong legs, and clawed zygodactyl feet, meaning that there were four toes on each foot, two pointing forward and two pointing backwards. The bird's brain-to-body size ratio was comparable to higher primates and hence he was an accomplished linguist, able to imitate a variety of human voices that he heard when people visited the apartment or from watching TV shows while Stanley was at work.

His imitations of Regis Philbin and Bob Barker were absolutely perfect, so much so that you would swear they were there in the apartment with you. The bird also liked to watch *Turner Classic Movies* and he could mimic older movie stars like Cary Grant, Gary Cooper, and Clark Gable. All told, his vocabulary exceeded ten thousand words, including some choice curse words he had learned while entertaining in a brothel in France that serviced soldiers of the French Foreign Legion. At times he answered the phone when it rang and pretended to be Stanley when his spikey-haired friend, Fiona, called him. She never caught on to the deception that she was speaking to a parrot.

The bird's diet consisted of eating fruit, flowers, nuts, seeds and flies. Unlike the cat, he didn't drink beer. But he did like to smoke cigarettes that the ORACLE pilfered for him from bar patrons who left their opened packs by their glasses when they went outside to smoke on Stone Street. Stanley always smelled the tobacco aroma in the living room when he got out of bed in the morning, however, he blamed it on the bar below and would often throw open the windows and angrily shout threats down at its owners before taking his shower. Of course, the bar didn't open until later at 11:00 A.M. so there wasn't anybody around to hear his idle threats.

The ORACLE employed a complex series of passwords and firewalls to protect his brokerage account data. Stanley was basically computer illiterate and only utilized the PC for e-mails and a little web surfing. The chance that he might learn of the cat's financial dealings was small; still, it was better to be safe than sorry. His account also required voice verification before Goldman Sachs processed any trades for him in Singapore. It was an extra precaution taken to deter Internet fraud and identity theft.

At the ORACLE's signal the parrot flew across the room to the PC table and spoke the verbal code words into the built-in speakerphone using his Cary Grant imitation. *"Polly picked a peck of pickled peppers and proceeded to pee prodigiously."*

The investment bank's voice analyzers in Asia processed the sentence pronunciation and quickly accepted him as the account holder. Details of his account positions appeared on the screen along with an automated good morning greeting to their esteemed high-net-worth client, Mr. Oracle, President of the Singapore Overseas Investment Corporation.

The cat sold all his emerging market and REIT stocks and shorted oil futures. He also sent the bank instructions to wire transfer $50,000 to the ASPCA in New York. It was his custom to donate a percentage of his profits earned every quarter to animal welfare societies. Last quarter his money went to PETA, next quarter it would be to NO PAWS LEFT BEHIND.

Before signing off, the ORACLE checked the various gold markets around the globe. He was heavily invested in gold bullion and gold futures as a hedge against the instability of the financial system and his fear that paper currencies might become worthless scraps of paper if the world economy collapsed, which it very well might the way things were going. Gold was a safe haven; it would retain its value when all other investments failed, including U.S. Treasury Bills.

The ORACLE had no interest in making money merely for the sake of making money; indeed, the concept of money was strictly an Earth thing and unique only to this planet in the entire Universe. Rather, he liked the great personal challenge that the financial markets posed, the skill and dexterity that it took for him, a lone investor, to go head-to-head against the large institutions with all their supercomputers, experts, and sophisticated financial models.

His singular advantage was that he had discovered long ago that the human brain was slow to adapt to change; that people were usually late in recognizing when a fundamental change in their environment had occurred. And change also fell outside the comfort zone of most people even though history had proven time and time again that all knowledge and progress comes from change; this was so because change generally brings with it some disorientation and discomfit. He, on the other hand, welcomed change as every change presented an opportunity for those who understood how to profit from it.

The cat also knew that stock market mavens liked to quote the Spanish philosopher George Santayana who had once said: *Those who cannot remember the past are condemned to repeat it.* Unfortunately for humans, they took this advice too much to heart when it came to change; people tended to study the way that change had occurred in the past in order to predict how change would occur in the future. They tended to look backwards rather than forward; it was like trying to drive a speeding car by looking only in the rearview mirror and not through the windshield in front of you. This was a terrible mistake and certain to end in disaster for both the driver and his passengers since every change is different; it never takes place in exactly the same way as it did before.

The parrot flew back to his stand and began to softly whistle the *Marseillaise*, the French national anthem. That was something he did every night before going to sleep. He made it a point to hit the hay by midnight because he was the building's alarm clock. Every morning at precisely 7:00 A.M. he went out on the fire escape and imitated a rooster; crowing so loudly that all the tenants knew it was time to arise and face the new day with all the trials and tribulations it held in store for them.

The ORACLE smiled. The two of them had been associates for almost 300 years, helping people to realize their dreams. Together, from this same building, they had witnessed the Financial Panics of 1857, 1873, and 1907; the Wall Street bombing in 1920; the Great Depression of 1929; the marvelous post-World War II expansion; the junk bond and insider trading scandals of the 1980s; the crash of 1987; the S & L crisis of the 1990s; the dot-com bust in 2000; the 9/11 terrorist attack in 2001.

They saw eye-to-eye on many of the political and social issues of the day: lower corporate tax rates, free trade, raising the drinking age to 25, the return to the gold standard, requiring all college graduates, without exception, to serve two years of military service, universal healthcare for all Americans, a strong national defense, amnesty and a path to citizenship for illegal aliens of reputable character, gay marriage, assisted suicide, women priests, a balanced budget, capital punishment, a strong dollar, legalized prostitution, medical marijuana, revising the personal income tax code to give the middle class a fairer shake, and on passing a law permitting only women with great legs to wear mini-skirts.

The ORACLE turned on the TV to catch the late BBC World News. He never watched U.S. news channels because he thought them to be biased in their reporting. Then he walked over to the large, opened window and went out onto the fire escape that he climbed to the roof. From the highest point on the roof he peered up at the dense star cluster located at the center of the Andromeda Galaxy, the nearest spiral galaxy to our own Milky Way, a mere 2.5 million light-years away. He blinked three times at the brightest star.

In response, a laser-like flicker of light danced for a millisecond on the dark horizon and then ricocheted far out into deep space. Any curious astronomer or astrophysicist who was awake and may have noticed this momentary aberration in the heavens would be inclined to dismiss it as a normal abnormality, most likely a pulsar from a distant neutron star.

═══════════════

The next morning, shortly after Stanley had left for the dance studio, their downstairs neighbor, Merle Pushkin, knocked on the front door of the apartment; then she let herself in with the key that the ORACLE had given to her in case there was ever a fire or another emergency in the building. Merle lived on the floor below with her pet black squirrel, Rocco, who drove everybody in the building crazy because he raced up and down on the fire escape all day long. She was a tall, gossipy, busty woman in her late forties with gray-black hair, Slavic features, and a wandering left eye that never looked at you when she spoke to you. Like many Russians of a certain generation, she had intense opinions about anything and everything.

According to Merle, she was a direct descendant of Merlin on her mother's side, the famous sorcerer-in-chief at the court of King Arthur and the Knights of the Round Table. Merle was also a genuine witch and she could make large objects like automobiles and airplanes appear and disappear at will. While this was mind-boggling and great fun, unfortunately, she couldn't predict the winning LOTTO or MEGA numbers; nor could she predict the outcome of baseball or NBA games, or whether the stock market was going to go up or down.

Thus, her magical powers, though very impressive, were highly impractical and that made it difficult for her to earn a decent living. She was hard up for cash most of the time and often borrowed money from the ORACLE to tide her over tough patches in her helter-skelter life. At one point, when she was younger, she had considered becoming a high-priced call girl and selling her body to politicians like Senators and Governors for big money; however this plan didn't work out because our elected officials didn't want to have sex with women who were tougher and smarter than themselves.

Lately, Merle had started a consulting business aimed at helping people who had lost their jobs and were behind on their car payments. For a fee, she would make their cars disappear so they could report them as stolen to the police; thus they could collect enough money from the insurance companies to pay off their bank loans and avoid the embarrassment of having their cars repossessed as well as irreparably damaging their credit ratings.

Merle had competitors who also made cars disappear for debtors -- they were thieves who stole them -- and then shipped them overseas to places like Bosnia and Albania where buyers asked no questions. However, dealing with these common thieves could be risky -- they were frequently arrested by the police while transporting the stolen vehicles to the docks -- and ended up squealing on the car owners who hired them in order to get shorter jail sentences. The car owners consequently went to jail themselves for fraud. With Merle's service, however, there was no such risk; when she made your car disappear it immediately ended up in another dimension where it would never be found.

"*Oy vey!*" Merle said, "I could use a stiff drink, maybe a double shot of *Stoli Strasberi* vodka or a *Jim Beam* neat with a beer chaser."

The parrot looked at the cat and then spoke for him. "The ORACLE never drinks hard liquor because it destroys too many brain cells; he only drinks Bud Light. Occasionally he will enjoy a little white wine if he has fish for dinner, but that's the extent of it. "

"Do you have any unfiltered cigarettes then?"

"I smoke one cigarette a day," the parrot said, "that the ORACLE bums off his friends at the bar for me when he hangs out with them at night. I'm afraid we can't keep cigarettes in the apartment because of Stanley."

"What a crappy day I'm having and it isn't even noon yet!" Her mischievous eyes noticed the beautiful blue Chinese vase resting on a credenza and she wrinkled her nose at it. The vase rose four feet in the air and hovered there. "I'm tapped out and I need to borrow $1500 this very minute."

"The ORACLE can't keep cash in the apartment because Stanley might find it. He requires two-business days notice for loans, and then he can only have funds wired directly into your account from Singapore. But you already know all this."

"I know, I know, but I'm desperate." Her wandering eye looked up at the vase and the other eye remained focused on the parrot. "That piece of crockery looks expensive, how much do you think it would it be worth shattered into a thousand itty-bitty pieces?"

The ORACLE blinked at her three times.

She began to whimper. "I'm sorry, O, please forgive me, I'm crazed, I don't know what I'm doing. You see, I met a handsome man and I'm desperately in love for the first time in my life. I need to get a manicure, a pedicure, my hair cut and colored, my butt toned, a facial, my legs waxed, my eyebrows threaded, and my teeth whitened. I also need to buy new mascara, lip-gloss, eye shadow, eyeliner, anti-aging cream, and body powder. "

The parrot tilted his head as though the different angle would give him a clearer understanding of her situation. "You've already been married three times, Merle, that's a fact."

She nodded. "Yes, it's true, but I never really loved any of my exes, not like the way I love my Vincenzo."

"Really?"

"Yes. He makes me feel like a young girl again when I was bursting with raging hormones. And his passionate kisses take my breath away; my heart flutters like a butterfly flying in the heat of the Sun; my knees go weak when he touches me and I collapse helplessly into his hairy, Italian arms. "

The parrot wanted to shriek but controlled himself. "Love has recently been diagnosed by scientists as a dangerous disease, Merle, it is a result of a fatal chemical imbalance in your biological system. And it often leads to addiction; you could be a love addict and not even realize it."

"I don't care about science; I'm in love with Vincenzo, that's all I care about, he's my drug-of-choice."

"You should know, Merle, that pharmaceutical companies have developed love potions that unscrupulous men can slip into the drinks of attractive women they meet at bars so they can have sex with them. You could be one of those women, I wouldn't put it past this Vincenzo guy."

"I didn't meet Vincenzo at a bar."

"That's good."

"We met in a strip club."

"That's bad."

"That's the way it is."

"Tell me, Merle, what is this Vincenzo's full name?"

She took out a piece of paper and read from it. "Vincenzo Garabaldi Tomasso Guido Sartuffomanganoto, Jr."

"Geez, that's a really long name, even for an Italian."

"Yes, it is; that's because he has royal blood from the royal family of Palermo, Sicily, flowing through his veins; so his friends just call him 'Vinnie Shots' for short."

The parrot shrieked loudly and glanced sideways at the cat.

"Would you call Lenny and ask him to lend me the money?" Merle pleaded.

The parrot shrieked again, this time directly at the cat.

"Pretty please with whipped cream on top," she begged, "I need you to do this for me. I am bonkers over this guy; it's my one chance at eternal happiness."

The ORACLE reluctantly went to the speakerphone. He hit the ON button and punched in a phone number with his paw. The parrot flew to the table to stand beside him.

After two rings a man's gruff voice answered. "Yeah, whatta you want? If you're selling something, I ain't buying; if you're giving something away, I don't want any; if you're looking for a donation, I'm flat broke; if you call me again, I'll get a restraining order against you."

The parrot responded in his best Gary Cooper imitation. "The ORACLE requests your presence, Lenny, at your earliest convenience."

"How about I meet him next Tuesday at noon by the telephone booth at the corner of Fulton and John Streets?"

"Now, Lenny, if you please!"

"Ok, if it's an emergency, I'm on my way."

The ORACLE hit the OFF button and Merle went to the door of the apartment and opened it. Almost immediately they heard the sound of the motorized wheelchair as it sped along the hallway and then burst into the living room, stopping inches short of crashing into the sofa.

The wheelchair jockey was a middle-aged man with brown, wiry hair, a creased forehead, and a pug nose. Mirrored sunglasses hid his eyes and a gnarled left hand operated the chair's throttle. A pitiful excuse for a goatee dangled from his cleft chin.

"That was fast," the parrot said.

Lenny spun the wheelchair around so he was facing everyone. "Time is money, birdbrain, money talks and bullshit walks."

Lenny Barber -- aka Lew Bookman, aka Leo Baskin, aka Les Baker -- had a real name but nobody knew what it was. A paraplegic due to a

NASCAR accident -- he wasn't driving one; he was struck by a racecar as he made a mad dash across a track in Daytona to get Mario Andretti's autograph -- worked for short-sellers in the stock market. Short-sellers made money when the price of a stock went down; they were basically betting against companies doing well. Lenny's job was to spread false rumors about companies being in trouble so that his clients would make fortunes as their stock prices dropped.

Earlier this morning he had been spreading the false rumors that United Airlines was on the verge of bankruptcy and that Bank of American was going to be taking another 50 billion dollar write-off on sub-prime mortgages. Lenny's cut was 0.000045 % of the net profit. What Lenny was doing was highly illegal; it was also immensely profitable.

The SEC was actively searching for edgy characters like Lenny and would nail his ass to the prison wall when they caught up with him. If he went to jail, he'd have to find a home for Leonard, the pet iguana who shared his apartment. Leonard looked like a large version of the green GEICO lizard that did all those TV commercials, except Leonard couldn't stand upright and he didn't speak with a Cockney accent. All he could do was look menacing and crawl up inside the leg of your pants and bite your genitals hard until they bled profusely.

"So what's up, O?"

The cat blinked three times.

"Me? You want *me* to lend Merle $1500 so she can look beautiful like a movie star for some joker she just met? Am I hearing you correctly?"

"Oh, Lenny, please," Merle pleaded, "you're the only person I can think of who keeps oodles of cash on hand because you don't trust banks and bankers. Everybody else stashes their funds offshore."

Lenny noticed the blue vase suspended in mid-air. "Are you doing parlor tricks again, Merle?"

She wrinkled her nose and the vase came down to rest once more on the credenza. "Please, Lenny, you're my last hope, I'll be forever in your debt."

"That's what I'm afraid of."

"Oh, Lenny, you know I'm good for it."

"What's your FICO score, Merle? I only lend money to people with strong credit ratings who score 700 or better."

Her face trembled like she was close to breaking out in tears. "I've had some problems in the past with eight or nine of my credit cards, however, I'm close to working that out and entering into payment plans."

"Uh-huh, so what's your credit score?"

She mumbled a response that was inaudible.

"Speak up, Merle, I couldn't hear you."

"32."

"32!!!! Did you say 32, like in a 3 with a 2 after it?"

Merle slumped down in her chair and buried her face in her hands.

"Holy Toledo! I bet that panhandler on the corner of Pine Street holding a paper cup in his hand has a higher credit score than that."

Now crocodile tears streamed between her fingers and down both her cheeks.

Lenny drummed the fingers of his normal hand on the metal rim of the wheelchair. "Merle, I love you like a sister, babe, but FUHGEDDABOUDIT! You're a deadbeat, there's no denying it."

The flow of tears greatly increased in quantity.

The ORACLE blinked at Lenny three times.

"Ok, that's the only way I'll make her the loan, O, is if you'll guaranty it." He reached into his pocket and took out a roll of hundred dollar bills that must have been four inches thick. After counting out $1500 he throttled the wheelchair to where she was sitting and handed her the money.

"Thank you, dear, precious, wonderful, pal of mine, Lenny."

"Yeah, yeah, yeah, yeah, yeah, don't mention it."

Merle jumped up from her seat and gave him a big hug and a kiss on the forehead. Then she picked up the cat and danced around the room with him, all the time singing -- *For he's a jolly good fellow which nobody can deny.* She put the cat down and headed for the parrot but the bird hopped back inside his cage before she could grab him.

Stuffing the bills down into her deep cleavage she went to the door and opened it. "I'm going to the beauty salon for the next twenty-four hours. "When you see me again you won't recognize me because I'll be such a piece of ass." Then she was gone.

The ORACLE smiled at Lenny. He knew that Lenny wasn't as bad or as tough as he pretended to be. He tended to shoot from the lip but under all that anger and cynicism he was a scared guy who needed help to combat the severe depression he suffered from. The folks at NOT

DEAD YET were a good support group for him. So too were the Iraq amputees he played wheelchair basketball with on Saturdays at the courts in Battery Park City.

The parrot hopped back onto his stand. "Lenny, you come into contact with a lot of unsavory people in your shady line of business. Do you know of someone named Vincenzo Garabaldi Tomasso Guido Sartuffomanganoto, Jr., by any chance?"

"Wow, that's a mouthful, how can you remember such a long moniker?"

"I'm blessed with a photographic memory."

Lenny tugged on his goatee. "Nah, I can't say that I know the dude."

"I am told that he is also known as 'Vinnie Shots' in some quarters."

The paraplegic almost fell out of his chair. "Stay away from that *goombah*, I'm warning you, or you'll end up as parrot soup in a pirate movie if you mess with that psycho. He's connected up to his eyeballs and he's a wiseguy."

"So he *is* in the Mob."

"Yeah, and he did time in the joint for armed robbery, extortion, and attempted murder. "

"I was afraid it would be something like that."

"In addition to being a three-time loser, the guy is also a three-time widower; it seems that all of his former wives had freak fatal accidents before their final divorce decrees came through and they could start collecting alimony from him."

"Oh, dear."

"Why do want to know about that creep for?"

"I am afraid that he is Merle's new boyfriend."

"Are you pulling my paralyzed leg?"

"No, but maybe there's another 'Vinnie Shots'."

Lenny shook his head. "Nah, there's only one 'Vinnie Shots', take my word for it."

The ORACLE blinked three times.

"Yeah, O, I agree, we got us a major problem. I think we need to talk to the Professor. I'll give him a jingle now. " Lenny took out his cell phone.

Humphrey Kincaid, 63, was a tall, solidly built man with heavy lidded eyes, brown hair, and pink, farm-boy cheeks. A retired Professor of Spanish at NYU, he disliked his first name as much as Humphrey Bogart had so he encouraged people to call him Professor instead, which everybody now did. He and his dog, Georgette, a Bull Terrier – Chihuahua mix lived downstairs in the apartment next to Merle. Since retiring he supplemented his university pension by authoring romance novels under the pen name of Rosa Santiago. Late in life he discovered that he had a natural flair for writing about large breasted young women in heat who had their bodices ripped off by well-endowed pirates with chiseled chests and vulnerable, handsome faces.

Upon entering the room the Professor bumped knuckles with Lenny, nodded to the cat and parrot, and then sat on the sofa so he could keep a wary eye on the door and windows in case a burglar might show up. His own apartment had been broken into 17 times; fortunately, nothing was ever taken. Still, it was strange because no other tenants in the building had break-ins. And Georgette should have been a strong deterrent as she was known to go after the postman and FedEx delivery people at every opportunity. A veteran detective from the NYPD unit investigating the case was known to have voiced the opinion to a colleague that he thought the break-ins were an 'inside' job.

"Professor, we got us a horrific situation here," Lenny said, and then brought him up to speed about Merle and 'Vinnie Shots'.

The Professor slapped his knee. "*Madre de Dios! Pensaba que bruhas eran mas intelligente que eso. Como pudo ser que aes maldito hombre la engano?*"

The cat and parrot understood eight languages, including Spanish; however, Lenny only had a weak command of English. "Huh?"

"I'm sorry, Lenny, when I get excited I slip into Spanish even though my first language is English. I said: Mother of God! I thought witches were smarter than that. How could she be fooled by that evil man?"

"That's what I thought you said."

"I guess the old maxim that love is blind must be true after all."

"We could tell Merle the truth about this guy," the parrot suggested.

Lenny twirled his wheelchair in circles. "Nah, that wouldn't work, Merle wouldn't believe us. A woman in love doesn't listen to reason."

"A former student of mine is an FBI agent," the Professor said, "I could ask him to send Merle a copy of 'Vinnie Shots' rap sheet. He could do it anonymously so she wouldn't know that we're involved."

"Nah, she's a witch, she'd know it was us."

"How about if we confront this 'Vinnie Shots' character directly," the parrot said, "and warn him to stay away from Merle?"

"Then we might as well shoot ourselves in the head now," Lenny said, "because it'd be a lot more humane than what that gangster would do to us."

"What do you think he'd do?"

Lenny considered the options. "My first guess is that he'd cut our tongues out with a razor and then pulverize our faces using a sledgehammer until our skulls caved in and our own mothers wouldn't even recognize us."

"Yikes!" the parrot shrieked.

"My second best guess is that he'd cut us up with a chainsaw and then dowse our body parts with gasoline and burn us until we looked like used charcoal."

"Egad!" the professor exclaimed.

"My third best guess is that he'd use an acetylene torch to burn our faces and fingerprints off; pull our teeth out with pliers so we couldn't be identified by our dental records; and then hang our charred bodies from a lamppost in front of the New York Stock Exchange as a warning to others living in the Financial District who might try to mess with his love-life."

The parrot shrieked again and rushed back into his cage while the professor ran to the bathroom with a bowel spasm.

The ORACLE yawned; he walked calmly to the channel changer to click on Bloomberg to see how the financial markets were performing.

════════════════════

"Now you stay right there, Mister Celebrity," Stanley said, "I've got a BIG surprise for you. I'm going to fix your wagon once and for all."

The ORACLE could tell from the sly grin on Stanley's face that it wasn't going to be a *pleasant* BIG surprise.

Stanley activated the speakerphone and dialed a number he read from a newspaper ad. The phone rang twice and then was picked up.

"Hello, welcome to my weekend morning free call-in program, this is Dr. Willy Williams, consulting veterinarian. What kind of a problem are you are having with your pet?"

"Doctor Williams, I live above a bar and my cat sneaks out at night to go down there to drink beer with the customers. I want you to recommend a medicine I could give him that will make him deathly ill whenever he drinks alcohol."

"Your cat drinks alcohol?"

"Yes, he drinks beer, and lots of it, from the smell of him."

"That can't be, alcohol is toxic to cats."

"I don't know about that, doctor, all I know is that he drinks beer every night. Maybe he also drinks scotch and whiskey too for all I know."

"Have you actually seen the cat drink beer in that bar?"

"Well, no, doctor, I wouldn't set foot inside that wicked place myself. You see; it caters to an arrogant Wall Street crowd that sneers at you if you don't earn at least a million dollars a year."

"Hmmm."

"I think I'm going to report the bar owners to *Animal Planet* and to the New York State Liquor Authority. Perhaps they can raid the bar with some kind of joint task force and catch the bartenders in the act of serving alcohol to animals."

"Hmmm."

"I smell his breath when he comes home at night and I can tell you for certain that he's definitely been drinking. He's always burping and one time he had the hiccups."

"Is he ever unsteady on his paws?"

"Well, no."

"Does he slur his meows?"

"No, not that I can remember."

"Does he become argumentative and start fights with other cats?"

"No."

"Does he throw up on the rug?"

"No."

"What does the cat look like?"

Stanley studied the ORACLE. "He's not much to look at, doctor, he's just a black and white alley cat with a dopey face, a birth mark of a star on his chest, and he weighs about fifteen pounds."

"I see."

"And there always seems to be a smirk on his puss, at least there is when he looks at me."

The parrot wanted to laugh out loud like Cary Grant used to in all those old comedy movies of his but couldn't because Stanley didn't know that he was able to laugh.

"What do you feed the cat?"

"That's another strange thing, doctor, he drinks water and eats a little dry food. But when he comes home from that bar I often smell onions, French fries, hot sauce, balsamic vinegar dressing, horseradish, mustard, chili, relish, guacamole, and garlic on his breath."

"Really."

"Yes, that's because I think he eats whatever the customers eat at that bar. And I know what I'm talking about because I have an educated nose; I come from a family of perfumers. I know scents when I smell them."

"Cats can't eat food with that kind of heavy seasoning; they'd get deadly ill if they did."

"I'm telling you that this one does! And he's never been sick a single day!"

"Where did you get the cat?"

"He came with the apartment."

"What do you mean?"

"The real estate broker told me that the owner of the apartment lived in Singapore and would rent it to me for only $1,000 a month provided I took care of the cat. It is an 1800 sq. ft. two bed-two bath loft fully furnished with expensive furniture and it has three-plasma 56" TVs. The owner also pays all the utilities."

"Man-o-man, you got yourself a real sweetheart deal there, that same apartment in my building would go for $10,000 a month or more."

"I have to take care of the bird too."

"There's a bird?"

"Yes, a large parrot, he also came with the apartment. And he also has a smirk on his face when he looks at me."

"Parrots can't smirk."

"This one can."

"Hmmm. Does the parrot talk?"

"Not when I'm in the room."

"What does that mean?"

"He talks to the cat *after* I go to bed. I heard him a few times when they thought I was asleep."

"I'm beginning to see a pattern here."

"The parrot also sings bawdy songs about prostitutes and soldiers fornicating with women and drinking to excess."

"But only when you're not in the room?"

"Yes. However, I'm too smart for him, doctor, I eavesdropped."

"Does the cat talk to the parrot?"

"No, not that I ever heard."

At this point the ORACLE figured it would be an appropriate time to meow loudly like a silly cat, which he did, so the vet could hear him.

"If I understand you correctly, sir, the parrot talks to the cat, however, the cat doesn't talk to the parrot. Is that correct?"

"I know it sounds weird, doctor, but that's the way it is."

"Is there anything else I should know?"

Stanley lowered his voice. "I'm pretty sure that the parrot smokes cigarettes."

"Cigarettes?"

"Yes. I'm not a smoker myself so I can't tell you what brand."

"Let me ask you, eh, sir …"

"My name is Stanley, doctor, please call me Stanley."

"Let me ask you, Stanley, how long have you been under psychiatric care?"

Stanley bristled with outrage and screamed at the speakerphone. "I'm not under psychiatric care! I have never been under psychiatric care! I'm as sane as you are! "

"I am a veterinarian, Stanley, I don't treat people; however, I strongly urge you to seek psychiatric help as soon as possible." The line went dead.

The cat and bird were both staring at him, both clearly smirking.

Stanley grabbed a jacket and fled the apartment. Part way down the stairs he stopped, came back up to the landing and put his ear against the door of the apartment. It was a thick door but he was sure he heard the parrot laughing.

═══════════════

It was Monday night in Ulysses, perhaps the quietest night of the week, and the ORACLE stood by the front door. The music was turned low; the crowds wouldn't begin returning until tomorrow; so it was a favorite time for beery musings, an opportunity for the regulars to pause and quietly reflect on the vicissitudes of life.

The cat's eyes swept the large oval bar and he confirmed that the next round of candidates who had been selected to receive his special service were present. He decided to sit down on an empty stool next to an elderly man with a gaunt frame and thinning yellowish-gray hair who had been nursing a brandy for the past hour.

"Hello, kitty," the man said, smiling for the first time since he had gotten out of bed that morning, "it's always nice to see you, you're the highlight of my day." Then he patted the cat affectionately on the head and the ORACLE purred while reading his mind.

Aloysius Hanratty, 76, known to the regulars as Al, had that very day received the worst possible news from his doctor -- he was pronounced fit as a fiddle and might well live to be a 100. Al had hoped the doctor was going to tell him that he had cancer or a fatal brain tumor that would kill him in the coming months.

Like many senior citizens today, Al found himself in the tough situation of trying to live on a modest fixed income in an inflationary environment. According to his own calculations -- and he should know because he had worked as an accountant all his life -- he would run out of money in exactly five months. Outliving his money was something that shouldn't be happening to him; after all, both his parents and his sole sibling had died in their middle sixties. With any luck, he should have passed away ten years ago. Having no family to fall back on now, and too proud to accept charity, Al was going to be evicted from his small studio rental and forced onto the streets just when the weather turned cold. The

ORACLE knew that Al had hoarded a lethal dose of sleeping pills in his room and was now considering suicide as the only way out.

The cat jumped from the stool onto the bar and walked twenty feet away to where a much younger man was feverishly stirring a scotch & soda with a swizzle stick. Seth Reich, 31, a foreign currency trader at an international private bank, was a heavyset roly-poly with brown eyes and a rapidly receding hairline that characterized the early onset of male pattern baldness. "What's up, buddy, would you like a beer?" He signaled the bartender, Paul, a die-hard Liverpool soccer fan, to put the Bud Light on his tab and the cat rubbed gratefully against his arm. The bowl of beer arrived and the cat lapped it up, all the while keeping his eyes on his benefactor's troubled face.

Seth focused once again on the middle distance separating them and on his own precarious situation. His younger brother, Jay, 27, had a PhD. in mathematics from Columbia University and was a whiz kid at a large hedge fund where he worked in the quantitative analysis group writing algorithms to predict the ups and downs in the precious metals markets. He had an *Excel* spreadsheet for a mind and last year the kid earned a $1.5 million bonus, whereas Seth had taken home a paltry $200,000. His parents were overjoyed at Jay's great success and boasted about him to all their friends. Of course, they said that they were proud of Seth too, though not with the same high degree of enthusiasm, or so it seemed to him.

That's when it had started. His bank imposed strict limits on the maximum long or short positions a trader was allowed to take on any given currency on any given day. It was to prevent a situation from happening like that which had occurred at a bank in Paris last year where a rogue trader lost $7.5 billion. Seth wasn't a math genius like his brother but he knew the deficiencies in the computer system his bank used to monitor the trading positions. He was also sure that the U.S. dollar was going to decline sharply against the yen and the euro because of the coming recession, the rising trade deficit and soaring oil prices.

In early March he was able to amass a $ 3.0 billion short position and mask it by inputting fake offsetting long positions utilizing the user codes of other traders. By the end of March he was $88 million ahead. His plan was to unwind everything by April 15 and then record the profit piece-meal over the remainder of the year so as not to arouse any suspicions on the part of his bosses. Come December he would be a hero to management for earning such a huge profit and his bonus would surely rival that of his brother; surpass it even.

On April 8 everything went kerflooey. For reasons the economists still couldn't explain, the dollar surged and by the time he had covered his short position he was $22 million in the red. He didn't know how much longer he was going to be able to keep this loss a secret. There was a good chance he might go to jail. His parents would be mortified and disgraced. Every morning he went to work he was in a panic as that could be the day he was going to be exposed. He desperately needed the trade of a lifetime to get even

The cat licked his lips and walked farther down the bar to where Amelia Mancuso, 27, a breakable-looking brunette with bow lips, hazel eyes and flared cheekbones, was drinking orange juice through a straw. Amelia was generally fun loving, bright-faced, and outgoing but tonight a somber aura shrouded her like a dark cloud. She tickled him under the chin and he rubbed up against her stomach. "You're such a sweet boy, not like some other guys I know." Her mind drifted back to her former fiance, Phil, the same guy she had caught in bed with her best friend when she returned a day early from visiting her parents in Hartford last week.

Amelia had broken off the engagement on the spot. The next day she sold her engagement ring in the Diamond District and donated the proceeds to a home for unwed mothers in the East Village. The ORACLE knew that Amelia had something in common with the girls who lived in that home -- she was also pregnant. In a short time she would have to decide what to do with the fetus growing inside her.

Pedro Morales, 19, had black curly hair, was 5'3" tall, and weighed 115 pounds. A busboy at the bar, he was taking his dinner break when the ORACLE approached him. *"Ah, como estan ustedas noche, mi amigo, no stmach su habitacion para tener algo de comida?"*

The ORACLE meowed that yes, he was still hungry.

"Le gustaria compartir mi cena? Es my sabroso."

The Oracle meowed that he would very much like to share Pedro's dinner.

"Muy bien, Estoy tan feliz."

Faith, the bartender, a curly-haired, dark head-turner, avid reader, and aspiring actress, knew to bring a fresh bowl and a bottle of Bud Light without the busboy having to ask.

"*El gato le da las gracias, querida senorita,*" Pedro said, thanking her and showing her his warmest smile.

Faith petted the cat gently. "Enjoy, my little buddy."

The ORACLE rubbed against her arm before she left to wait on another patron.

"*Pedro esta enamorado de la Faith,*" he confided to the cat, "some day Pedro like to marry Faith. But she is too tall for Pedro, that is problem."

The cat meowed that he thought Pedro could overcome the big difference in their heights.

"*Eres un gato muy estranyo.* Yes, you are a very strange cat, I am thinking." Pedro put a pork slider on a paper plate along with three French fries and the cat began to eat alongside him. "Is delicious, *amigo,* no?"

The cat purred.

"*Coma despacio y mastique bien sus alimentos.*"

The ORACLE didn't need to be told that, he always chewed his food well.

Unbeknownst to everyone else who worked at Ulysses, the ORACLE was aware that Pedro had an I.Q. of 159, which made him more intelligent than 99.9% of the 6.5 billion people who lived on the planet at the present time. Pedro shared a one-bedroom apartment in Elmhurst, Queens, with fourteen other young Mexican workers. They slept in three shifts and used each other's shoes. Like his roommates, Pedro sent money home to his parents back in Mexico every week so his brothers and sisters could stay in school through the eighth grade. The ORACLE believed that Pedro could accomplish great things in life, if given half a chance.

Wanda Pearlmutter, 44, a raven-haired woman with a round face, sensuous lips, and sparkly green eyes, sipped a white wine and nervously checked her watch every few minutes. Her babysitter couldn't stay past 8:00 P.M. on school nights. She was a widow and the sole support of her twelve-year old son. The cat smelled her huge purse and could tell that she had been to yoga class at lunchtime. "There's nothing in there for you, sweetie, only my sweaty leotard and sneakers."

The ORACLE sat between her and her drink so he could stare into her eyes. Wanda was still in excellent shape for her age and possessed the voluptuous figure of a much younger woman, thanks to her strict diet and vigorous exercise regimen. Her new boss at the insurance company she worked at thought so too; and that was the problem. The sexual harassment was escalating and Wanda was afraid she might lose her job if she didn't give him what he wanted. She was fully vested and desperately needed the job. Maybe she should let herself get fat and sloppy so he wouldn't want her anymore.

Bobby Rankle, 22, also drank Bud Light so when the cat showed up at his table by the window he asked for an extra bottle when ordering his second round. "Ah, it's finally my turn, it it? Don't think I didn't see you schmoozing all those other folks, working the room like a pro. I'm on to you, you little politician." The young man stood 5'7" and had the lithe body of an athlete. His blonde hair was parted in the middle and his gap-toothed smile was charming and disarming. Aside from a two-inch pink scar under his left ear, his angular face was handsome and his complexion flawless.

Tonight Bobby's tie was askew and his white shirt was wet with perspiration even though the air-conditioning in Ulysses had been cranked up and the bar was comfortable temperature-wise. A stockbroker working for the family brokerage firm, Bobby was following in his dad's footsteps, just like his dad had done with his own father, and his father's father before him. The ORACLE knew that Bobby hated his job; that he really wanted to be a professional dancer, that's where his passion lay. The ORACLE also knew that Bobby was deep in the closet, secretly gay, living a double life and feeling terribly guilty and ashamed for doing so.

But Bobby didn't have the guts to tell his dad any of those things; he loved his dad and had always wanted to please him; his dad was an ex-marine, a great guy, and a man's man; they were not only father and son but best fiends too; the Rankle name was stenciled on the firm's door; he was expected to carry on the long family tradition; doing otherwise would break his dad's heart.

Last, but not least, the ORACLE walked to a hook in the bar where Artie Finch, the oldest bartender in Ulysses, was using this quiet time to try and read the novel of the same name, *Ulysses* by James Joyce. Many critics ranked it the best English-language novel of the 20th. Century but the author's stream-of-consciousness style was obviously giving Artie problems and he was being forced to re-read every paragraph three or four times before moving on to the next one. At this rate of progress the ORACLE calculated that it would take Artie a year and five months to read the entire 250,000-word scholarly book. The cat plopped down on the opened page so Artie would be forced to take a break from the arduous task he had set for himself."

"Good evening, you little vagabond," Artie said, removing the half-moon glasses from the bridge of his nose, "are you up for another beer?"

"Meow."

He reached into a bin of ice and extracted a cold bottle of Bud Light for the cat. "Here you go, buddy, one for the road."

Artie Finch, 49, was of average build and had black hair, blue eyes, a dimpled chin, and large teeth that sometimes overpowered his warm smile. A bartender since the age of 18, he could mix any drink you could name as well as a few dozen concoctions you never heard of. Unlike many other bartenders in New York, however, Artie had no desire to own his own bar some day. Originally from Rhode Island, he had come to New York as a young man fresh out of high school to make it as a novelist here. Thirty years of writing later he found himself the author of ten books, all of which had been rejected for publication by a multitude of editors and agents both domestically and abroad.

Although Artie didn't realize it, the ORACLE knew that he had achieved the unenviable distinction of having accumulated more rejection notices than any other writer in the United States. Artie lived with his invalid wife in a rent-stabilized, one-bedroom apartment in working-class Astoria, Queens. She remained his staunchest supporter and had always encouraged him over the years, holding his hand and rubbing his neck when his spirits were low, telling him that he wasn't a failure as the rejection notices piled up, reassuring him that one day the world would recognize him for the great writer that he was.

Artie's faith in himself had just about shriveled up with the passage of so much time, however, he still desperately wanted to get one of his manuscripts published, not for the money he might earn, but to justify his wife's unswerving belief in his talent. He had saved all the rejection notices and kept them in neatly labeled cardboard boxes in a storage facility near his home. One day, when he finally did get published, he planned to incinerate them in a celebratory bonfire and invite all his friends and neighbors. If that day never came, then upon his death he intended to have them shipped to the same crematorium where his own body was to be incinerated. That way his body and his words would go up in smoke together.

The ORACLE delved into Artie's eyes and saw that behind his warm, welcoming smile that Artie was about to give up and throw in the towel, never to write another word for the rest of his life. That would be a great tragedy because the cat knew that Artie had one last book left in him, and that book, if ever written, would be ranked, fifty years from now, as one of the best novels of the first half of the 21st. Century.

Meanwhile, up in the apartment, Stanley locked the door of the birdcage and threw a sheet over it so the parrot wouldn't be able to see what he was going to do next. The bird shrieked loudly and Stanley smiled; he was going to show that vet that he wasn't crazy, that everything he said was true. No dopey cat and goofy bird were going to make him a laughingstock and get away with it.

He went into his bedroom and re-emerged with a small, expensive camera/ voice recorder that he positioned between books on a shelf near the TV. From that spot it had a clear view of the entire living room. It was battery operated and voice activated. Governments used it to spy on suspected terrorists and working mothers used it to check up on the nannies minding their children. Satisfied with its placement, he took the sheet off the birdcage and unlocked its door. The parrot shrieked again but had no idea what had taken place.

The following day the four of them -- Lenny, the Professor, the parrot, and the ORACLE -- were huddled together in a follow-up meeting regarding the 'Vinnie Shots' problem when there was a knock at the door and then it was suddenly flung open. A statuesque, platinum dyed blonde posed flirtatiously in the doorway wearing dark glasses and a skimpy beaded-ivory dress that barely covered her. It was low cut in the front, revealing everything but the nipples of her massive boobs, and also in the back so you could see the tattoo of a butterfly above the crack of her ass when she twirled on her toes in the black patent leather high heeled shoes. Her eyelashes were long and dark; her pouty red lips glossy and moist, her milky skin radiant, like her collagen-free legs. When she spoke it was with a slight French accent and her perfectly white teeth glistened in the daylight. "*Bon jour,* boys, can you tell me how to get to Versailles from here?"

A loud wolf whistle roared up from Lenny's throat followed by the words, "Hubba! Hubba! Ding Dong!"

"Merle, is that you?" the Professor asked.

"*Oui, ces't moi.*"

"Oh, Merle, look what you have done to yourself!"

"Do you like my new dress?"

"There isn't much to it," the parrot observed dryly, "it leaves absolutely nothing to the imagination."

"I'm letting it all hang out, boys, I want my Vinnie to see exactly what's in the package he's getting."

"Merle, please come in and take a seat," the Professor said, "we need to have a talk with you about your new boyfriend."

She sat on the sofa. "Ok, I'm listening."

The Professor cleared his throat, then hemmed and hawed, finally saying nothing.

Lenny squirmed in his wheelchair, opened his mouth several times as though he was about to speak, then closed it again.

The parrot hummed the ominous opening notes of Beethoven's Ninth Symphony then retreated back into his cage.

The ORACLE, exasperated with his companions, looked Merle in the eyes and blinked three times.

"Ahhhhh!" she cried, "that's not true! My Vinnie isn't any of those dreadful things that you say he is."

The Professor, recovering his courage, handed her a copy of her boyfriend's lengthy rap sheet.

She read it and cried out again. "It's not true! It's all lies!"

"I'm sorry," Lenny commiserated, "I know exactly how you feel, I once had a girlfriend who was a rotten, thieving piece of scum like this dirt-bag, slime-bucket, schlub of a 'Vinnie Shots.'"

Merle angrily rocked to her feet and headed for the door. "I'm going to tell Vinnie what you said, Lenny, every single word." The door slammed behind her.

Lenny started to shake uncontrollably. "I ... I ...I was just trying to do a good deed for the first time in my life ... and now I'm screwed ... a marked man with a gangster out gunning for him."

Every morning the ORACLE and parrot did yoga for thirty minutes together while watching the Fitness Channel on television after Stanley left for work at the dance studio.

The ORACLE, as was his habit, then meditated on the inevitability of change taking place in both life as well as in business and the necessity to embrace it, while he sat motionless on the windowsill, basking in the warm morning sunlight.   In particular, he reviewed the events of the past twenty-four hours to see if he could detect the early signs of any fundamental change occurring that he might have not picked up on in the heat of the moment.   Change typically occurred when it was least expected and his antennas were always up.

The parrot also thought about change; he was perfectly comfortable with change as long as it didn't affect his little daily routines, the scheduling of his favorite TV programs, and the way he lived his life. As he sat on his stand he then considered the 'Vinnie Shots' problem and wondered if he should also take precautions against being kidnapped and tortured to death the way Lenny and the Professor had.

Lenny had started wearing an eye-patch and had changed his name to Lee Bugaloo. That was easy enough for Lenny to do; all he had to do was print up business cards with that name on it and tell all the shady characters he knew that he was no longer Lenny; that Lenny had skipped town without leaving a forwarding address. The Professor had begun to dress as a woman and changed the name on his doorbell downstairs to Rosa Santiago, the pseudonym he wrote his romance books under.

But the parrot didn't have a name to begin with; so what was there to be gained by him doing the same? And wasn't it easier to track down a person who had a name than someone who didn't have a name? Besides, there was nothing in Vinnie's rap sheet about him ever torturing birds.

The ORACLE possessed a unique gift; he was able to sense the advent of change; that was one reason why he was such a successful investor. Perhaps that was also why he noticed something different about the apartment today; somehow it had changed.

He blinked three times at the parrot.

"Yes," the parrot replied, "now that you ask, something unusual had happened the other night. I meant to tell you about it but I forgot, maybe because I was so worried about getting killed by a psycho I don't even know." Then he told the cat about Stanley throwing a sheet over his birdcage.

The ORACLE walked slowly around the apartment, looking everywhere and sniffing like a bloodhound. It took almost ten minutes for him to find the camera/ recorder hidden between a book on quantum physics and a book on differential calculus on the shelf.

"Is that what I think it is?" the parrot asked.

The cat nodded.

"So, we've been on *Candid Camera*, that's what Stanley was up to."

"Thank you for coming, Lenny," the parrot said, "I know it took great courage for you to leave your apartment under the circumstances."

"My name's not Lenny, it's Lee."

Both the bird and the cat sighed.

The Professor sat sheepishly on the sofa wearing a yellow dress with a full skirt and black flats. Long curls from the brunette wig almost reached his shoulders. He must have realized how silly he looked because he didn't try to deny who he really was.

The parrot flew to the bookshelf, picked the camera up with his claws, and then deposited it on the coffee table before returning to the stand.

Lenny immediately grasped the situation. "The place is bugged!"

"Could it be 'Vinnie Shots'?" the Professor asked, a tremor in his voice.

"No, it's Stanley," the parrot replied, and he told them all about the call to the veterinarian.

Despite their fear of imminent death, the two men laughed out loud and the tension in the room seemed to dissipate considerably.

"That's the funniest thing I ever heard," Lenny said, "I wish I coulda been a fly on the wall during that conversation."

"Very funny," the Professor agreed, "it sounds like Stanley was so embarrassed that he's trying to get the evidence to prove to that vet that he isn't a nut case."

"Stanley embarrassed himself," the parrot said, "he arranged the call and did all the talking. Still, he's not a bad person; he's just narrow-minded, sanctimonious, has low self-esteem, and is very judgmental like most insecure people are."

"I know Stanley doesn't approve of me," Lenny said, "but I don't hold that against him. Lots of fine people don't approve of me; sometimes *I* even don't approve of me."

"What are you going to do about the camera?" the Professor asked. It has probably already captured some incriminating video and dialogue."

"We want you to hide the camera in your apartment."

"What happens when Stanley goes to check on the film and finds the camera is missing?"

The parrot tried to shrug but couldn't because he had no shoulders. "It will be interesting to see what he does; if he accuses us of taking it then he has to admit that he was spying on the ORACLE and me. Somehow, I can't see Stanley doing that; it would make him even more embarrassed."

The professor picked up the camera/ recorder and inspected it. "One of my hobbies is photography so I know a fair bit about cameras. I can tell you that this is a very expensive piece of surveillance equipment that is generally only used by professionals like private detectives or intelligence operatives."

"I'm surprised, Stanley is so frugal."

"I woulda said that he was a cheapskate, or a skinflint," Lenny said.

The Professor read a label on the underside of the camera. "Stanley leased it, he didn't buy it; the leasing company's name is here."

"That explains it then."

"Still, I bet it was expensive to lease, even for a few days. And he would have had to sign a contract making him responsible for its loss or for any damages."

"That's going to make it more interesting," the parrot said, "when he realizes that it has disappeared."

"By the way, Merle ain't been back to her apartment in two days," Lenny said, changing the subject.

"Are you certain of that?"

"Yeah, I woulda heard her; the walls are so thin I always hear her crying or cursing in there. It's usually one or the other with her."

The parrot winced. "That's so sad."

"I gave Rocco some acorns and water so he's ok."

"That was nice of you, Lenny."

The ORACLE mentally added Merle's name to his mission list."

The ORACLE had returned early from Ulysses because the TV program, *So You Think You Can Dance*, was coming on at 9:00 P.M. It was the one show that he, the parrot, and Stanley watched together as a quasi-family unit. Being a choreographer, Stanley was able to offer expert commentary on the various dance routines performed by the contestants. The cat and parrot found this very enlightening since neither of them could dance. When a particular couple's routine was very spirited the parrot often got caught up in the action and in the heat of the moment he would hold one foot high in the air and jump up and down on the other foot; however, this didn't constitute real dancing on his part, he was just having a fun time pretending that he was dancing.

Stanley usually sat on the sofa during the show; flanked by the parrot on one armrest and the cat on the other armrest. Tonight, half way through the program, however, he arose from the sofa and drifted very nonchalantly, or so he thought, to the shelf where he had hidden the camera/recorder. His plan was to pocket the unit and inspect the film later in the privacy of his bedroom.

The parrot and cat continued to watch the show and took no notice of Stanley's absence. They heard the sound of books being moved, carefully at first, then more frantically, until a bunch of books fell from the shelf and crashed to the floor. They both turned to the source of the noise.

The look on Stanley's face passed from bewilderment, then to concern, and finally to panic as it dawned on him that the very expensive camera/recorder was missing.

The cat meowed as though to ask what was going on.

"Eh, I was looking for a book," Stanley said, in a strained voice, "but I couldn't find it, it's disappeared." He hurriedly picked up the fallen books from the floor and replaced them haphazardly on the shelf, checking again to make sure that the camera/ recorder still wasn't there.

The cat and parrot turned back to the TV screen where a young couple was doing an energetic hip-hop dance number.

Stanley backed towards his bedroom door. "I … eh …I just remembered that I have to make an important phone call."

Once the bedroom door had closed the bird flew to the speakerphone and waited for the extension light to come on before he hit the LISTEN button with his beak. In the meantime the cat went to the channel changer and muted the sound volume on the TV.

The telephone rang several times before a female voice answered. "Hello."

They both recognized the voice as belonging to Fiona, Stanley's only close friend. Neither of them had met Fiona in person because under the terms of Stanley's lease he was forbidden to bring women under the age of 45 into the apartment unless they were chaperoned.

"It's gone, Fiona, it's gone!"

"Stanley, is that you?"

"Yes, it's me, who else were you expecting to hear from tonight?"

"I have a life, Stanley, it's not all about you."

"I apologize; I'm in an agitated state."

"Calm down, tell me what's wrong."

"That camera/ recorder you told me to get, it's missing, gone, disappeared."

"I didn't *tell* you to get it, Stanley, it was only a suggestion since my girlfriend Heather successfully used one to catch her sleaze-ball husband frolicking with that meter-maid."

"Well, it's vanished."

"Are you sure, maybe you misplaced it. You know how careless you are sometimes, Stanley."

"I didn't misplace it, Fiona, somebody took it!"

"That doesn't make sense; you and I were the only ones who knew about the camera/ recorder. Who could have taken it?"

Stanley looked at his bedroom door to be certain that it was shut and held his mouth closer to the receiver, lowering his voice. "I think *they* took it."

"Who is they?"

"The cat and bird, that's who."

Laughter came from her end of the line. "Are you listening to yourself? Do you know how crazy that sounds?"

"They are devious, I tell you; I wouldn't put anything past them."

"They're not devious, Stanley, they're too dumb to be devious."

In the living room the cat and parrot nodded at each other; yes, it was true; they were very devious.

"Stanley, let's think about this rationally for a moment. I remember you telling me that there have been break-ins in your building."

"The Professor's apartment was broken into 17 times, but that doesn't really count because the police think it was an inside job."

"The guy broke into his own apartment?"

"No, the police think his dog, Georgette, did it."

"I never heard of anything so absurd."

"In any event, Fiona, nothing was ever taken in those break-ins. That's not the case with me, the camera/ recorder is definitely gone."

"Is anything else missing?"

"No, not that I can see."

"And you think your cat and bird took it?"

"They're not *my* cat and bird; they belong to the owner of the apartment who lives in Singapore."

"Do you have Tenant's Insurance?"

"No, of course I don't have Tenant's Insurance, why on earth would I? Nothing in this place belongs to me except for my clothes and the food in the refrigerator; it all belongs to the owner."

"That's a very strange rental set-up you have there, Stanley."

"Never mind that now, Fiona, I'm in a real bind here. That camera/ recorder costs $17,000 and I have to return it three days or I have to pay for it."

"Boy, I'd say you have a major problem."

"Tell me something I don't know, Fiona, that's why I'm calling you! Of course I have a major problem! I know that all too well!"

"Relax, Stanley, let me think."

Almost a minute passed.

"Stanley, are you still there?"

"Barely, I think I'm slipping into cardiac arrest."

"Don't be such a baby."

"Did you hear me before, I said $17,000, that's a fortune to someone like me."

"The first thing you have to do, Stanley, is to search the entire apartment thoroughly."

"Ok, that makes sense; I can tell them I'm doing a Spring cleaning."

"Tell who?"

"The cat and the parrot."

Stanley, stop it, they're animals."

"You don't know them like I do."

"All right, have it your way."

"But what happens if I can't find the camera?"

"Cross that bridge when you come to it, Stanley."

"I want to cross it now, Fiona, because I know it's going to be there staring me in the face after I finish cleaning and don't find the camera."

"Then the best thing you can do is to be extra kind to the cat and bird."

"What the hell do you mean by that?"

"Feed them their favorite foods, pay more attention to them, play with them, speak baby-talk to them."

Stanley was shouting now. "You're saying I should kiss ass! I won't do that, Fiona, I'll never do that, never in a million years!"

"You said so yourself, Stanley, $17,000 is a whole lot of money."

Ten minutes later when Stanley slunk back into the living room the cat and parrot were still resting on the armrests watching a couple do the tango. Stanley sat down on the couch in his usual spot; crossed his legs one way, then the other; cleared his throat; rubbed his neck; ran a hand through his hair; squeezed his nose; took a deep breath and finally forced a smile towards the parrot. "Does Polly want a cracker?"

The next day Stanley used a duster and a damp sponge to clean every nook and cranny in the loft apartment. Three hours later, exhausted and defeated, he slumped in despair on the couch. He was now certain that the camera/recorder had been somehow spirited out of the apartment by a thief. The cat and parrot were staring at him and this made him feel guilty and ashamed.

"I owe you two guys an apology; I hid a camera/ recorder on that shelf over there so I could spy on you. I was sure that you could talk, parrot, and that you were some kind of mastermind, cat." He laughed a little too loud and too long as though he was finally losing his mind.

The cat and parrot continued to stare at him.

"I think I'm cracking up. Maybe that vet was right; maybe I do need to see a shrink. There is definitely something wrong with me, I can feel it. Some days I'm so hyper that I think I'm having heart palpitations; I get the sweats and my hands shake. Other days I'm so listless that I can barely get out of bed in the morning, and when I do I'm mean to people, I blow them off, even those people that I like. That's probably why I have so few friends, that along with the fact that I have zero personality and no sense of humor. I don't know how to network socially; it explains why I'm not a more successful choreographer, it's a people business and I'm not a people person. I'm no Balanchine or Robbins, that's for damn sure."

The parrot made a sad cooing sound that no human being in New York ever heard before.

"I didn't used to be a misfit, when I was young I was a happy-go-lucky kid and I was funny, people liked me, I had plenty of friends. But somewhere along the line a bad thing happened, that funny kid got lost or smothered and I took his place. Stan became Stanley, a lonely and bitter man, envious of others who are popular and lead interesting lives."

He reached over and petted the cat for the first time since he moved into the apartment two years earlier. "That's why I was always yelling at you, cat, I was jealous of all those friends you have at the bar. To you I owe the biggest apology of all, I'm truly sorry and ashamed of my actions. If I could take back the last two years and make amends, I'd gladly do it, I'd do it in a second. "

The ORACLE blinked at him three times.

Stanley's eyes widened to saucer size and he clutched his throat, gasping for breath "I ... I don't believe it ...that can't be true."

"It's true enough," the parrot said, "I *can* talk, the ORACLE *is* a mastermind, and we *are* very devious."

"What?"

"And I *do* smoke cigarettes, but only one a day, I'm not a chain-smoker."

Stanley slapped himself hard across the face. "I must be having a dream, I need to wake up."

"From now on, Stanley, we are going to call you Stan, the name you had as a child. If you're going to change your image, you'll have to change your name back to when you were a happy and gregarious person."

"That makes sense in a nonsensical kind of way," he said feebly, still dazed but slowly coming around.

"Next, you'll need to lighten up your personal appearance; shave those long sideburns off and stop wearing all those black, grungy clothes. Green is the new black, Stan, the whole world is going green."

"Uh-huh."

"As to your camera/ recorder, the Professor has it in his apartment, Stan, although he dresses like a woman now and calls himself Rosa Santiago."

"Huh?"

"You can pick it up tomorrow and return it to that leasing company."

"Thank you, I am so relieved."

"And by the way, our neighbor, Lenny, is no longer known as Lenny, he calls himself Lee Bugaloo now, and he wears an eye-patch because the Mafia may be out to kill him."

"The Mafia!"

"Yes. In fact, the Mafia may be after all of us because Merle told 'Vinnie Shots' what Lenny said about him. The guy is apparently a psycho, so each of us could be murdered in our beds while we sleep, and incidentally, that includes you too, Stan, since you live in this apartment and are thus guilty by association."

His face contorted in disbelief. "Me, I could be murdered in my bed?"

"Yes, Stan, I know it must come as a great shock," the parrot said, "ten minutes ago you were worried sick about a lousy $17,000 camera, now you've got something much bigger to worry about."

"My God!"

"Life is strange, Stan, and the occupants of this building are a bit strange too; don't you think so?"

━━━━━━━━━━━━━━━

The next afternoon Leonard slipped into the top floor apartment from the fire escape through the partially opened window and silently made his way to the middle of the living room.

Stan looked up from reading the paper. "Leonard, don't sneak up on people like that, it's very nerve wracking."

The iguana flicked his tongue ten inches into the air and snatched a fly that was buzzing around the room.

"Yes, Leonard, you're a very impressive reptile," the parrot said, "Lenny is fortunate to have you as his pet."

Leonard was about a foot and a half long and had scaly green skin, a short, thick neck, a third eye on the top of his head, and a row of spines running down his back to his long tail. There were five toes on each of his four limbs and he was an excellent climber and sprinter.

"I prefer to be called an iguana," Leonard said, "not a reptile or a lizard, if you please."

"My mistake," Stan replied, "it won't happen again."

Leonard looked at the parrot. "And I'm not Lenny's pet; I prefer to be described as his confidante."

The parrot shrieked. "How is poor Lenny bearing up under all the strain?"

"Not well," Leonard said disgustedly, "he's so uptight that I had to leave the apartment for a while to protect my own nerves. He never turns the lights on anymore and all he does is peak out the window to look for strangers on Stone Street. I can't even watch TV at night because he's afraid that it gives off too much light and people will know that he's holed up in the apartment. And he won't cook any real food anymore because he's afraid the aroma will give his presence away."

"That doesn't sound good."

"No, it isn't and …" The iguana paused in mid-sentence as his acute sense of hearing detected a sound beyond the closed front door. "There is someone in the hall, he's trying to be quiet but I can still hear him."

Then they heard a faintish scratching at the door.

Stan walked over to it. "Yes, who's there?"

The voice was equally faint. "It's me, Lee Bugaloo."

"I don't know any Lee Bugaloo."

"That's Lenny," the iguana said, "you had better let him in."

Lenny manually wheeled his chair into the apartment before the door was fully opened and immediately went to the window where he carefully parted the curtains. "The gangsters are finally here, I just spotted them."

The parrot, Stan, and the iguana rushed to the other window and carefully peered down at Stone Street.

"See that guy, the one with the sunglasses in the dark suit with the black shirt and the white skinny tie over by the entrance to that deli across the street; he's one of them."

"He certainly doesn't look like a Wall Street investment banker or trader to me," the parrot said, "he sticks out like a sore thumb in this neighborhood."

"There's another one sipping a beer at a table in front of our building."

Sure enough, another swarthy man in sunglasses, a dark suit, black shirt, and skinny white tie was sitting there, taking notice of the people who went in and out of Ulysses.

"The third guy is hiding in the doorway of that small bank building near Hanover Square. He remains hidden most of the time but sticks his head out every minute or so to check the street."

They all stared at the doorway for what must have been thirty seconds until a man in sunglasses, a dark suit, black shirt and skinny white tie suddenly popped his head out to look around and then quickly pulled it back."

"I wonder why gangsters all dress like that," the parrot said, "it is such a stereotype."

"They're casing the street," Lenny said, "the next thing you know, they'll be kicking my door down and dragging me out by my hair."

"No, there are too many people on the street now for them to do that," Stan said, "they'd be afraid that somebody would call the police."

The lunch hour passed and only a few people were to be seen on

Stone Street. All three men were sitting at the same table now; they seemed to be communicating in grunts and hand gestures.

"I'm gonna be swimming with the fishes soon," Lenny said, "please take care of Leonard for me after I'm gone."

The iguana rushed over to where Lenny was sitting in his wheelchair and wrapped himself tightly around his left leg. "If they take you, Lenny, they'll have to take me too."

Lenny tickled the spikes on the iguana's head. "You're such a dear boy, Leonard, I'm gonna miss you."

Stan's eyes welled up at the plight of the two buddies.

"Where's O?" Lenny asked, "I'd like to collect on that guaranty he made of my $1500 loan to Merle before her boyfriend kills me. It don't seem fair that I'm going to lose both my life and my money because of her."

"I don't know," the parrot answered, "he disappeared without telling me where he was going."

"Maybe 'Vinnie Shots' has got him."

The parrot, puffing up the feathers on his chest, boldly walked out the open window and perched conspicuously on the top edge of the fire escape so he would be clearly visible to anyone on the street below.

"Hey!" the iguana said, "they'll see you out there."

"That's the general idea, Leonard, I'm not hiding out like a coward anymore. I'm a parrot with a courageous heart."

Stan clenched his jaw, opened the window fully, and joined the parrot on the fire escape; the iguana followed close behind. Lenny tried to poke his own head out the window but the best he could do was get his nose over the windowsill.

They looked down at the three men and were surprised to see the ORACLE was now sitting with them and drinking a Bud Light.

The cat looked up at them and blinked three times.

"My word," the parrot said, "those guys aren't gangsters; they're actors in a *Law & Order* episode that is being filmed a block away."

"Actors!!!"

"And look, here comes Merle, she's back, she's entering the building."

Merle sashayed into the living room, made herself comfortable on the sofa, and faced her anxious audience -- the cat, parrot, Stan, the iguana and Lenny. She was wearing a chic but sensible red dress and much less makeup than when they last saw her. Her skirt was modestly tucked down below her knee and her bosom was completely covered so that she displayed no cleavage whatsoever. All in all, she looked like an attractive, prim and proper, confident businesswoman.

"Merle, we were worried about you," Lenny said, "we thought you might be dead; or worse, that you ran off and married 'Vinnie Shots'."

"I'm sorry for all the trouble I've caused. After I stormed out of this apartment three days ago, I took a hard look at myself in the mirror and I didn't like the person looking back at me."

"You didn't?"

"No, I discovered that I don't look like me anymore; sure, I'm getting older and I've gained a few pounds; well, to be honest, more than a few pounds; but that's not what I mean; I mean I don't like to look at myself because I see all the chances I missed in life; all the time I've wasted; all the promises I made to myself that I never kept; and it hurts."

"Uh-huh."

"And there's something else about me that you all should know; I can't stand pain; which is another one of my personal problems, because you can use pain to change your life; which I never did, and probably never will, if you catch my drift."

All eleven eyes, including the iguana's three eyes, were focused on her. So far, none of them could see what she was driving at.

"Anyways, to make a long story short, I came to realize that there could be no future for me with 'Vinnie Shots'. It was all a fantasy on my part; you see; I'm also fantasy prone; that's another personal problem I have."

Stan glanced at the cat, iguana, and parrot and wondered if he was living a fantasy.

"So I broke it off with 'Vinnie Shots', we're not going steady any longer."

"Weren't you scared that he'd ring your neck and pluck out your eyes if you dumped him?" Lenny asked.

She nodded. "I was a little concerned about that so I had my fifth cousin on my father's side call his Godfather to square things. There's no problem, in fact, 'Vinnie Shots' has already got himself a new girlfriend. Her name is Tiffany; she's a dental hygienist in the Bronx."

"Wow, Merle, your fifth cousin must be a powerful person; who is he?"

Merle lowered her head. "I have another confession to make, my name isn't Merle Pushkin; that's the stage name I adopted when I was young and in my belly dancing phase. My real name is Mariska Tatiana Alexandra Anastasia Putin."

"Putin!" Stan gaped, are you by any chance related to Vladimir Vladimirovich Putin, the President of Russia and a former spymaster in the KGB?"

She nodded again. "Vlad and I used to play spy games when we were kids. I was always the CIA agent he captured and tortured for information."

"I'll be a monkey's uncle," said the parrot.

"Did you tell 'Vinnie Shots' all the bad things I said about him?" Lenny asked.

"No, I never did."

"Holy mackerel, Merle, and here I was frightened out of my wits for the last three days. It was all for nothing; I was never in any real danger."

"I'm sorry, Lenny."

"It just goes to show you," Stan said, "our worst enemy can oftentimes be our own imaginations. This should be a lesson to us all."

Everyone in the room nodded in agreement.

"That's a fact," the parrot said, "what appears to be obvious is not always true; and what is not true is not always obvious; what is false is sometimes obvious; and what is not obvious is sometimes false. So I ask you all, where does that leave us?"

Lenny, the iguana and Stan had no idea. The cat yawned.

Merle looked at her watch and stood up to leave. "I must be going, I have a heavy date and I have to apologize to Rocco for deserting him."

"A date!" Lenny said, "what's this new guy of yours do for a living? He's not another gangster, is he?"

"No, his name is Floyd O'Donnell and he's a beautician."

"Where did you meet him?"

"I met him at the beauty salon that I went to for my makeover. That's where I was for the last three days; they rent rooms for difficult cases."

"Floyd is a cool moniker," Lenny said, "the next time I take an alias I'm going to call myself Floyd."

"Floyd is actually changing his name because he wants to be a teacher."

"Why does he gotta change his name to be a teacher for?"

"He wants to become a guru, which means teacher in Sanskrit." She took a piece of paper from her pocket. "His new name is going to be Swami Chakra Shankara Ramana Maharshi. And I'm going to be his first pupil."

━━━━━━━━━━━━━

Stan went with the cat into Ulysses later that evening and followed the ORACLE to the rear of the bar. He had shaved off his long sideburns and was wearing a spinach green sports shirt, beige slacks and penny loafers. With his new preppy look he blended easily into the downtown crowd and could pass for a Wall Streeter provided he kept his mouth shut and his opinions to himself.

The excitement of financial panic gripped the barroom. Ulysses was abuzz with loud talk about the collapse of Bear Stearns and Washington Mutual, the bankruptcy of Lehman Brothers and the takeovers of Freddie Mac, Fannie Mae, and AIG by the U.S. Government. Rumors were running rampant about which bank or broker would be the next to fail. More than a few patrons looked to be shell-shocked after losing large amounts of money for their customers as well as for their own accounts in the past few days. Others were saying that this was the end for Wall Street and that the U.S. would shortly lose its hegemony as a superpower in international finance to the City of London.

All of the TVs were tuned to CNBC Business News. Reporters were interviewing a panel of finance experts about the $700 Billion bailout of Wall Street by the Government using taxpayer money. Many in the bar expressed hope that the Treasury would inject the funds into the banking system quickly before the credit markets shut down completely. Most of the older drinkers seemed to think that a bailout wouldn't work and that the country was headed into a very severe recession like we had in 1981-82. A few talked openly of another Great Depression like the 1930s.

The scene on the TV screen then shifted to the front of the New York Stock Exchange building where a picket line marched on Broad Street holding up signs while being closely observed by a phalanx of heavily armed police.

**GREED KILLS WALL STREET
DOOMSDAY IS HERE
THE END OF CAPITALISM
HANG'EM HIGH
NATIONALIZE THE BANKS
DEATH TO SWINDLERS
AMERICA IS SOCIALIST NOW**

The ORACLE had lived through many financial crises in the past and he knew that the most important thing for people to do was not to panic; the person who keeps his cool will come out whole in the end. Those investors who cut and run generally end up selling their stock at precisely the worst time and at the lowest prices, ensuring themselves of large losses. If he had his druthers, the cat would have enjoyed listening to the many conversations taking place around him but he was on a different mission tonight. So instead, he jumped up on the table where Bobby Rankle was sitting alone drinking a beer.

"Hey there, buddy," Bobby said, and rubbed his ears, noticing that the cat had brought him a visitor.

"Hello, I'm Stan Kane, the cat lives with me upstairs. He wanted me to come down to Ulysses with him tonight and meet some of his friends."

"Hi, I'm Bobby Rankle, please pull up a chair."

"Thanks, I will."

A chorus of boos suddenly erupted in the barroom as the Secretary of the Treasury and the Chairman of the Federal Reserve appeared on television.

"Do you work on Wall Street, Bobby?"

"Yes, I'm a stockbroker."

"I confess that I don't know much about Wall Street," Stan said, "but I can almost taste the doom and gloom in this place."

Bobby nodded gravely. "We are living in very perilous times, Stan, it has all the makings of a perfect storm."

"I tried watching some of those business shows to learn more about what the problem is but I couldn't understand what they were talking about most of the time. Sub-prime mortgage loans going bad, now that I can understand, but that stuff about derivatives and credit default swaps is way beyond me."

"You put your finger on the crux of the problem, Stan, it turns out that the Masters of the Universe on Wall Street didn't understand them either."

"I heard one regulator complain that the people who opposed Government regulation of the market when times were booming are the very same people who now want the Government to bail them out when times are bad."

"That's true."

Stan chuckled. "This guy phrased it eloquently, he said that these people are capitalists on the way up and socialists on the way down. I thought that was well put."

Bobby smiled. "I'll have to remember that one."

The ORACLE hissed at those people, he was a free-market capitalist -- first, last, and always.

Behind them, a tipsy tourist from Seattle at the bar yelled, "Don't worry, folks, be happy, it's gonna be all right, Butch Harris promises you; and you can take that to the bank."

A trader who had lost $ 6.5 million earlier in the day became so infuriated by the alcohol-fueled remark that he had to be physically restrained by his drinking buddies from punching the visitor in the mouth.

"Things are getting ugly," Stan said, looking up at a TV screen that now showed the picketers in an altercation with police outside the NYSE. A commentator reported that they were the victims of another giant Ponzi swindle that had unraveled as stock prices nose-dived; cheated out of all their savings. Many were openly distraught and appeared to be elderly, in their seventies and eighties, well-to-do last week and suddenly penniless this week.

"I'm afraid we ain't seen nothing yet, Stan, this is only the tip of the iceberg."

"Bobby, let me ask you, as a financial guy are you in favor of the taxpayers bailing out Wall Street?"

"No, I think the banks and insurance companies have to be held accountable for their recklessness. In my book, nobody is too big to fail."

"I agree with you. If the little guy fails, the Government isn't going to toss him a lifeline. And it's not only Wall Street that's looking to be bailed out, now the auto companies, their parts suppliers, the regional banks, real estate firms, and even ordinary people delinquent on their prime mortgages and credit cards all got their hands out."

"I know, Stan, and it doesn't stop there, many of the states like California, Ohio, Michigan and Massachusetts are in danger of going bankrupt too, they don't have the cash to meet their payrolls or pay any more unemployment benefits."

"Where is it all going to end, Bobby, I mean, can the Federal Government afford to bail everybody out?"

"Intelligent question, Stan, I wish I had an intelligent answer."

"The Government is already straining to support Medicare and Social Security. These entitlement payments are going to skyrocket as the baby boomers retire over the next few years."

"Yes, that's a hard fact."

Stan watched the screen as some demonstrators were handcuffed and led into police vans. "Am I going to have health insurance and an income when it comes time for me to retire twenty-five years from now?"

"That's another good question I can't answer."

The ORACLE knew the answers to both of these questions; however, he also realized that people wouldn't like the answers if he told them.

"And who is going to pay for all this?"

"Now that's a question I do know the answer to, Stan, your kids and your grandkids will get stuck with the bill. Their tax rates will be astronomical by today's standards."

"The country needs to get back to traditional values, Bobby, that's what we need to do."

"I agree; the era of conspicuous consumption is over. You're not going to be seeing any more people renting out Yankee Stadium for *bar mitzvahs* or hosting birthday parties for ten thousand of their closest friends at Madison Square Garden. Those days are gone."

"How bad is New York City going to get hurt?"

Bobby grimaced. "There's bound to be a ton of layoffs here in the Financial District, probably a hundred thousand or even much more."

"My God! What are all those people going to do?"

"They're going to have to reinvent themselves because Wall Street, as we know it, will never be the same again. Most of those lost jobs are gone forever."

"And they were well-paying jobs, Bobby, you're not talking flipping burgers for minimum wage work."

"Correct. And it gets worse; the shortfall feeds on itself. The amount of money the city collects in taxes will decline dramatically because so many banks and investment firms have taken horrific losses; that means they won't be paying taxes again for years to come."

"I see."

"City coffers will be bare; services will be cut back sharply and the infrastructure will deteriorate due to lack of maintenance and new construction."

"Hmmm."

"We are all going to be waiting much longer for subways and buses in the future; our garbage isn't going to be picked up as often; we're not going to be seeing as many cops or firemen; hospitals will be swamped with indigent patients; the numbers of homeless will rise precipitously; the prisons will be overflowing and the court system will be clogged. New York could have another budget crisis much worse than it had back in the mid 1970s when the city almost went bankrupt."

"That's an ugly scenario to contemplate."

"And there's the ripple effect to consider. Many of the surrounding suburban towns like Darien, Ridgewood, and Oyster Bay are going to also get hurt badly because so many of their residents work down here."

"I forgot about the commuters."

"My firm will probably have to lay off brokers. We're a small shop, the employees are like family; it will be gut-wrenching."

"Do you see any bright spots in all this bad news, Bobby?"

"Church attendance will rise, people always pray more when they're frightened."

"Anything else?"

"Liquor and beer sales will jump; people will also smoke more."

Stan smiled weakly. "Maybe I should buy stock in companies like Coors and Philip Morris. What do you think?"

"Take my advice and keep your money in the bank where it's insured by the FDIC. Now is not the time for amateurs to be dabbling in the stock market, Stan, you need to lay low and preserve your cash so you can make some great buys when the economy starts growing again."

"You're older than your years, Bobby, how does such a young man like yourself know so much?"

He shrugged. "I've been hanging around my dad's brokerage firm since I was six years old after my mom died. You learn a lot about the market and about human nature as the Dow zigs and zags all over the place and people earn or lose serious money."

"I don't doubt it."

Jill, a pretty, savvy brunette bartender stopped by the table and petted the cat. "Will it be the usual, handsome, a Bud Light in a bowl?"

"Meow."

"And what will you have, sir?"

"I'll have a ginger ale," Stan said.

"Be back in a minute, guys."

"I'm surprised you're not a beer drinker, Stan, I figured that's where the little fella learned to drink beer."

"No, he didn't learn it from me. For many years I was a dancer. Dancing is a very stressful profession and requires great strength and coordination. So I was on a strict diet -- no alcohol, no red meat, and no junk food. I lived by the rule: *If something tasted good in my mouth, I had to spit it out.*"

"No kidding, Stan, you were a professional dancer?"

"Yes, I received my formal training in Ballet and Modern Dance at NYU's Tisch School of the Arts. I danced in a number of Broadway musicals and also in Las Vegas, Miami and in Europe. Now I'm a choreographer; mostly freelance."

Jill brought the bowl of beer and the ginger ale.

The cat began to lick up the beer as the three of them watched.

"Jill," Bobby said, "Stan, here, is a also a dancer and choreographer."

"No kidding."

"Yes, he danced on Broadway." He turned to Stan. "Jill works with a dance troupe in Brooklyn, in fact, she's just back from a tour in Italy."

"I'm happy to meet you," Stan said, "where are you dancing now?"

"I'm not, I hurt my foot while jogging at the beach. The doctor tells me that I won't be able to dance again for another six months or so."

"Oh, that's a shame, I know how that feels. I've had my share of bruises and fractures over the years; it's an occupational hazard."

"It is, but it's worth it. I can't think of myself doing anything else in my life."

"I can hear the commitment in your voice."

"Well, I have to run, it was interesting meeting you, Stan."

"Yes, Jill, me too, I'll see you around."

The ORACLE finished off the beer and licked his paws. "I shouldn't be drinking beer," Bobby said, "as I do some dancing myself."

"Wow, so many dancers in one establishment; Ulysses must be putting something in the water."

"I really wanted to study dance but I ended up at Tufts University in Boston instead and studied business administration. My dad graduated from there and so did my grandfather. I'm not complaining; it's a great school; I even danced in a few college shows. But it's not what I would have picked for myself if it had been my choice."

"So you're a stock broker now."

"Yes, I work for my dad, he has plans for me to take over the firm one day."

"Have you always done what your dad wants?"

"More often than not. He's the greatest dad a guy could have; he loves me and has always done what's best for me."

"There is nothing wrong with having dreams of your own, Bobby, maybe you're old enough now to know what is best for you."

"I understand that; I intend to talk to him about it when the time is right."

"When do you think that might be?"

"Soon, very soon," he said unconvincingly.

"You mentioned that you were doing some dancing earlier."

"I am, it's nothing like Broadway, you understand, just some off-off-off Broadway venues and a few clubs in the East Village."

"Really, well, I'll have to come see you dance one night."

"I'd like that, Stan, I'd really like that."

"As a choreographer, I'm always on the lookout for new talent."

The young man fidgeted with the label of his beer bottle and then furtively glanced around the bar to make sure that other patrons wouldn't be able to hear what he was about to divulge. "I …I don't dance under my own name because …because I'm gay … and my dad doesn't know that I am."

"I see, that must be very difficult for you."

Bobby nodded and looked away quickly. "My dad is an ex-marine and a military buff. I think he's the only guy on Wall Street who is a member of the National Rifle Association. You wouldn't believe the large gun collection he has up in our summer house in New Hampshire."

"Guns scare me," Stan said.

"They scare me too but I forced myself to learn to shoot because I knew it would please him."

"I don't happen to be gay, myself," Stan said, "although many dancers assume that I am. That's because I'd estimate that nine out of ten guys in my business are. I don't know why that's the way it is, but it is."

"It would shatter my dad if he ever found out about me."

"Don't underestimate him, Bobby, he might surprise you."

"Maybe."

"I think you need to do a little soul-searching."

"I do."

Jill came by and saw that the cat's bowl was empty. "Two more Bud Lights, Bobby?"

He handed her his empty beer bottle. "No, Jill, just bring one for the cat. I'll have a Diet Coke this time around."

Stan smiled approvingly at him.

Bobby slapped his stomach. "I'm a little heavier than I want to be; I'll need to get in better shape if you're going to come see me dance."

━━━━━━━━━━━━━━━

The next evening Stan returned to the bar, this time with the parrot sitting proudly on his shoulder. His eyes panned the faces of the many customers until he located the individual that he had been sent there to talk to. Al Hanratty was sitting quietly by himself, nursing a brandy, and occasionally looking up disinterestedly at one of the many TVs in the bar that were all tuned to a Yankee game. Ulysses seemed much quieter than it had been the night before.

Stan sat down on the empty stool next to him. Jerry, a cheerful, talkative young bartender from Ireland who had quickly transformed himself into a dyed-in-the-wool New Yorker, immediately approached him. "What can I get for you and your fine feathered friend tonight?"

"I'll have a ginger ale and the parrot will have some peanuts."

"Good choice, I'm thinking."

The parrot turned his head in Al's direction. "Hello, sir."

"Why, hello," the elderly man responded, "you can speak, I see."

"I can whistle too." The parrot produced a wolf whistle, so loud that all the men at the bar turned to see which beautiful babe merited such attention.

"I must warn you that he is quite a talker," Stan said, "some days you can't shut him up."

Jerry arrived with the soft drink and the peanuts in a saucer. "Here we are, enjoy."

Stan cracked the shell of the largest peanut and the parrot plucked it out of the palm of his hand with his beak.

"How old is the bird?" Al asked.

"I am informed that he is 76," Stan said, telling a white lie.

Al was stunned. "I'm 76 years old."

"Really. Now that's some coincidence, isn't it?"

"Let me introduce myself, I'm Al Hanratty."

"Hey, Al, I'm Stan Kane; I rent an apartment upstairs in this building."

"I didn't know that parrots could live that long."

"They can live to be a 100 years old if properly taken care of."

"That's another coincidence, Stan, my doctor told me the other day that I could live to be a 100."

"That's great."

The older man made a sour face. "Is it?"

"You don't look too happy about that, Al."

"Frankly, I'm not."

"How come?"

Al swirled the brandy in his glass. "My family is all dead and my pals are all gone too. My cell phone never rings anymore unless it's a wrong number and the only correspondence I get these days is bills and junk mail. Except for the few people I talk to in Ulysses some evenings, I'm basically alone all the time."

"I see."

"I think there comes a point when people have lived long enough, Stan, a point when they have outlived their usefulness and it's time for them to make a graceful exit. The world is getting too crowded; resources are stretched too thin; too many old people like me have overstayed their welcome."

"Older people have collected much wisdom over their years, Al, that they can pass on to younger generations."

"I have nothing to contribute and nothing to say. And to be brutally honest, I'm tired of life. Death would be an answer to a number of problems."

"Maybe you are just bored, Al."

He shrugged his frail shoulders.

"My grandfather used to say that you're not old unless you think you are."

"I'm thinking your grandfather didn't look in the mirror very often."

"He also told me that you have to work very hard not to be old."

"In my experience, Stan, the older you get, the less you care."

The ORACLE and Rocco sat high in the bar's rafters above the two men. Rocco read their lips and repeated the conversation word for word to the cat.

"Do you fear death, Al?"

"Believe me, Stan, I am not afraid of dying; I'd even welcome it at this stage."

The ORACLE knew that Al was going to get his wish much sooner than he had been led to believe by his physician.

Stan ate a peanut. "I've heard it said that some people are in love with death."

Al shook his head. "I'm not one of them; it's just that there comes a time when enough is enough."

"I see."

"And the older you get, Stan, the more you think about death."

"I had a near-death experience as a kid."

"Tell me about it."

"My parents rushed me to the hospital for an emergency appendectomy and my heart stopped beating while I was on the operating table. They told me that I was technically dead for almost a minute. The doctors had to resuscitate me."

Al looked up at the TV. "What was it like being dead?"

"Are you asking if I saw bright lights, angels, deceased relatives, that kind of thing?"

"Yes."

Stan shook his head. "No, there was nothing."

"I didn't think so."

"On that depressing note, Al, I think we need some cheering up." Stan caught the attention of the bartender. "Another ginger ale for me, Jerry, and bring Al another of whatever he is drinking."

"Coming up."

"Thank you, Stan, I appreciate it."

"Don't mention it."

"You know, I don't recall seeing you in Ulysses before."

"That's because I've only been in here once. But I think I'll start coming in more often in the future. I don't have very many friends myself, Al, and this place seems to attract an interesting crowd."

"It does. Ulysses has a subtle ambience, whoever designed the lighting system did a masterful job. We all look much better in here than we do out on the street in the stark sunlight, even old farts like me. That's because the cones of light from the overhead lamps make it harder to see the wrinkles, blemishes and scars."

Stan laughed.

"Boy meets girl, that's what places like this are mostly about."

"Agreed."

"I enjoy being around young people, Stan, they allow me forget how ancient I am; and I like to eavesdrop and listen to what they think and do. I can tell you one thing, it's a very different world today than the one I grew up in."

"Is that a good thing?"

"Yes, by and large, I think it is."

"Would you like to be young again, Al?"

The elderly man creased his brow and stared at the liver colored age spots on his hands. "Yes, I'd love to be a young man again. And I'd do things much differently in my life, I can tell you that."

The fresh drinks arrived.

"A toast," Stan said, "to better times ahead." They clicked glasses.

"So what kind of work did you do before you retired, Al?"

"I used to be an …"

The parrot suddenly began to sing.

I'm a rambler; I'm a gambler
And a long way from home
And if you don't like it
Just leave me alone
I eat when I'm hungry
And I drink when I'm dry
And if whisky don't kill me
I'll drink till I die

The patrons around them clapped loudly and the parrot shrieked at receiving all the applause.

Stan rubbed his beak. "I wasn't talking to you, silly."

Al laughed heartily. "He's a real character, isn't he?"

"You don't know the half of it; he can curse like a trooper when he doesn't get his way. And most of the tunes he sings are so bawdy they'd make a nun blush."

"Did you teach him all that?"

"No, I think he picked it up from soldiers of the French Foreign Legion. I'm told that one of his previous owners ran a bordello in France."

"No kidding."

The parrot jumped from Stan's shoulder to the bar, then walked up the elderly man's arm and perched on his shoulder.

"I think he likes you, Al."

Al tried not to show how pleased he was but couldn't quite pull it off; his eyes gleamed and he smiled from ear to ear.

The parrot shrieked; Al laughed; Stan looked pleased with himself.

"Hey!" a customer cried out, "Al's got himself a new drinking buddy."

Al stroked the bird's chest. "Us old-timers need to stick together."

After a few minutes the bird walked down Al's arm and pecked at the peanuts in the saucer.

"Did you ever have any pets when you were a child, Al?"

"No, my father was allergic."

"You were going to tell me what kind of work you did."

"After I came back from Korea, I worked as an accountant."

"What were you like as a young man?"

He squeezed his eyes and his mind traveled back almost six decades. "I was average, I guess; no great student or athlete, nothing like that. Come to think of it, I have only a single photograph of me when I was very young. It was taken when I graduated from Manhattan College in 1953. The remainder of the family photos were destroyed by a fire that later broke out in my parents' apartment in the Bronx. Fortunately, none of us was hurt but all our possessions burned up. I don't even have a picture of my mother and father. As the years go, by their faces become fuzzier and fuzzier."

"That's a shame."

"It's strange that I should remember this now, but, whenever I looked at myself in those old family photos, I was never the person I saw myself as being."

"Yeah, Al, I hear you, my kid photos never captured the person I believed myself to be either."

"Still, they say the camera doesn't lie."

"I guess we deceive ourselves."

"Probably."

"You never married, Al?"

"No, I came very close once though, her name was Maureen Ryan. It wasn't her fault; she was a wonderful woman. I suppose I wasn't ready to raise a family. Eventually she got tired of waiting and married someone else; they had five children together."

"That's a lovely family."

"I kept track of her over the years, from a discrete distance. I don't know why I did, but I did."

"I see."

His face became pained. "That's a lie, Stan, I never stopped loving her, that's the real reason."

"So you regret not marrying her."

He nodded. "I really do, it was the worst decision I ever made in my life. I don't know what I was thinking at the time, I must have been brain dead. That's the only explanation I have."

"Is she still alive?"

"No, Maureen died eight years ago and I went to her funeral. All her children and their families were there in the church. Looking at them from a back pew, I couldn't help but think that those children and grandchildren could have been mine. As it is, when I die, my branch of the family tree will die with me. And there won't be anyone to mourn me when I go, that's a fact."

"I take it that not marrying her was one of the things in your life that you would do differently."

"If I could live my life all over again, I'd get down on my knees in the middle of Times Square during a tsunami and beg Maureen to marry me."

"All of us make mistakes that we wish we could take back, Al, you're not alone in that regard."

"I guess."

"Tell me," Stan asked, "did you always want to be an accountant?"

He smiled and shook his head. "No, you'll laugh if I told you what I really wanted to do."

"I promise I won't."

Al moved the brandy glass in circles on the wooden bar and blew out his breath. "Well, I wanted to be an artist, a painter; my art teacher in high school told me I had real talent."

"That's a far cry from being a number cruncher."

"I know it, and that's the second thing I'd do differently. But at the time I didn't have the *chutzpah* to become a struggling artist. After earning next to nothing in the service for three years, the attraction of having a decent job with a steady paycheck was too hard to resist."

"I completely understand."

"What's your line of work, Stan?"

"I'm a choreographer now; I was a professional dancer for many years."

"Dancing is something creative, Stan, that's worthwhile. It sure beats pushing papers for a living."

"Do you still have any of your old paintings, Al?"

"A few that I did after the fire."

"I'd like to see them."

"You would?"

"Yes."

He thought about it for a few seconds. "Ok, I'll bring them in one of these days."

"Fine, I look forward to seeing them."

Al smiled at the bird. "I'd also be curious to find out what the parrot thinks of them."

The bird looked up from eating the peanuts and shrieked.

The next night Lenny and the green iguana sped into Ulysses, the lizard sitting defiantly on his lap, and they parked the wheelchair next to where Seth Reich was incessantly stirring another scotch & soda with a swizzle stick.

The bar manager, Mike, approached warily, eying the lizard's large, sharp teeth. As a former resident of tropical climes he was well aware of how dangerous these creatures could be if provoked.

"I'll have a double tequila martini with olives and limes," Lenny said, "but hold the tequila because I'm driving." He spun the wheelchair in a tight circle to demonstrate his driving prowess.

"What will *it* have?" Mike asked, nodding at the lizard.

"*It* is an iguana and he is partial to ice water with a dash of lemon."

"If you say so."

Leonard climbed up onto the bar and sniffed Seth's drink.

"Don't worry," Lenny said, "Leonard doesn't imbibe alcohol; he only wants a whiff to clean out his sinuses."

"He's a large iguana."

"Yeah, he's a big boy; a burglar is in for a nasty surprise if he tries to rob my apartment. Once Leonard sinks those teeth into you, you're a goner."

"I believe it."

"I'm Lenny; a pleasure to meet you."

"Hello, Lenny, I'm Seth."

Leonard flicked his tongue ten inches into the air and zapped a fruit fly fluttering over the beer taps.

"Now that was impressive," Seth said admiringly.

"Yeah, there are no flies or insects of any kind in my place, thanks to Leonard."

"How old is he?"

"I'll be damned if I know. I've had him ten years, ever since I ended up in this chair." He rapped the rail of the wheelchair with a knuckle.

"What happened to you, an accident of some kind?"

Lenny pinched his lip. "Nah, no accident," he lied.

The bar manager brought the two drinks and the iguana started knocking the ice cubes around with his tongue.

"Sorry, I didn't mean to pry, " Seth said, "forget I asked."

"It's ok, I don't mind telling you. It happened when I was a tobacco-chewing commodities trader."

"No kidding, it's a small world, I'm a currency trader."

"You don't say?"

"Yes, it's true. "

"Well, I don't know that much about currencies, but, I can tell you that trading commodities is a very risky business. You never know when the military in some underdeveloped country is going to stage a coup or whether it's going to rain too much or to little in the grain fields of Iowa or Australia. Prices can soar into the stratosphere or drop like a stone in less than an hour. And if you're on the wrong side of the trade, forget about it; you can lose your shirt and get totally wiped out."

Seth thought about his own debacle and nodded soberly. "I know exactly what you mean."

"It's like shooting craps in Las Vegas; it's pure gambling."

"It sure is, Lenny."

"But if you're on the right side of the trade, the sky's the limit, there's no telling how much money you can make. You can get filthy rich in one afternoon. It's a monster adrenaline rush, a higher high than you can get from any drug; you're on top of the world. "

"I know that feeling too, Lenny, I've been there myself."

"Well, kid, one day greed got the better of me and I made a huge bet that crude was going to drop by $10 a barrel based on what some hotshot oil analyst who had recently come back from Saudi Arabia told me. In those days that was a huge price move for oil; it's not like today where oil can fluctuate by that amount in a couple of days. "

"I remember."

"I bet the kitchen sink and the market moved against me; some Islamic terrorist group in the Middle East attacked a refinery and disrupted supplies, oil went through the roof, and I lost big time."

"I'm sorry to hear that."

Lenny shrugged. "Things happen."

"Tell me about it," Seth said, his own bitter experience forefront in his mind.

"I lost all my own dough and a large chunk of a major customer's money as well. The guy got very pissed off at me even though I had made him a pile in the past."

"I see."

Lenny moved the wheelchair closer to him and lowered his voice. "The guy got so pissed off, in fact, that as I was walking home a few nights later I took two shots in the back. The shooters left me for dead on the street."

"Oh, my God!"

"One of the bullets damaged my spine and I've been numb from the waist down ever since."

Seth finished his drink in a single gulp. "I never heard of such a thing happening on Wall Street."

"My customer turned out to be an international arms dealer; he was hooked up with very bad people; they'd kill you if you looked at them cross-eyed."

"Did you tell the police who shot you?"

Lenny shook his head. "Nah, because I knew that if I did, the shooters would come back to finish the job. I figured that life in a wheelchair was better than no life at all."

Seth held up his empty glass to the bartender for a re-fill.

"I got myself into a jam, kid, that's what happens when you get overconfident and take crazy risks. Learn from my mistake, don't you ever do what I did."

The currency trader swallowed deeply. "That's great advice, Lenny, however, in my case it comes a little too late; I'm already in a jam and hiding a big loss from my bosses at the bank."

"Tell me what happened, kid."

Seth recounted in detail his massive, unauthorized, shorting of the U.S. dollar; the initial huge profits; the subsequent dollar surge that materialized out of nowhere; his resultant net loss of $22 million."

In the rafters the ORACLE frowned as Rocco repeated what Seth had said. In today's volatile markets the cat knew that a trader needed to take his profits sooner rather than later because profits can turn into losses in a few seconds.

The iguana stopped licking the ice cubes long enough to swivel his three eyes and give Seth a shocked look; then he made a loud whistling sound to underscore the enormity of the loss.

"I don't know why I'm telling all this to a complete stranger," Seth said, "when I haven't told any of my close friends or family. Maybe it's because you were in a similar situation once; because you'd understand what I'm going through; or maybe because my head is going to explode if I didn't tell someone about it."

Lenny propped his chin on a fist. "This is for real, kid, you're not jerking my chain, you actually are left holding the bag for $22 mil?"

Seth's re-fill arrived and he took a swig. "Yes, it's the truth, I wish it wasn't so, but it is."

"Bartender, I think I could use that shot of tequila now."

"Coming up."

"And there's nobody to blame but me," Seth said, "nobody twisted my arm; it was all my own doing; I was always very competitive with my brother. Pride was a large part of it, I think."

"Hmmm."

"In the *Book of Proverbs* it tells us that 'pride goeth before a fall.'"

"Yeah?"

"It was the primeval sin of Satan. And pride also caused the fall of Adam and Eve."

"It sounds like you know your Bible, kid."

"I do."

"Religious, huh."

"Yes, and I have no excuse for my actions, Lenny, I deserve to be severely punished for what I did."

"Hold on a minute, kid, don't be so eager to throw yourself under the bus."

"This thing is eating me up inside."

"You're absolutely sure that nobody else knows about the loss?"

"I'm sure but I don't know how much longer I can keep it a secret. The auditors could find out at any time. Every morning before I go to work I puke my guts out thinking this will be the day they discover the loss and arrest me."

"If I were in your shoes, kid, I'd be scared shitless."

"I am scared out of my wits; I'll be arrested and probably go to jail. That's not what my parents were looking forward to when they sent me to Wharton. They'll be disgraced in front of all the relatives."

"Me, I only got a High School Equivalency Diploma."

"I think I'd gladly trade places with you, Lenny, sitting in that chair doesn't seem so bad in comparison."

"Don't say that, kid, you don't know what you're talking about."

"I'm sorry, I'm not thinking straight these days; I'm not sleeping well at night; eating very little; drinking mostly coffee and booze; I'm a wreck emotionally."

"I can see that."

"The truth is that I was never cut out to be a trader; I should not even be working on Wall Street; it's too rough-and-tumble, I don't do pressure very well; making a lot of money is not something that I daydream about."

"Then you are definitely in the wrong business, kid, Wall Street is all about pressure; the pressure to succeed, the pressure to be King of the Hill, the pressure to have everything now."

"I always wanted to be a chef and open my own restaurant one day, nothing fancy, a friendly family kind of place."

"So why didn't you?"

He shrugged. "Everyone in my family is a professional of one kind or another; lawyers, doctors, bankers, architects, politicians, college professors."

"No chefs, huh?"

"No."

"That's too bad, kid, I think we need more chefs in this country and less lawyers, politicians, and bankers. It was those guys that brought on the Credit Crisis and the sub-prime mortgage mess we're up to our eyeballs in."

"You make a valid point, Lenny."

"I suppose you know that the restaurant business is the riskiest kind of business you can get into; more restaurants fail than any other kind of business."

"I'm aware of that but it doesn't scare me. I can succeed, I know I can."

Lenny folded his arms and pursed his lips. "So, to sum things up in a nutshell, all you have to do in order to live happily ever after is find a way to come up with $ 22 mil. Then you can ditch the banking job with a hoop and a holler; put on a white chef's hat, and cook to you heart's content behind a hot, smoldering stove."

Seth smiled wanly. "Not such a small order; is it?"

"I think I might be able to help you out of this predicament you're in. Let me tell you about the racket that I'm working now." Lenny outlined his false rumor mongering activities for short-sellers and how lucrative a business it was.

Seth's face grew darker the more he heard.

"I'm really an expert at my job, kid, there's nobody better at spreading false rumors than me. My lies are so believable that they make the truth seem like a lie. In fact, a rumor travels much faster and farther than the truth. Only yesterday morning I started a false rumor about IBM losing a bundle in Malaysia. In the afternoon I got a call from a trader in Turkey repeating the same rumor back to me. Can you believe it? IBM's price dropped $6 a share in a day. My clients were ecstatic."

"I believe it."

"As a favor to you, I could start a rumor that Iran is going to demand that buyers of its oil pay for it in euros going forward instead of in U.S. dollars. The dollar will crash and if you're already short dollars; you'll earn enough dough to cover the $22 million. Then you can ride off into the sunset and cook all you want. How does that sound?"

"I appreciate the offer, Lenny, but what you're doing is illegal, you're manipulating the market."

He twitched in the wheelchair. "I guess you could say that if you want to split hairs; but think of it as *spin*, the hedge fund guys and politicians do it all the time."

"It is out-and-out securities fraud, Lenny, that's what it is; you're destroying a stock's value and hurting investors. It's worse than insider trading."

"It's no different than what all you over-educated guys with your fancy degrees are doing; securitizing junk securities and assigning triple-A ratings to it; securities that you know are worth shit; screwing mom-and-pop investors out of their life savings; causing union pension funds to be unable to fund retirement payments to their members; all so you guys can earn huge bonuses and buy that fabulous beach house in Southampton or Fire Island. Am I telling it like it is?"

"You're mostly on the money; I'm not going to argue with you about that."

"You bet you're not, kid, because you haven't got a freaking leg to stand on."

"If the Feds catch up with you, Lenny, you and I might be sharing the same cell."

The iguana looked worriedly at Lenny and made a soulful sound that prompted Mike to bring him more ice.

Lenny rubbed the spikes on its back. "Don't worry, pal, I'm not gonna be caught. I'm an Urban Legend, like the *Scarlet Pimpernel* was."

"Who?" asked Seth.

"I'm sure you remember the famous lines:

They seek him here
They seek him there
Those Frenchies seek him everywhere
Is he in Heaven?
Or is he in Hell?
That damned elusive Pimpernel"

"No, Lenny, I never heard them before."

Lenny sighed. "Never mind, kid, I won't hold your very young age against you, I'll still help you get your bacon out of the fire."

"Thanks, but two wrongs don't make a right," Seth said, "I'm going to have to find another solution to my problem."

"So what are you going to do?"

"That's the $64,000 question, isn't it?"

The Professor and Georgette sauntered into Ulysses the next evening and circled the bar until they found two empty stools next to Wanda Pearlmutter, the person the ORACLE sent them there to strike up a conversation with. He wore a blue blazer, yellow buttoned down shirt, and tan slacks. Wanda was in a white blouse and dark business suit, sipping a white wine that she always treated herself to after work on the days that she did yoga. The Professor lifted Georgette up and sat her down on the stool closest to Wanda so the dog's head was level with the surface of the bar.

"What kind of mutt is that?" the bartender, Artie Finch, asked, a puzzled expression on his face.

"She is a genuine Bull Terrier – Chihuahua mix and her name is Georgette."

"I never saw one like her before, she's ... she's a hoot."

Georgette was gray and had an egg-shaped head, flat at the top, and a Roman muzzle sloping down to the end of her nose like a typical Bull Terrier. She was also thickset, muscular, and had a jaunty gait like that breed of dog was known for. Her ears were huge, however; her feet tiny and dainty; her eyes large and round like a Chihuahua's. She weighed 25 pounds; about half what a typical Bull Terrier would weigh; but four times the weight of the small Mexican dog. A mean-spirited person might be tempted to call her a freak of nature.

"Yes, I like to think that she is one-of-a-kind."

"What can I get you?"

"I'll have a Manhattan and she'll have a tonic water, no ice."

"Very well," Artie said.

Georgette nuzzled Wanda's arm with her wet nose and made a whining sound.

The woman petted her head. "You are so precious."

"I'm very sorry," the Professor apologized, "she has no manners sometimes."

"No, that's ok, I don't mind in the least, I love dogs."

Artie brought their drinks. Georgette put her two front paws on the bar and began to slurp the tonic water.

"She's so cute," Wanda said, "my son would adore her."

"Georgette is playful with kids, her favorite game is hide-and-seek."

"I haven't seen her in here before; are you new to the neighborhood?"

"No, actually we've lived upstairs in this building for a few years."

"You're so lucky; I have to schlep all the way out to Brooklyn every night."

"By the way, my name is Humphrey Kincaid, however, people call me Professor."

"Hello, I'm Wanda Pearlmutter."

"Hi, Wanda."

"So, tell me, are you a real professor?"

"I used to be, I taught Spanish at NYU; then I took early retirement. Now I write romance novels when I'm not taking Georgette out for long walks."

"That's wonderful," Wanda said, "I'm a voracious romance reader. Maybe I've read some of your stuff, although your name isn't familiar to me."

"It wouldn't be, I write under a pseudonym; I use the name Rosa Santiago."

"Oh, my God!" she said excitedly, "I've read all your books, I'm a big fan."

The Professor glowed. "Well, that's amazing."

"You know, I always suspected that Rosa Santiago was a man, there is a definite masculine undertone to the writing."

"You don't say?"

"I wonder if I could ask a favor, Professor, would you autograph some of your books for me?"

His chest expanded two inches. "I'd be delighted; it would be my great pleasure."

The dog howled for no reason.

"Easy girl, they'll throw us out of the place if you keep that up."

Artie came over. "What's the matter, does she want something to eat?"

"She probably does, please bring her some nachos, but without the hot peppers."

"She really eats nachos?"

"Yes, it must be her partial Mexican heritage."

"Ok, nachos it is; hold the peppers, coming up."

Wanda laughed. "My son will crack up when I tell him about her."

"How old is your boy?"

"Allen is twelve. A baby-sitter watches him after school until I get home from work."

"I see."

"I'm a widow, my husband, Dan, died seven years ago."

"I'm sorry to hear that."

"It was a slow death from cancer; Allen really misses his father."

"I'm a widower, my wife, Sarah, died from leukemia almost twenty years ago. It was also a drawn out ordeal, a very painful way to go."

"Do you have children, Professor?"

"No, it's only me and Georgette."

The dog barked as Artie placed the platter of nachos on the bar in front of them. "I brought three plates so all you guys can share."

"Thanks."

"I don't think I'll have any," Wanda said, "I have to watch my figure."

"Oh, come on; eat a few," the Professor said, "take it from me, your figure is absolutely perfect; I've been noticing."

She blushed and accepted a plate from him.

The dog bit into a tortilla chip covered with cheese and immediately made a moaning sound.

Rocco and the ORACLE salivated up in the rafters, they both craved nachos.

"You are right, Georgette, the nachos are excellent," Wanda said, munching one, "I had forgotten how tasty they can be."

"So tell me, Wanda, what kind of work do you do?"

"I'm an underwriter for an insurance company on Maiden Lane; we do fire, marine, and casualty."

"That sounds interesting. Do you like your job?"

Her eyes clouded over. "I do, but I've been having a problem lately."

"Oh, anything you can talk about?"

She took a sip of wine and dabbed at her mouth with a napkin. "I've worked at my company for ten years and everything was fine until a few months ago when my old boss retired. The new guy seemed fine at first but lately he has been hitting on me; making improper advances; talking dirty."

Georgette growled loudly and bared her impressive array of sharp teeth.

"I don't know what to do, Professor, I really need the job but I also have my self-respect."

"Can't you report him to your Human Resources Department?"

"It would just be my word against his; and he's a VP. I don't know if they would believe me."

The Professor smashed the bar with the bottom of his clenched fist, rattling their glasses and plates. "I'd like to punch that guy's lights out."

The dog growled again and then laid his head on Wanda's lap.

"Thank you both for listening," she said, petting the dog.

The Professor finished his drink and had a determined look on his face. "Wanda, I think you should meet Lenny and Stan."

The ORACLE made a practice of going up onto the roof of the building every night at precisely one minute to midnight to do *tai chi* as today becomes yesterday and tomorrow becomes today. After completing his Zen-like introspection he climbed up to the highest point on the roof and blinked three times at the brightest star in the star cluster at the center of the Andromeda Galaxy. In response, a laser-like flicker of light danced for a millisecond on the dark horizon and then ricocheted into deep space.

He meditated on the complexity of the rapidly expanding Universe and on the many marvels that existed beyond its boundaries in the seven other dimensions. On this particular occasion, however, the ORACLE was forced to cut short his nightly reflections because he had an important visitor. He jumped down and walked over to where a spectral figure patiently waited for him, arms folded, in the darkest corner of the roof.

"A very good evening to you, O," said the man in a deep, gravelly voice. He wore an immaculate white linen suit that had last been all the rage in aristocratic European circles of the 1930s and was of indeterminate age and height; not old or young, both short and tall, depending on one's vantage point. His blue eyes were penetrating, yet distant, and there were no laughter lines to mar his smooth, elegant face. It was apparent from the way he lingered in the shadows that he was much more comfortable in the darkness than in the light.

The ORACLE sat down in front of him and blinked three times to initiate the life-or-death negotiation process.

═══════════════════

It was 6:45 P.M. when Merle breezed into Ulysses with Rocco, her pet black squirrel, sitting in her hand. She spotted Amelia Mancuso sipping an orange juice and sat down beside her at the bar. Rocco scampered over to the young woman and stood on his hind legs in a classic begging position. His large, bushy tail thumped loudly on the wooden bar as he waited for a handout.

"Oh, I'm sorry, " Amelia said, "I don't have anything to give you, I wish I had."

"Rocco, you little moocher, leave that lady alone." Merle picked the squirrel up and placed him by her. "I apologize for his rudeness."

Amelia smiled. "He is so unusual, you don't see black squirrels very often in New York."

"Yes, they are rare in this part of the country."

"Did you purchase him in a pet store?"

"No, I found him in Central Park; that is, he found *me* in Central Park."

"He did?"

"Yes. One day I was shopping at *Bergdorf's* and afterwards I went to the park to sit on a bench by The Pond off 59th. Street. It's such a peaceful spot on a sunny day and I find it relaxing to watch the ducks and the egret."

"I agree, I know the place," Amelia said, "it's like being in the country. Deep down I'm a tree-hugger, I love it there."

"Well, I had two shopping bags with me and I placed them on the ground near my feet. After about a half hour I left the park and took the downtown train at Columbus Circle. When I arrived home and began to unpack the bags, the squirrel jumped out. That was two years ago and he's been with me ever since."

"That's an amazing story."

"He must have sneaked into the shopping bag when I wasn't looking and played possum under the packages."

"How old do you think he is?"

"I have no idea." Merle petted him. "Sometimes I think he is very old ... and very wise."

"Wise?"

"Yes, I know it sounds silly but that's the feeling I get when I look into his eyes."

The squirrel resumed his begging pose in front of Amelia.

She waved down Mike. "Could you bring this little guy some peanuts?"

"Absolutely. We get all kinds of animals in here," Mike said, "but never a rodent before, at least not one that ever sat at the bar."

Merle rubbed the squirrel's tummy. "I live upstairs in the building but this is my first time in Ulysses."

Mike looked closely at the squirrel. "Wait a second, is this the same black squirrel that runs up and down the fire escape like crazy all day long?"

"Yes, I'm afraid he has an obsessive-compulsive problem when it comes to the fire escape. It drives my neighbors batty too."

"The poor thing probably misses climbing the trees in Central Park," Amelia said, "don't you, sweetie?"

Mike flipped two peanuts to the squirrel and Rocco began to expertly crack the shells with his enlarged front teeth. "

"What can I get for you, Miss?"

"A vodka gimlet, please."

"Be back in a jiff."

"By the way, my name is Merle."

"I'm Amelia, pleased to meet you."

"And you've already met Rocco, Amelia."

The squirrel began to attack another peanut.

"Yes, he's such a sturdy boy."

"Actually, Rocco is a female."

"Really?"

"Yes, after I decided to keep him I had a vet check him out to be sure he was healthy and didn't have any diseases. That's when I found out that he is a she. By that time, however, I was so used to calling him Rocco that I never changed his name."

"That's so funny."

Mike brought Merle's drink.

"I don't even know how to tell the difference between male and female squirrels. Do you, Amelia?"

"No, I don't either."

"Now I just have to worry that Rocco doesn't get knocked up. I haven't seen any other squirrels on Stone Street but I guess a male could find his way over from Battery Park. That's all I'd need, another five squirrels running madly up and down the fire escape. My neighbors would kill me."

Amelia paled noticeably.

"Hey, you look a little queasy; are you ok?"

She hugged herself. "I'm fine."

"I don't think you're fine, Amelia, there is definitely something wrong. I'm a witch, I can always tell."

"You're joking."

"Am I? Watch this." Merle glanced around to be certain nobody else was watching then she wrinkled her nose at Amelia's glass of orange juice and it rose three inches into the air before settling back down on the bar."

"Oh, my God, you really *are* a witch."

"You'd be surprised at how many of us there are here in New York City."

Amelia picked up the glass to verify that no trick was involved.

"So out with it, Amelia, what's wrong?"

She took a deep breath and blew it out. Then she told Merle about her ex-fiance, his infidelity, the cancelled wedding, and her surprise pregnancy.

When she finished, Merle signaled Mike to bring her another vodka gimlet.

Amelia rubbed her forehead. "I can't believe that in this modern day and age that I managed to get myself into this situation."

Mike brought the fresh drink just as Rocco decided to climb the partition that separated the rear and side bar areas. In no time he was about twenty feet off the floor up near where the music speakers were hung. "I hope he doesn't chew on the speaker wires," Mike said, "he could get electrocuted."

"Rocco, come down here this instant," Merle pleaded to no avail. The squirrel ignored her and munched on a peanut shell, pieces of which rained down on her.

"I'll keep an eye on him," Mike said, "and if worst comes to worst, I'll send one of the busboys up on a stepladder."

"Thanks."

Amelia sighed wearily. "So that's my tale of woe."

Merle nodded. "There are eight million stories in the Naked City, Amelia, and that's the most common one."

"I know it."

"Have you decided what you're going to do?"

"No."

"Does the ex-fiance know that you're pregnant?"

"No."

"Do you plan on telling him?"

"No, this will be my decision and mine alone."

"I agree; don't tell the cheating bastard anything."

"Do you have any children, Merle?"

"I've had three husbands and countless loser boyfriends over the years, but no children, thankfully. I'm not the mothering kind; I'm too selfish, too self-absorbed, too neurotic, and too narcissistic."

"You're exaggerating."

"No, I'm not; Amelia, ask anyone who knows me, they'll tell you I am all those things."

"What kind of work do you do?"

Merle considered how to best answer the question. "Um, I'm a kind of debt consultant to people who are having trouble making their car payments; I make their financial problems disappear, so to speak."

"That sounds like such a very noble thing to be doing."

"Believe me, Amelia, it's not as noble as it sounds. What do you do?"

"I work for a charitable foundation; we fund education projects for children living in low income neighborhoods."

Merle was impressed. "Now *that's* a worthwhile job; everybody down here in the Financial District is so much into the money-making thing that it's disgusting."

"I like my job, it's rewarding, though not financially; non-profits don't pay very well."

"Do you come from a large family, Amelia?"

"No, I am an only child."

"Me, I have two brothers and three sisters living back in Russia."

"I miss not having brothers and sisters. I was lonely growing up. And that's something else I'll have to consider. If I keep the baby, he or she may be an only child too. I wouldn't want them to go through what I went through."

"Are you a religious person?"

"Not really, I was raised a Presbyterian but I haven't been to church in a long time."

"It's the same with me. My family is Russian Orthodox and I haven't been to services since I came to this country twenty-seven years ago."

The ORACLE entered the bar, stopped, and blinked three times up at Rocco who was now making chattering noises while atop one of the bar's SONY TVs that was suspended from the ceiling. The squirrel immediately slid down the partition head first at a tremendous rate of speed and landed with a thud between the two women.

"Oh, look," Amelia said, "it's the little kitty without a name that drinks beer in here all the time."

"Oh, he has a name, Amelia, he is the ORACLE and lives upstairs in this building with a talking parrot and a choreographer."

"Hmmm, that's a strange name for a cat."

Merle smiled enigmatically. *I never said he was a cat.*

The conclave with Wanda on her sexual harassment problem took place in the ORACLE's apartment.

"What's this schmuck's name?" Lenny asked, after hearing Wanda's story.

Wanda hesitated for a second then told him. "Rodney Herkimer."

"Rodney!" Lenny spun the wheelchair in a tight circle, almost knocking down a floor lamp. "I hate that name, I'd never take it as an alias; never in a trillion years; not even if my life depended on it; not even if it meant going to jail and they were going to throw away the damn key."

The parrot shrieked his displeasure at the name too and Leonard made a hissing sound, swinging his long tail hard against the leg of the coffee table where Wanda had placed her knock-off *Gucci* purse. Outside on the fire escape, Rocco was running up and down the steps while Georgette made goo-goo eyes at him every time he passed the window. Only the cat and Stan made no sound.

Wanda gave the Professor an alarmed look and began to have second thoughts about what she had gotten herself into.

"I despise that name," Lenny continued, "I hope the bastard chokes on it the next time that he has to tell someone his name."

"Never mind about his name," the Professor said, "what we need to do now is come up with a plan to get this guy to stop sexually harassing Wanda. Anybody have any bright ideas?"

Lenny looked at Stan who looked at the parrot who looked at Georgette who looked at Rocco who looked at Leonard; no one had any suggestions. Then they all looked at the cat.

The ORACLE blinked three times.

"Of course," Stan exclaimed, "I should have thought of that myself." He bounded to his feet and raced into the bedroom, returning with the camera/ recorder in his hands. "I was going to return this thing to the leasing store tomorrow but instead we can use it to get this Rodney character on film."

"Great idea," the Professor said, "the Human Resources people at her company will have to believe Wanda once they see this guy *in flagrante delicto*."

"Professor, you know I don't speak Spanish," Lenny said, "what's that mean?"

"It's not Spanish, Lenny, it is Latin and it means 'to be caught red-handed'."

"Yeah, now that I understand, I've been caught that way a few times myself."

"Well, *I* don't understand," Wanda said.

Stan explained to her how the voice activated camera worked and how she could use it to get the goods on her boss.

"I ... I'm not a technical person," she said when he had finished, "I'm afraid that I might put it in the wrong place ... or worse, that he might find it and fire me."

"Wanda, you can do it," a voice that sounded exactly like Regis Philbin said, "I know you have it in you, girl."

She was startled and looked up expecting to see the diminutive game-show host there in the apartment, however, only the parrot was to be found where the voice had emanated from.

"The parrot does imitations," Stan explained.

"Oh."

"I can set up the camera/recorder up for you," Stan said, "the people at the leasing company showed me how to obtain the best results with it. I could meet you in the lobby of your office building early on Monday morning, then you could get me through Security before too many of your people show up for work."

"Monday would be the best day because Rodney spends the weekends in the Hamptons and doesn't get in till late."

"Where does he 'hit' on you, Wanda?"

"Mostly in my own office. The walls are glass so he doesn't get physical; he only talks dirty after he closes the door."

"That's great, it's a confined space; it should take about two minutes for me to set up the camera. Just remember, when he comes on to you, don't say anything that might be construed as encouraging his advances; make it plain that you are offended by them; ask him to stop; give him enough rope to incriminate himself. If he threatens to fire you when you won't give him sex; that's all the better, then we'll have what the lawyers call a 'smoking gun.'"

"I'm still nervous," Wanda said, tensely wringing her hands.

The ORACLE blinked at Stan three times.

"Wanda, what are your plans this Sunday?" Stan asked.

"I don't really have any."

"Professor, why don't you take Wanda to brunch downstairs in Ulysses on Sunday; it'll help take her mind off things."

The Professor beamed. "Yes, that's a wonderful idea, I'd love to."

Wanda seemed to like the suggestion as well. "I'm afraid that I don't have anyone to watch Allen, my son."

"Bring him with you," the Professor said, "I'd very much like to meet him. And after brunch, maybe he could come up here and meet Leonard and Georgette, and the rest of the Stone Street menagerie."

"Oh, he'd really like that, he loves animals."

"Fine, it's settled then."

The ORACLE blinked at Stan three times.

"On second thought," Stan said, "let's *all* go to the brunch on Sunday. And we'll invite Al, Bobby, Amelia, and Seth to join us as well."

"The more the merrier," the Professor agreed.

Sunday was the only day of the week that the ORACLE ever ventured into Ulysses before 6:00 P.M. That's because Sunday was Brunch Day and the bar - restaurant offered an all-you-can-eat large spread plus a free drink for $20. The ORACLE was especially fond of the roast beef, ham, turkey, sausages, and shucked oysters they served. Unlike the weekdays when Ulysses catered to its regular customers who readily bought him beer and food, the people who came for the indoor/ outdoor brunch were mostly day-trippers from New Jersey or Long Island and assumed that the ORACLE was merely another bar mouser; they didn't realize that he was the celebrated mascot of Wall Street and a beer drinker *extraordinaire*. As a consequence, the pickings on some Sundays could be slim and the ORACLE was forced to use all his cuteness and considerable powers of persuasion to obtain free food and drink.

On this Sunday, however, the cat had no such worries because all his friends were at the brunch. Lenny, Leonard and Seth sat at one table together while the Professor, Wanda, Georgette, and Allen sat at a second table. Merle and Amelia occupied a third table by themselves; unfortunately, Rocco had been barred from Ulysses by the management after his first visit for chewing on the sound system's electrical wires. Stan, Al, Bobby and the parrot sat at a fourth table.

The ORACLE happily spent the afternoon flitting from table to table eating a bit of this and a bit of that as the iguana and parrot each vied for the attention of the tourists -- Leonard by hanging upside down from a ceiling beam, snickering at them and winking his three eyes at the same time; the parrot boldly singing racy ballads in French as he knew that people from the suburbs couldn't speak foreign languages.

Georgette didn't participate in entertaining the crowd because she was miffed that Rocco wasn't allowed to be present. To show her displeasure, she silently flashed her many sharp teeth at Jimmy, the intense General Manager of Ulysses, every time he walked by her table.

While Wanda and Allen became engrossed in a conversation with Lenny about the joys of keeping iguanas as pets, the Professor decided to visit with Artie Finch who was tending bar that afternoon.

Artie was speaking with a young man who looked like he was suffering from a migraine headache and could use a Tylenol so the Professor waited within earshot for them to finish their business.

"I think I left my credit card in here last night," the young man said, "at least I hope I did. To tell you the truth, things got fuzzy after 2:00 A.M."

"Let me check." Artie went to a tin box and extracted a bundle of about forty credit cards that were wrapped in a rubber band. "What's your name, son, and what kind of card is it?"

"Kramer, Richard Kramer, and it's a Chase Visa card."

Artie sorted through the cards and found it. "Can I see some I.D., please?"

The young man took out his wallet and showed him a driver's license.

Artie handed him the card. "Here you go."

"Thanks a lot, I was afraid that I lost it."

"You're very welcome."

"I was running a tab last night for some people from the office, do you know if it was charged to the card?"

"It would have been, we close out all the outstanding tabs at the end of every night. You'll see the charge on your next bill."

He nodded. "Did you happen to be on duty last night?"

"No, it was my night off."

The young man rubbed his eyes. "That's too bad, I was hoping you could tell me what I was up to."

"I couldn't say but it looks like you got home in one piece."

"I did, but I don't remember how I did. My friends must've given me a ride."

"Then you were lucky last night," Artie said, "no harm was done"

"I guess so."

"But you don't want to go making a habit of getting blotto, one day it might not turn out so well. Know what I'm saying, son?"

"I do and it's smart advice, I'll be more careful in the future." He pushed a ten-dollar bill across the bar. "For your trouble."

Artie pushed the money back. "No trouble, the advice is on the house."

"Thanks, again." The young man picked up the bill and left.

The Professor moved in and nodded at the pack of credit cards still in Artie's hand. "You have quite a bundle there."

Artie shuffled the stack like they were playing cards. "This is just from the last few days."

"Are you serious?"

"I am, we've got a whole drawer full of cards that go way back."

"That's an eye-opener for me."

"Yeah, people drink a bit too much and get careless with their possessions."

"I had no idea."

"Customers leave all sorts of things behind -- coats, jackets, eyeglasses, briefcases, ties, cufflinks, watches, pens, bracelets, cell phones, rings, gloves, PCs, you name it, we got it in our Lost & Found. One time we even found a ten-foot surfboard some dude left in the Men's Room. We've got so much stuff downstairs that I could open up my own thrift shop."

"Wow."

Artie slipped the rubber band around the credit cards and put them back into the tin box. "So, Professor, how are things with you?"

"I can't complain."

Artie looked over to the table where Wanda was sitting next to his empty chair. "She's a fine looking woman, I can see why you have no complaints."

The Professor reddened. "What's up with you, fellow writer?"

"I'm not a real writer," Artie replied, "I've never been published, you're the only real writer around here, Professor, as far as I'm concerned."

"I don't kid myself, Artie, the stuff I write is fluff; muscular, moronic pirates ripping off the blouses of big breasted, vapid women. I will never win any awards for it. Ernest Hemingway and John Steinbeck can rest easy in their graves."

"You sell books, people pay money for them, I'd gladly settle for that."

"I'm a hard-working hack, Artie, but I'm still a hack. I've seen some of your material, it is literary fiction, deep, sensitive; it makes you think."

Faith, the second bartender on duty that day, walked by them on the way to her station at the other end of the bar.

"Faith," the Professor called to her, "you're an avid reader, have you read any of Artie's books?"

She shook her head. "No, I only read dead authors."

The two men looked agape at each other.

"Artie, I still say your writing is worthy of being published."

"My books have been rejected by every publisher in the world, Professor, what does that tell you?"

"It tells me that maybe you need to shift gears and write about what you know best."

Artie wiped the bar down with a damp cloth. "I don't know much about anything, I grew up in a small town out in the sticks of Rhode Island and now I live in Queens, that's it. I've never traveled to Europe or Asia; I haven't even been to Florida or California. I was in New Jersey once to go to Ikea, the Swedish furniture store. My knowledge about the world is very limited, I only know what I read in books and watch on television."

"You know about the bar business, Artie, write about that."

"What do you mean?"

"Maybe write about all the oddball characters that you've come into contact with in bars over the years, write about this urban subculture that you know as few other people do. You must have a thousand interesting stories to tell. Your words will ring true, you'll get published, I'm sure of it."

Artie looked dubious.

The ORACLE jumped up onto the bar between the two men and blinked three times at Artie.

The bartender seemed befuddled for a second, however, a second later he looked like he couldn't remember what he had been befuddled about.

"Artie, are you ok?" the Professor asked.

"Huh?"

"Are you feeling all right?"

"I feel fine now, I just lost my bearings there for an instant."

"You do look a bit tired."

He rubbed his eyes. "The truth is that I haven't been sleeping very well and I've been having crazy dreams."

"What kind of crazy dreams?"

"Annoying stuff. Like I park my car and then when I look for it later I can't find it even though I know precisely where I left it. Or I come home from work and get off the subway at my usual stop but then I can't find my apartment building on the street where I've lived for almost twenty years. I search for hours and hours in vain until I wake up in the morning exhausted."

The Professor nodded. "I know exactly what you mean, I used to have the same kind of dreams. But with me, I'd lose my briefcase that was filled with important test papers and I'd end up searching the entire NYU campus without finding it. I'd wake up in a panic, my undershirt soaking wet."

"It's uncanny that we both dreamt that."

"I finally figured out what was happening. You can blame it on all those rejection letters you've been getting, Artie, you've been frustrated so long in trying to get published that your subconscious mind is acting out. All this fruitless searching of yours will stop once you get your first book published."

"It will?"

"Yes, and I know what I'm talking about, that's exactly what happened with me."

"I'm trying not to get depressed, Professor, I really am."

"I know it's tough to keep going in the face of all that rejection, Artie, but you gotta roll with the punches for a while longer."

"Some days I'm so beat up I feel like going to bed and not ever getting up again. If it weren't for my wife's support, I'd give up. "

"Remember what I said, Artie, write about what you know." The Professor gave him an encouraging poke on the arm and returned to his table.

Artie scanned the barroom and his eyes skipped from the parrot to the iguana to the squirrel to the dog to the cat. The seed of an idea began to germinate in the deep creative recesses of the right side of his brain.

Afterwards, the contingent marched upstairs to the ORACLE's apartment where Bobby and Stan talked dance; where Amelia, Merle and Wanda talked girl talk; where Lenny and Seth talked high finance; where Al, Allen and the Professor tried to play Scrabble in spite of a certain iguana who, from time to time, stuffed game tiles into his mouth and pretended to chew them to bits; where Georgette sat in the window alternately snarling and making moon-eyes at Rocco outside on the fire escape.

The ORACLE and the parrot observed the goings-on and were pleased that everyone was having such an enjoyable time.

Later that Sunday night, after his guests had departed, the ORACLE went down to Ulysses for a nightcap. Sunday nights were typically slow so he was forced to rely on the generosity of the bartenders for a freebie or two. Sunday night was also when the bar conducted its weekly Trivia Q&A Quiz. Patrons were given a pencil and a scorecard and Keith, the tall, imposing, lightly bearded bartender, used a microphone to read aloud a series of multiple-choice questions, each with four possible answers. The winners received fun prizes.

As usual, Lenny was present and, as usual, he was getting all the correct answers. Each time a question was read aloud, Leonard would slap his tail on the bar either once, twice, three times, or four times to correspond with the correct answer. Leonard had acquired his extensive trivia knowledge from a previous owner who had designed crossword puzzles for the *Los Angeles Times*. Of course, Keith was aware that it was Leonard, and not Lenny, who was supplying the correct answers. Since iguanas were not eligible under the house rules to enter the trivia quiz, Lenny was never actually awarded a prize for his efforts. Nevertheless, he still showed up dutifully every Sunday night to participate.

Sunday night was also the ORACLE's least favorite night of the week; there was something lonely, even foreboding, about it. While he didn't have to rise early on Monday morning and squeeze himself into a slow-moving, crowded subway car to go to work uptown, he still dreaded

Monday mornings as much as many workers did. But by 11:00 A.M. the feeling would usually pass; he would be back in the swim of things, ready to face whatever the new week held in store.

═══════════════════

On this particular Monday morning, however, the ORACLE was excited from the moment he woke up because they were going to 'sting' a sex bully by the name of Rodney Herkimer. *The Sting* with Paul Newman and Robert Redford was one of the ORACLES's most favorite movies of all time, along with the first *Star Wars* and *Close Encounters of the Third Kind*. At 6:55 A.M. there was a knock on their apartment door while Stan was still in the process of shaving.

"Come in," the parrot said, sounding like Clark Gable.

"I'm sorry to disturb you at such an early hour," the Professor apologized, entering the room, "but I couldn't sleep a wink last night because I was so worried about Wanda."

"There's nothing to worry about," Stan replied, "she's not going to be making a parachute jump into Afghanistan in the dark, you know, she's only going to do a bit of acting, that's all."

"Still, I'd like to go with you so that I'm nearby in case anything goes wrong and I'm needed. I'll beat that guy into a pulp if he so much as touches her." He smashed a fist into the palm of his hand to stress the point.

The cat and parrot exchanged amused glances.

"Professor, we've known each other for two years now and I've never seen this side of you before. Since when are you going about rescuing damsels in distress?"

"I … I know it's not like me, especially in light of the cowardly way I behaved in the 'Vinnie Shots' affair, however, I have turned over a new leaf. I will do whatever it takes to protect Wanda, no matter the risk to my own person."

Stan was tempted to laugh out loud but he kept a straight face. "Do I detect the sweet scent of romance in the air?"

The Professor stretched his neck as though his shirt collar was suddenly too tight. "Wanda is a much younger woman, she'd have no interest in an old fossil like me."

"I'm not so sure about that, I took notice of the special way she was looking at you yesterday at brunch. I'd say she is very interested."

His face turned crimson. "You would, Stan, you think she likes me?"

"Yes, I do, and I'm not the only one who noticed." Stan turned to the parrot for confirmation.

"The lady in question is definitely hot to trot," the parrot opined in his Cary Grant voice.

The Professor cleared his throat and threw his shoulders back. "Eh, I'd like to tag along and be your backup, Stan."

Stan realized that it was futile to argue. "Ok, partner, let me finish dressing and we'll hit the bricks together."

The two men walked up William Street and were waiting for Wanda when she entered the lobby of her office building on Maiden Lane.

"Why, Professor, I didn't know that you'd be coming along this morning."

"Yes, well, Wanda, I thought I'd cover Stan's back, you know, like friends do for each other in difficult situations."

"That's so wonderful of you." She squeezed his arm and his blood pressure spiked dangerously high.

"I'll stay down here in the lobby and keep my eyes peeled for this Rodney character in case he returns from the Hamptons early. If he does, I'll stall him, maybe bump into him accidentally and knock him flat on his back. Don't worry, Wanda, he won't suspect a thing."

Wanda squeezed his arm again. "You make me feel so safe, Professor."

"Your safety is important to me my dear, I'm glad to be of service."

Stan shook his head. "Professor, you don't even know what this Rodney guy looks like; how are you going to identify him?"

"Then I ... I'll think of something else," he stammered.

"Oh, Professor, you're so gallant," Wanda told him.

"You have my cell number, Wanda, call me and I'll be up there in a shot."

"You can't get through Security," Stan said, "the guards won't let you up."

"If I have to, I'll steamroll the guards."

Stan rolled his eyes. "Come on, Wanda, let's go upstairs before I make a rude remark to Sir Galahad here that I'm going to regret later on."

Wanda showed her I.D. card and the guards processed a guest pass for Stan. Then the two of them went into a waiting elevator.

Stan sighed. "There's no fool like an old fool."

Wanda smiled coquettishly. "He's not so old; not so old at all."

The long awaited telephone call from Wanda finally came at 3:15 P.M. and the Oracle put it on the speakerphone. Stan, the Professor, Lenny, Leonard, the parrot, Georgette, the squirrel, and Merle were also present in the apartment.

"Hello, this is the Kane residence," the parrot said, imitating Stan's voice perfectly.

"Stan, it's me, Wanda."

"I'm glad it's you, Wanda, the Professor has been pacing up and down so much that he's almost worn a hole in the oriental carpet."

"That's so sweet of him."

"How did things go with Rodney, Wanda?"

"I'm a better actress than I gave myself credit for, Stan, I think we have our 'smoking gun.'"

"Hallelujah!" the parrot shouted.

"Listen and judge for yourself." She played the recording that lasted for almost fifteen minutes. In it, Rodney Herkimer clearly came across as a vile lecher and several times he threatened to fire Wanda if she didn't 'service' him whenever he was in the mood. He went into graphic detail as to the kind of kinky sex that he expected, including 'doing her' on his desk during office hours. When Wanda told him that she would complain to Carolyn Schmitt, the head of HR, he called that woman a lesbian bitch and said that her days at the company were numbered. He also described the existing CEO as a senile, doddering idiot who should be euthanized for the benefit of the stockholders. The recording ended with Herkimer telling Wanda that time was running out and that if she was smart she'd come into his office immediately and give him a sample blow job as a token of her good intentions.

All during the recording the Professor kept his eyes closed; his jaw and fists tightly clenched. To show her support, Georgette growled during the more salacious parts of the recording.

"That's all of it," Wanda said, "what do you guys think?"

"I think I'm going to break both his arms and legs," the Professor answered, "after I smash his damn face in."

The telephone line crackled. "Oh, that's so sweet of you."

"This Rodney guy is toast," Lenny said with assurance, "he won't have a legal leg to stand on in court."

"Are you sure about that?" the real Stan asked.

Lenny nodded. "Yeah, very sure, he did everything short of physically attacking her. Now all that Wanda needs is a smart attorney who's not afraid to play hardball with her employer. Based on my many encounters with the legal system, I think it should be a woman, just in case it goes to a jury trial, and preferably someone who used to be a prosecutor at one time. Prosecutors are experienced at going for the jugular."

"I think I know such a lawyer person," Merle said, "a woman in my kickboxing class, her name is Svetlana Brutalefsky."

"I like her name," Lenny said, "it kinda rolls off the tongue."

"Svet is 5'3" and weighs 300 pounds; all muscle. We give her the nickname the 'Pit Bull' because she keeps coming at you, slashing and ripping at your body and face until you collapse from the punishment. And when you fall down she doesn't stop, she stomps on you, especially if you're a man, because she hates men for some reason."

"I never heard of the woman but I'm liking what I hear about her," Lenny said, "I think Rodney will like her too."

"She sounds really frightening," Wanda said over the phone line.

Merle nodded. "Yes, she is, she used to prosecute Russian Mafia in Brooklyn; they threatened to kill her; so she threaten to cut their gonads off. Believe you me, nobody messes with Svet Brutalefsky and comes away un-bloodied."

Lenny looked at the cat. "What do you want us to do, O?"

The ORACLE blinked three times.

"I'll tell her." Lenny spoke to the speakerphone. "Wanda, you and me and Merle are going to meet with the 'Pit Bull' as soon as Merle can set it up. You should make a copy of the recording and bring it to the meeting with the lawyer. In case this Rodney character 'hits' on you again, get it all on film. The more film we have, the easier it will be to prove a pattern of persistent and severe sexual harassment. Are you copasetic with that?"

"Yes, Lenny, I'll do as you say."

"And bring the film here to the apartment tonight after you finish work. We'd all like to see this Rodney character in action."

"Ok, I'll be there around 6:15 P.M. Bye for now."

Lenny looked at the Professor. "Everybody will be here except for you, Professor, O wants you to take Wanda downstairs for a drink while we run the recording. He's concerned about your emotional state of mind and objectivity in this here matter."

The Professor reluctantly agreed. "If you insist."

"We'll all come down to join you at Ulysses after we've seen the recording and discuss our strategy going forward."

"Fine."

━━━━━━━━━━━━━━━━━━━━

Stan had set up the camera/ recorder so it would play on the plasma TV in the living room. When Rodney Herkimer's image first appeared on the screen the parrot shrieked; Leonard swung his tail ominously from side to side and made a sickening sucking noise usually only heard in a rain forest before a nasty storm; Georgette snarled louder than she ever had before in her life; Rocco scraped his nails on the metal apartment door that made everyone who had dental fillings cringe. The cat took it all in stride and yawned.

━━━━━━━━━━━━━━━━━━━━

As was their routine on Tuesday nights, Stan, the parrot, and the ORACLE watched *So You Think You Can Dance*; but on this occasion they had a guest, Bobby Rankle, join them. After the TV program had ended, Stan and Bobby moved all the furniture in the living room back against the walls. Stan performed a series of Ballet and Contemporary Dance moves demonstrating pirouettes, lifts, jumps, turns, glides, kicks, spins, leaps, and a variety of box steps.

There was a loud knock on the door.

The parrot spoke: *"S'il vous plait venire a entrer, mais a vos propres risques."*

Merle and Amelia came into the room. "What do you mean that I enter at my own risk? What kind of shenanigans are you all up to? I thought my ceiling was going to come crashing down on our heads."

"Sorry, Merle," Stan said, pausing in his demonstration, a bit out of breath, "I was showing Bobby some dance moves."

"Don't let us interrupt you, go ahead, we'll watch." The two women took seats on a sofa.

Stan resumed his solo dancing for another ten minutes. When he finished Bobby and the two women clapped enthusiastically. The parrot shrieked: *"Bravo! C'etait au-dela des mots, Stan, J'ai adore."*

"Thanks, guys, I'm not as agile as I once was, age takes its heavy toll, I'm afraid. Now I do mostly cardio dancing."

Amelia's eyes took in his sinewy torso as he glistened with perspiration in the tight black leotard.

"My best dancing days are behind me. What I'd like to do now is choreograph for one of those entertainment type reality shows on television."

The ORACLE stored the comment away in his memory banks.

Then it was Bobby's turn to show them what he could do.

The young man had been far too modest about his abilities; after a few minutes it was evident to all present that he was an accomplished dancer. His jumps were higher than Stan's; his leaps were longer; his kicks were stronger; his spins were faster and his glides smoother. The applause he received was almost thunderous and surely caused a few heads down on Stone Street to look up at the window. Leonard slapped his tail so aggressively against the credenza that the valuable blue Chinese vase resting on it began to move dangerously towards the edge.

"Bobby, that was wonderful," Merle told him, "I once saw Rudolf Nureyev dance in *Don Quixote* in Leningrad when I was a child and he had nothing on you."

"That is more praise then I deserve," he replied, drying his face with a towel.

"Are you certain that you haven't had professional training?" Stan asked.

"No, I only took a few private lessons on the sly."

"You have real talent, young man, there is no question about that. A talent like yours doesn't come along every day. Even in my prime I wasn't in your league as a dancer."

"You're too generous, Stan, but thank you."

"And you've also lost some weight since I last saw you."

"Yes, ten pounds, I've been going to the gym every morning before work. You put me back on the right track; I needed that push to get back in shape."

"I'm very impressed," Amelia said, "you should definitely pursue a career in dance. I wish I had a marvelous talent like yours."

Stan nodded. "You're 22, Bobby, there's still time for you to make it as a professional. You could be in the big time."

"Um … I don't know about that."

"Well, *I* do, dance is my business."

Bobby didn't reply.

"Listen, a former colleague of mine is a Professor in the Dance Department at Juilliard. From time to time, I've recommended a few young people to him who, in my judgment, had exceptional talent. He respects my opinion; I can't get you into Juilliard, Bobby, but I *can* get you an audition. And I'll even choreograph a number for you. I personally think you have a decent shot at being admitted into the Fall dance program there."

"You do?"

"Absolutely. So shall I call him and set it up? What do you say?"

Bobby stared mutely at the floor.

"Look, Bobby, let's not get ahead of ourselves and project too far in advance; let's take it one step at a time. Don't say anything to your dad about the audition, just go to it and give it your all. If you don't cut the mustard, no damage is done; you continue to work as a broker and dance recreationally as you have been. If, on the other hand, Juilliard accepts you into their program, then you tell your dad about your desire to change careers. You don't have to tell him you're gay, he doesn't need to know that yet."

"He'll be hurt and upset if I leave the firm."

"Yes, there's no question that he will be disappointed, however, his dream is not your dream. He will get over it in time. If he is the great dad that you say he is, he'll want what's best for you."

"I guess."

"Does that sound like a plan?"

Bobby exhaled deeply and sat down on a chair. "Yes, it does."

"That's the spirit. Now I think we all should all go downstairs to Ulysses to celebrate," Merle said, "then, after a few vodkas, I will tell you about one of my old lovers who danced with the Kirov in St. Petersburg, and what a really naughty boy he was. You will be grossly shocked and scandalized, I guaranty it."

━━━━━━━━━━━━━━━

Svetlana Brutalefsky's one-woman law office consisted of two drab rooms situated above a pizza parlor on Avenue A in the East Village. Photographs of Russian SWAT teams hung on the orange painted walls. Her many kickboxing trophies occupied a large bookcase in the reception/waiting room. Adjacent to it, inside a bulletproof glass case, there was a small collection of medieval instruments of torture, including nail-studded whips, testicle crushers and fingernail rippers. Merle and Lenny were impressed; Wanda was aghast and didn't know what to think.

"*Zdravstvujte, prijatno poznakomits,*" the lawyer greeted Merle effusively, kissing her on both cheeks.

"This is Wanda and Lenny who I told you about on the phone."

"*Dobro pozalovat!* Please to call me, Svet," the lawyer said, "all my clients have that permission." The lawyer was 47, with dirty blonde hair tied into a bun and held in place with rubber bands, had pale blue eyes, and wore a tight-fitting sleeveless orange dress that emphasized her three hundred pound frame and all her other bad physical features, of which there were many. A concave indentation on her forehead was a souvenir from when she had been attacked and almost raped by a drunken Communist Party official while still a teenager. Her knuckles and elbows were heavily calloused and on her left bicep there was a tattoo of a skull. Her size 14 feet were encased in steel-pointed leather walking shoes that looked comfortable but also very lethal.

Her visitors wasted no time and played the Rodney Herkimer video recording for Svet on the office TV to give her a quick understanding of the nature of the sexual harassment case they had come to consult her about.

At the film's conclusion, the lawyer stood up; shouted something nasty sounding in guttural Russian; and then drove her fist into the wall beside her desk, creating a large hole in the sheetrock. Next a vicious leg kick from her tripled the opening.

Wanda was rattled; Merle grunted; Lenny laughed.

The secretary rushed in, already knowing what to expect. "Oh, Svet, not again, that's the third time this month. I'll have to call the contractors back."

Wanda then asked the question that the Professor had told her to ask. "Svet, what do you think our legal strategy should be? Do we take the high road or the low road?"

The lawyer's face twisted with rage and huge dollar signs flickered in her fiery eyes. "We gouge his eyes out, Wanda, we castrate him, we rip him a second asshole, that is going to be our legal strategy in this case!"

"Oh, my God."

"And we sue every deep-pocket in sight: your employer, the Board of Directors, senior management, the owner of your office building. If Svet can think of any more deep-pockets to sue, we sue them too."

Wanda grew concerned. "But I really like my employer, Svet, they've always been fair with me, they've given me raises, allowed me extra time off when Allen was ill, paid for the education courses I needed. I don't want to sue them."

Svet picked a brick up from a pile in the corner and split it in two pieces with a vicious karate chop. "There is no being nice today, Wanda, being nice is interpreted as a sign of weakness. Large companies only understand toughness; they take you serious only if you scare the living shit out of them."

"Svet is right," Merle concurred, "Vladimir Vladimirovich always said to me that power respects only power."

"*Da.* Svet knows what she is talking about, trust me."

"I guess I will have to."

"When Svet finish with your employer, Wanda, you will get a big promotion, a big raise, and a big cash settlement. Svet know what she is doing; Svet is Cossack; violence and mayhem is in blood."

"I love you, Svet," Lenny said, "you're my kind of broad."

The lawyer fluttered her fake eyelashes at him. "When the Nazis invaded Russia, my grandfather slit the throats of all our livestock on our farm, he blew up our houses and barns, poisoned our wells; burned our fields of crops. Then he fled to the woods and became a partisan where he tore out the hearts of six SS troopers and ate them for dinner because they had nothing else to eat during the cold Russian winter."

"My Lord!"

"And that's how Svet will treat this Rodney no-goodnik when Svet get him on the witness stand for cross-examination. Svet will cut him here, then there, and after an hour or two he will have a thousand cuts, his blood will flow all over the courtroom like a raging red river."

"Ugh, that revolts me, I've always hated the sight of blood."

"Then you know what Svet is going to do to him, Wanda?"

Wanda shook her head with some trepidation. "No, I'm afraid to ask."

Svet took out a photo of Rodney Herkimer that Wanda had given her and dropped it on the floor. She arose from behind her desk and stood by it. "Svet do this to him." She jumped as high as she could and all 300 pounds of her stomped on it repeatedly until the photo of Rodney was totally unrecognizable and torn to shreds."

Her secretary came running in again. "Not again, Svet, you promised the pizza guy you wouldn't do that because it causes asbestos from the ceiling tiles to fall down into his tomato sauce."

Lenny smiled. "You will be my lawyer the next time I need one, Svet, I'll give you a retainer before I leave today."

Wanda, though shaken, was encouraged by the rabid enthusiasm of her counsel.

"I come from KGB family," Merle said approvingly, "I know about such harsh tactics, they always get results."

"I must tell you, Svet, that I don't have a lot of money," Wanda said, "how much do you charge for your services?"

"Not to worry your pretty head, Wanda not pay Svet anything unless Svet wins case. Then Wanda pays Svet one-third of what you collect from sex harassment lawsuit."

"So you are taking my case on a contingency basis."

"*Da*, if Svet loses case, Wanda pays nothing."

"That's very fair of you. We have a deal."

"But Svet no lose case, Wanda, Svet promise that on grave of her beloved grandfather, Ivan Igorovich Brutalefsky." The lawyer looked around for something to punch, kick, karate chop, or stomp on as they left her office.

━━━━━━━

"Al, I asked Amelia to be present," Stan explained, "because she majored in Art History at Barnard and her charitable foundation sponsors art projects so she knows many art teachers in the city."

"Hello, Amelia."

"Hi, Al."

"I've seen you in Ulysses."

"Yes, I've seen you also."

"I'd value your opinion." He had three canvasses under his arm. "Where shall I put these?"

"Let's use the dining room table," Stan suggested, "lay them down next to each other."

Al removed the paper wrapping and did so. Each oil painting was unframed and measured 3'x 4'. Each was painted in different styles: an Impressionist landscape scene, a Cubist horse, and a Photo-Realism scene of a telephone booth on a crowded urban street.

"Amelia, help me here," Stan said, "what are we looking at?"

Amelia pointed to the landscape. "This is an example of art from the Impressionist Movement in France that began in the 1870's."

"Ok."

"Impressionists create sensory depictions of real world objects as opposed to traditional painters who seek to create an objective reality where the object looks like it does to our naked eye. See the bright primary, unmixed colors used to simulate light. Degas, Renoir, Cezanne and Van Gogh were some of the prominent artists of the time. This work is in the style of Van Gogh, in fact, while I'm no expert, I'd say this *was* a painting done by Van Gogh, if I didn't know that you painted it, Al."

Al smiled proudly.

She pointed to the horse next. "Cubism was an avant-garde art movement that dates back to about 1900. It stresses abstract structure and was pioneered by Picasso and Georges Braque."

"We've all heard of Picasso."

"Yes. Cubism breaks up an object into geometric shapes and reassembles it into an abstract form. It tries to show all sides of a 3-dimensional object on a 2-dimensional canvas by displaying several views of it simultaneously. Notice the flat, two-dimensional surface; the actual intent here is *not* to imitate nature. Again, Al, if I didn't know that you painted this, I would swear this was a Picasso from his Rose period."

Al nodded.

"The last oil painting is a great example of Photo-Realism, a hyper-realistic art style that began in the United States in the late 1960's as a counter to Abstract-Expressionism. Simply put, it is based on making a painting of a photograph."

"It does look like a photograph," Stan said.

"Estes, Flack, Chen and Blackwell were some of the artists credited with its rise. Photo-Realism attempts to capture precisely what a camera would if it took a picture of an object. Look at the meticulous attention to detail of the aluminum telephone booth, the way it shines in the light, the reflection in the glass, the instrument itself. Notice the incredibly intricate texture and fine brushwork. Again, Al, if I didn't know better, I'd say this work looks like it was painted by Richard Estes."

"Thank you, Amelia, I'm flattered to hear that."

She stepped back and considered the paintings again from a distance. "Your paintings are all wonderful, Al, and in my opinion many of today's art experts would be fooled. They are not merely painted in-the-technique-of these great artists, they are indistinguishable from paintings those artists would paint today."

"I'm pleased that you think so."

"You'd make a great art forger, Al, one of the best."

Stan had a puzzled look on his face. "Amelia, can a forgery be so good that it, too, is also a masterpiece?"

Amelia shook her head.

"But why not? I mean, if Al can paint exactly like Van Gogh, Picasso, and Estes so that even the best experts can't tell the difference, why isn't Al's work a masterpiece too?"

"I don't think the art world would look at it that way."

"Doesn't it take just as much talent to do an undetectable forgery as it did to do the original work of art?"

"There is the question of originality, each of those artists created a new style. The world never saw anything like it before."

Stan frowned. "I bet Lenny knows people who could sell Al's paintings tomorrow for lots of money by passing them off as originals. The art market is still hot now even though the economy stinks."

"That wouldn't surprise me at all."

"Maybe I should show them to Lenny," Al said, "I'm hard up and could use the money now that the doctor has told me that I'll probably live to be 100. Social Security doesn't go far in this day and age; after I pay the rent there's hardly anything left."

Stan put a hand on the elderly man's shoulder. "We'll find you a better way."

"I was joking about doing forgeries, Stan, at least I think I was."

"Al, you need to develop your own, unique style," Amelia said, "to paint your own vision, to show people the world the way you see it."

"I don't know if I have a style, Amelia, and at this late stage in my life, I'm not sure that I can create one."

"Grandma Moses didn't start painting until she was in her seventies, Al, it's never too late. And like you, she had no formal training, only raw talent. I know you can do it if you set your mind to it."

"I've always been a glass-half-empty kind of guy, Amelia, I never really believed in myself. You might have more confidence in me than I deserve."

"I do believe in you, Al, now you have to believe you can do it."

Al seemed energized by Amelia's faith in him and clenched his jaw with determination. "I'm going to give it my best shot, I'm going to start painting again."

She gave him a high-five. "That's the spirit!"

"Thank you for getting the old juices flowing again, Amelia, I can't wait to get started."

"I'm so excited for you, Al, I know this is going to turn out great."

"I'm excited myself, suddenly life seems worth living again."

Stan rubbed his chin. "So, Amelia, what can a guy with Al's fabulous painting talent do to earn some pocket change?"

"Hmmm."

"Is there a legitimate market for great art forgeries? Could he be an Art Restorer or an Art Teacher of some kind? How about him painting murals for restaurants or office building lobbies? Or maybe doing billboards or stage sets?"

"I'm going to have to do some research and get back to you on that, Stan."

━━━━━━━━━━━━━━

Stan answered the telephone on the second ring. "Hello."

"Stan, it's Doug Fowler at Juilliard."

"Hi, Doug, hang on, let me put you on the speaker." He hit the button. "There are some other folks here who will want to hear what you have to say. Ok, shoot, what does Juilliard think about Bobby Rankle as a dancer?"

"His audition was positively brilliant, Stan, I can't remember when the Dance Department panel has been so impressed. He's a natural, as they say, it's hard to believe that someone with so little formal training can be so accomplished."

"That's wonderful to hear."

"And that routine you choreographed for him was astonishing, Stan, all the panel members thought so too."

"Thanks for the compliment."

"The Board intends to offer him a full scholarship and a spot in the Fall class. I wanted to let you know before I called him with the news."

"I appreciate the heads-up, Doug."

The parrot shrieked. The cat yawned.

"What was that strange noise, Stan?"

"Pay no attention, Doug, it's a parrot that I'm babysitting for my landlord who lives in Singapore. The bird thinks he can sing but he's not Juilliard material, I can assure you of that."

The cat meowed, corroborating Stan's evaluation.

The parrot pouted.

"I see."

"Doug, I can't thank you enough."

"No, it's *I* who should thank *you*, Stan, Mr. Rankle will be a great addition to the Juilliard family. I'll speak with you soon; take care."

Stan hung up the speakerphone. "Well, guys, I'd say that we're good Samaritans and have done our good deed for the day."

===============

Trying to keep up with Lenny in his wheelchair was a problem for Seth as he raced after him down Hudson Street in the West Village, weaving in and out of the pedestrian traffic.

"Lenny, where are we headed? Where are you taking me?"

"It's a surprise, kid, we'll be there in a minute."

Lenny was about thirty feet ahead when he turned a corner and disappeared entirely from view. Seth reached the corner and saw that Lenny was waiting for him in front of an Italian bistro named *Adagio*.

"We're expected," Lenny said, "I made a dinner reservation for us."

"Really."

"Yeah, really. What's the matter, kid, don't you like Italian food?"

"I love Italian food."

"Great, let's go eat then. And there's someone special I want you to meet."

Seth opened the door and Lenny sped inside to where an older man with a toothbrush mustache and gray hair was standing by a reservation book.

"*Come stai?*" Lenny said to him.

"*Benvenuto*, Lenny, *bene grazie. E tu?*"

"I'm fine. Marko, this is Seth Reich, the young man I told you about."

"*Piacere di conosceria*," Marko said, bowing, "any friend of Lenny's is a friend of mine."

"Hello, Marko."

"Come, I'll show you to your table."

They followed Marko to the rear of the restaurant and out to a garden where some ten tables had been set up amidst plants and flowers.

"This is lovely," Seth said, "it's so relaxing to be able to dine outdoors like this in the city."

Marko bowed again. "*Grazie mille.*"

"Yeah," Lenny said, "Marko comes from *Venezia* where they know a thing or two about dining alfresco."

When they were seated Marko took their drink orders and left them menus.

Seth looked around. "This is such a charming restaurant, Lenny, it's exactly the kind of place that I'd like to have one day."

"Yeah, that's why we're here tonight, kid, to talk a deal for you."

"What? I don't understand."

"I've been coming here for years," Lenny said, "me and Marko got to be buddies. Marko has been in this location for thirty-five years and he has built up a profitable business. Customers come down here from all parts of the Tri-State area because the food and service is so excellent."

"I have read reviews of this place, it has a fine reputation."

Lenny lowered his voice. "You wouldn't know it to look at him, but Marko isn't well, he's got bad angina."

"Oh, that's too bad."

"Yeah, it is. Anyway, he's almost seventy now and wants to return to the old country to spend his retirement years; he's got family over there that will take care of him."

"I see."

"That's where *you* come into the picture, kid."

Seth eyes bulged in their sockets. "Me?"

"Yeah; you. I told Marko about how you hate working on Wall Street and that it was your ambition to become a chef and open your own place. I laid it on real thick and told him what an honorable, person you were and how you could be counted on to carry on the tradition of hospitability and great food at reasonable prices that he has established here."

"I certainly would."

"If you pass his interview, kid, I think Marko would work out a deal with you where you gradually take over the place and pay him off over time out of the future profits. That way you wouldn't have to come up with a lot of cash upfront. He wants me to become your silent partner as added insurance that you'll run the place the way he has."

Seth seemed uncomfortable. "I ... I don't know what to say."

"You can cook, kid, isn't that so?"

"I'm a superior cook, Lenny, don't worry, I know my way around the kitchen."

"So what's the problem?"

"The problem is that I can't run the restaurant from jail. Did you forget about the $22 million dollar loss that I'm sitting on?"

"No, kid, I didn't forget. Have you given any more thought to letting me work my rumor mongering magic on your behalf? You could make some serious money and get out from under."

"I haven't changed my mind about that, Lenny, like I told you before, two wrongs don't make a right."

"Then do your parents happen to have a spare $22 mil laying around the house that they can lend you?"

Seth put a knuckle to his mouth. "No, of course not."

"Well, if that's the case, there's no way in hell you can make restitution."

"That's true, Lenny, unless I can find the trade of a lifetime."

"Wrong, kid, terrible mistake! That's what got you into this jam in the first place."

The waiter brought a carafe of the red house wine and some homemade Italian bread with olive oil.

Lenny poured the wine. "I think maybe it's time for you to take the bull by the horns."

"What do you mean?"

"I've been reading up on that rogue trader in Paris who worked for the French bank and lost $7.0 billion dollars a couple of years ago."

"He actually lost $7.35 billion."

Lenny shrugged. "A lousy $350 million bucks is hardly worth mentioning."

"Go on."

"Anyway, the guy's free; he did no real jail time. In comparison, your $22 mil loss is chump change. If that frog walked, you should be able to as well."

"This is the United States, Lenny, not France. Given the crash and all the scams, down-on-their-luck Wall Streeters don't get any sympathy from the public. The media would crucify me and the authorities would be forced by the politicians to seek the maximum penalty."

"Look, kid, it's not like you stole the money and spent it on wine, women and song. You took a calculated risk and tried to make your bank a bundle to recoup their losses, your intentions were pure."

"I also had a big ego and I was jealous of my brother."

"All traders have big egos; and people are always jealous of somebody else who is smarter, better looking, or richer than them. That's only human nature."

"I exceeded my authority."

"Unfortunately for all concerned, you made a business decision and it didn't work out, but deals crater every day on Wall Street, much larger deals than yours."

"Lenny, I broke the rules."

"Kid, you need to step back and look at the big picture here."

"I don't follow."

Lenny took a swig of wine and pooled the alcohol over a painful canker sore in his mouth before swallowing. "The country is in tough economic times today, banks are writing off billions and billions of bad loans left and right; they are being forced to go overseas with their hats in their hands begging foreign sovereign wealth funds to bail them out. Traders like you are under intense pressure to earn large profits to offset these losses. Isn't that true?"

"Yes, that's true."

"The last thing a bank wants today is to get the media's spotlight shone on them because of a rogue trader. Rogue traders mean their risk management systems are lousy and that bank managers are incompetent. Take that bank in Paris, the rogue trader went free but the CEO and a bunch of manager types lost their jobs in the shakeup that followed."

"I don't consider myself a rogue trader, Lenny."

"Of course, kid, you're not, I wasn't implying that you were. My point is that banks can't afford any additional bad PR now; their stocks have been hammered; their capital has been depleted; the regulators are all over them; their stockholders have lost their shirts and are mad as hell. The last thing they want to do today is hang more of their dirty laundry out to dry in public. When that happens, heads in the executive suites are definitely going to roll."

"Go on."

"I think you need to go to the senior management of your bank, kid, and tell them about the trading loss before they discover it for themselves."

Seth finished his wine in one gulp and refilled his glass.

"Offer the bank your resignation, pledge not to work again in the securities business for the rest of your life, and agree to sign a confidentiality agreement not to ever disclose the loss to the media. In exchange, you want their agreement not to prosecute you for the trading loss or to seek restitution."

"Hmmm."

"In effect, you want a get-out-of-jail card so you can wave bye-bye to Wall Street and come here to operate this restaurant."

Seth tore off a piece of bread and dipped it in the oil. "That sounds like it could be one tough negotiation, Lenny, I'm not sure I could pull it off."

"You couldn't, kid, you'd need a shrewd, tough lawyer to represent you; someone who could point out in gruesome detail all the pitfalls to the bank and its senior management if they prosecute you."

"Hmmm."

"This lawyer would basically have to be able to intimidate your employer into letting you off the hook."

Seth rubbed his forehead. "All the lawyers I know are with white-shoe firms that have banks as their clients; they wouldn't dare represent me. Besides, they are corporate lawyers; it sounds like I need a criminal lawyer."

"Yeah, you do."

"I don't know any criminal lawyers."

Lenny smiled. "Lucky for you, I do, and she's the best."

"She? It's a woman."

"Uh-huh."

"Are you sure she's tough enough?"

Lenny burst out in boisterous laughter and slapped him on the shoulder. "People call her Svet, it rhymes with sweat, that's because she makes rival counsel perspire so much in court."

Marko reappeared at their table.

Lenny looked up at the owner from his chair. "Seth is anxious for the interview to start, Marko, and from the little he's seen so far he tells me he thinks he can run this restaurant much better than you are. Maybe you could show him the kitchen."

"I swear I didn't say that, Marko, Lenny is kidding."

Marko nodded. "Yes, Lenny is great kidder, I only hope that one day his sense of humor doesn't get him killed."

Stan entered Ulysses and found Amelia sitting alone at the bar sipping her usual orange juice.

"Do you mind if I join you?" Stan asked.

"Hi, Stan, no, please sit down, I'd enjoy the company."

"Thanks." He ordered a ginger ale from Artie.

Amelia saw that Rocco was hanging upside down by his tail from the fire escape outside on Stone Street and watching them very closely.

"You've been followed, Stan, if you hadn't noticed."

"I know, Rocco's a lot of laughs but he can be a nuisance sometimes."

Artie brought Stan's ginger ale and lingered nearby, cutting up some limes.

She smiled. "I heard the great news about Bobby, kudos are in order, Stan; you've changed his life."

"No. I just finagled him the Juilliard audition and designed a dance routine for him, Amelia, Bobby did all the heavy lifting."

"You motivated him, Stan, without you Bobby never would have reached out for it."

"Maybe; maybe not."

"You should feel proud of yourself."

"No prouder than you should feel for getting Al interested in painting again. I think you may have saved his life, Amelia."

"Al has so much talent that it would be a great waste if he didn't use it."

"I agree, the world needs to see what he can do."

"Bobby is also equally talented."

"Yes, there's no question about that. I just hope he accepts the scholarship offer from Juilliard."

"He hasn't accepted it yet?"

Stan shrugged. "I don't know, he won't return my phone calls or e-mails."

"It's such a sweetheart deal."

"It certainly is."

"Come to think of it, Stan, I haven't seen him in Ulysses for several days."

"That's not a good sign, this place is like a second home for him."

"He'd have to be crazy to turn down Juilliard, Stan, it's the best in the country and so hard to get into."

"Bobby might be terrified, Amelia, afraid to face his father."

She blew out her breath. "So many people I know today are scared, life can be so damn scary sometimes, especially these days."

"Listen, Amelia, don't be mad but Merle told me about your ... eh ... problem. She thought I might be able to help."

"I know Merle means well, Stan, but this is one problem that I'll have to face alone."

"Anyway, I told her I'd chat you up."

"Chat me up? Now you sound like a Brit."

"I lived in London for several years when I was a dancer, a few idioms stayed with me when I came back to the States."

"I've never been to London; I understand it's a great city."

"It is, it's a walking city like New York; I'd love to show you around some day. There are some great pubs I'd want to take you to."

"That would be wonderful, Stan, I'd really like that."

"Getting back to your situation, Amelia, is there any chance that you and your ex-fiance might patch things up and get back together?"

She shook her head firmly. "No, I can forgive a lot of things but not infidelity; it's too serious a betrayal. He might as well be dead as far as I'm concerned."

"I see."

"I'm sure this attitude on my part reflects a deep flaw in my own *psyche*, but so be it, that's the way I feel."

"Yeah, I think I'd feel the same way if my fiancée cheated on me, I wouldn't be able to forgive her or trust her again."

"Have you ever been engaged, Stan?"

"No, I've never been much of a ladies man."

"I find that hard to believe, you are an attractive guy."

"Women always made me nervous, I was always tongue-tied around them."

"I see."

"Besides, when I was young, all I had time for was dancing, it consumed me."

"There's nothing wrong with being passionate about your work."

He placed his elbows on the bar and clasped his hands together. "I became too passionate about it, too focused; I sort of lost touch with myself for a long while. It wasn't until recently that I found myself again."

"Well, I'm glad you did, Stan, because you're a nice person."

"So are you, Amelia."

She brushed away a strand of hair that had fallen over her face. "I am pregnant, respectable girls don't get pregnant, not unless they have husbands they don't."

"That's a bit old-fashioned, don't you think? There are many single-moms today, there's no stigma anymore."

"I grew up without brothers or sisters; that was hard, I was very lonely, but at least I had a father. Every child needs a father, especially girls."

"You're still young, Amelia, you will meet someone."

"I doubt that; let me ask you, Stan, how many men do you know who would want to raise some other guy's kid?"

"I can't speak for other men, Amelia, but I'd say that having a family and being loved by a woman beats having no family and being alone by myself."

She cupped her face in her hands and stared deeply into his eyes. "What are you trying to say, Stan?"

"I guess I'm saying that if you want to keep the baby, Amelia, I'll marry you so he or she will have a father."

Her mouth fell open. "You hardly know me, Stan, we only met a few weeks ago."

"It doesn't matter, I know that you're a good person and have positive energy. You'll make a wonderful mother. My instincts about people are rarely wrong. And I also happen to find you very desirable, very sexy."

"I turn you on?"

He nodded. "Oh yeah, you do, I'm gonzo about you, I think you're a foxy lady."

"Nobody ever called me that before."

"I never said that to a woman before."

"I ... I'm at a loss for words, Stan."

"It gets more personal, I've been having erotic dreams about you, extremely lusty stuff."

Red blossoms appeared on her cheeks.

"I don't mean to offend you, I'm just putting all my cards on the table."

Amelia took a drink of her OJ because she didn't know how to respond.

"You're surprised, huh?"

"Yes, to say the least."

He nodded. "I am 44, a lot older than you, Amelia, which is something you'll have to take into consideration. And I also have to warn you that my biological clock is ticking."

"I thought only women had biological clocks."

"No, some men have them too."

"I see, go on."

"Like you, I'm also an only child, so I can relate to your lonely experience growing up. I was lonely too. Maybe that's why I like kids so much; I want to have a large family myself."

"How large?"

"Six kids would be perfect."

Her mouth fell open again. "Six!"

"Well, at least three kids then."

At that moment a young woman passed by them carrying a crying baby in her arms as she headed for the door of Ulysses so that the other people at her table would be able to eat their meal in peace.

"I'm not sure I'd be good with kids, Stan, I don't have the right temperament, I'm high-strung and I might snap. The kid could be traumatized for life."

He laughed. "You'll do no such thing."

"How can you be so sure?"

"I just am."

"I'm not the person you think I am."

"Yes, you are. And you're also beautiful."

"I'm a complete mess on the inside."

"Don't be so hard on yourself."

She looked away. "At Barnard I was a LUG."

"What's that?"

"A Lesbian Until Graduation. I was a dyke, I dated strictly women for four years, I didn't even like men."

"You're not a lesbian now, are you?"

"No, that's obvious, isn't it?"

"It's not an issue then, the past is the past, what's important is the present and the future."

"Oh, Stan, grow up."

He touched her wrist with a finger. "I know that this isn't a very romantic way for a man to make a marriage proposal to a woman. You deserve better; but it comes from my heart."

"I can sense that."

"And I'm not proposing just because you're in the situation you're in, Amelia, I'd want to marry you even if you *weren't* pregnant."

She forced a sad smile. "You would, would you?"

He made a face. "That didn't come out exactly the way I meant to say it."

"I think I know what you meant."

"Look, Amelia, you could do better, I'll be the first to tell you that. I'm not the handsomest guy in the world and, Lord knows, I'm certainly not the smartest. And I'm no stud, I've only been with two women in my whole life, it was socks-on sex, and neither of them would give me rave reviews on my performance. Then again, I didn't love any of those women so I might be a great lover with a woman like you who I was deeply in love with. Does that make any sense?"

"A little."

"Well, anyway, will you think about my proposal?"

"I will, Stan, I promise."

When Stan got up to leave Rocco was still watching them from the fire escape.

<hr>

The parrot gave Al the bad news about his health straight and without any sugarcoating as the ORACLE looked on compassionately.

"You are destined to die on this Saturday evening, Al, I'm sorry."

"But that can't be, my doctor recently told me that I was going to live to be a 100 years old?"

"Your physician was mistaken; the medical tests missed a lateral weakness in the main artery leading to your brain; you're going to have a fatal stroke on Saturday night while you're asleep in your bed. If you have to die, it's probably best to die in your sleep; it's quick and virtually painless."

"How can you be so sure that I'm going to die on Saturday?"

"The ORACLE knows these things."

Al covered his face with his hands. "Boy, this is a real bummer. A few weeks ago I would have been happy to get handed a terminal sentence. My life was pointless then and I had nothing to live for. That's all changed now, I have pictures to paint, a real reason to go on living."

"Yes, Al, we believe that you are a major talent, it's a terrible shame. The timing here really sucks."

The elderly man sagged back on the sofa and shrugged his frail shoulders despondently. "I guess that's that then, my new lease on life is over."

"Not necessarily, Al, you could negotiate with Death; you may be able to come to an arrangement with him."

His eyes widened. "Death is a *him*?"

The parrot shrieked. "It is best not to get bogged down in the details, Al, the point is that the ORACLE has arranged for you to sit down with Death so that you can try and hammer out a deal to buy yourself more time."

"Me ... you want me, Al Hanratty, to bargain with Death?"

"That's the general idea, after all, you're the party of the first part."

"This can't be happening, the whole thing is unreal!"

"Nevertheless, Al, it is the way that things are."

"But I was never proficient at negotiating; I've always ended up getting the short end of the stick in the past."

"The stakes are much higher now, Al, your life was never on the line before. That should make a big difference."

Al took a deep breath and exhaled slowly to calm himself. "How soon must I meet with Death?"

"His schedule is extremely tight, however, he has agreed to move his appointments around so that he will sit down with you on Friday night in Ulysses."

"That's too soon, I'll need more time to prepare."

"There is no more time, Al, you are destined to die on Saturday night. Remember?"

"What will I say to Death?"

The ORACLE blinked three times at the parrot.

"Be truthful and be yourself when you plead your case to him, Al, but whatever you do, don't get him mad."

"Huh?"

"That's very important, I can't stress that point too much."

"Death gets mad?"

"Oh, yes, he has a rotten temper, and when he gets mad, bad things happen."

Al massaged his frontal lobe. "I'm totally screwed, I tell you, that's what I am!"

"Like I said before, Al, it is best not to get bogged down in the details. Merely treat it as an ordinary business meeting."

Al's chin fell to his chest. "I ... I am afraid."

"I thought you told Stan that you weren't afraid of dying, that you'd even welcome it."

"That was before, when I had nothing to live for; this is now, when I have everything to lose."

"Don't get down on yourself, Al, the ORACLE has paved the way for you, it should be fine."

Al looked gratefully at the cat. "Thank you."

The cat yawned.

"Just remember, Al, whatever you do, don't get Death mad."

"I won't, I'll be on my best behavior; I'll grovel if I have to, I'll call him sir, I'll hang on his every word, I'll buy him drinks, I'll kiss his ass, whatever it takes, Al Hanratty will do."

"That's the proper attitude to have."

"I'll even tell him jokes and sing him a song."

"Don't go overboard, Al."

"Oh, one other thing, how will I find Death in the huge crowd at Ulysses? It is wall-to-wall people in there on Friday nights. "

"Death is very recognizable." The bird described him in detail.

"I still might miss him in the crowd."

"Don't be concerned about that, Al, Death will find you."

Al went white as a sheet. "That's what I'm afraid of."

"You'll charm him, I know you will."

"I hope I don't pee in my pants."

It was 4:45 P.M. and the stock market had closed at a loss for the tenth straight day as Stan took up a position in front of the office building on Broad Street where Bobby Rankle worked. Bobby still hadn't returned any of his calls or text messages so Stan decided to force the issue. He had to wait about half an hour before Bobby came out of the building.

"Hey, Bobby, do you have time for a Diet Coke?"

"Hello, Stan, I've been meaning to call you."

"Sure you have. How about that drink?"

"I can't. We landed a large account and my dad is having a cocktail party and dinner for the new client up at the Yale Club. I'm on my way there now."

"Have you told your dad about Juilliard yet?"

"Not yet, he's all excited about the new piece of business and I didn't want to rain on his parade. I'll tell him next week."

"Would it help if I was present when you told him? I could answer any questions he might have about the dance business."

"No, Stan, this is something I have to do by myself."

"Ok, Bobby, whatever you say. I hope you realize what a great opportunity this is. It's harder to get into Juilliard than it is to get into Harvard."

"I know."

"Call me when you've told him."

"I will."

"And call me if you don't tell him too."

"You got it." Bobby disappeared down the IRT subway steps.

Wanda had a view of the neon pizza parlor sign from her lawyer's office as she gazed out the window onto Avenue A.

"Svet use private detective to take close look at this Rodney Herkimer no-goodnik. Nicky find out interesting things."

"Who is Nicky?" Wanda asked.

"Nicky is Nikita Ilyich Gordunov, former KGB and FSB agent until he was retired early because he was too aggressive in his interrogations of suspects."

"What does 'too aggressive' mean, Svet?"

"Well, very many peoples have heart attacks during questioning by Nicky."

"Oh, my Lord, how did someone like that manage to get into the United States?"

"Svet sponsor him, naturally. He is from my village in the Ukraine; we are all Cossacks there. Wanda know about Cossacks?"

"No, not really."

"We are all warriors, we fight and kill our enemies on horseback; we loot and pillage, drink and raise hell everywhere we go. Like the Japanese Samurai, we not afraid to die; death is our companion, we cherish it."

"But you are a woman, Svet, surely the women Cossacks don't kill?"

"Wrong, women are best killers, we use sex to seduce our enemies, then we cut off their balls in middle of the night when they are asleep and feed them to the pigs so they cannot be reattached, they bleed out."

Wanda shuddered. "Oh, that is so horrible, I think I'm going to be sick."

Svet smiled. "Not to worry your pretty head, Wanda, in this case Nicky not interrogate anyone, he just snoop around like only sneaky secret policeman can do."

"What did this man find out in his investigation?"

The lawyer opened a manila folder and perused some papers. "Your pervert of a boss lives in mansion in Scarsdale, drive Cadillac and Porsche, also has beautiful beach house in Southampton."

"I know, around the office he is constantly bragging about how wealthy he is."

Svet lifted an eyebrow skeptically. "Nicky discover that houses and cars are registered in wife's name, not in his name. In fact, all family assets are in wife's name. She is what you Americans call a 'trust fund lady'."

"You mean a 'trust fund baby'.

"Baby ... lady ... no matter ... she inherit big bucks from her very rich, very dead papa."

"That comes as a surprise to me. Rodney always talked like the money came from his.side of the family."

"Also, wife's lawyers insist that Rodney sign prenuptial agreement before he married wealthy wife, so he get chicken feed if they get divorced."

"I had no idea."

"Rodney not only sex masher, he is liar too."

"How do we proceed, Svet?"

"Wife is another deep pocket because of her inheritance, we also name her in our lawsuit against Rodney and your employer."

"But the woman is innocent, Svet, and we can't collect from her; can we?"

"No, but we make her angry as hell after she sees films of her husband, Rodney, hitting on you for sex on top of desk."

"I see."

"Poor man who lives off wealthy wife is always secretly afraid of her."

"I suppose you know what you're doing, Svet, however, I'm very reluctant to drag his family into this sordid mess."

"Please to trust Svet on this point."

"Ok, if you say so, but I reserve the right to change my mind later."

"Nicky also find out that Rodney joined Ashley Madison dot-com in order to use Internet to find women to have sex with."

"What is Ashley Madison dot-com?"

"It is website on Internet for married peoples who want to have affairs and cheat on their spouses. For women it is free to join; men pay fee and receive a secret password. Their profile is then posted on website and men and women members send them messages to meet and have sneaky sex."

"That's disgraceful, Svet, it sounds like a website for adulterers."

"Not everyone think is so terrible, Wanda, website have over three million members; lots of hanky-panky going on in this country."

"Well, I think it should be against the law to do that. Think of all the marriages that could be ruined."

"Company claims that it saves many marriages. Spouses not getting enough hot sex at home now can get it from Internet dates."

"I am disgusted by the idea."

Svet shrugged. "Legal; illegal; website not our concern. Nicky will hack into Rodney's computer to find out his password. Nicky is nerd-head, he take KGB courses on how to subvert Western computer systems."

"I think the technical term is tech-head, Svet, not nerd-head."

She shrugged again. "Then we give his password to wife so she can see who his sex partners are. Rodney will never know what hit him when her lawyers attack."

"That reminds me." Wanda opened her purse and took out a film chip. "He hit on me again yesterday, this time he told me that I had to put out by next week or he would make up a reason to fire me."

Svet stood up and mouthed a long string of curse words in Russian, then drove her fist into the wall, creating another hole in the new drywall."

Her secretary came running in. "Oh, Svet, not again, the contractor just fixed that wall last week."

Wanda was not stunned at her behavior this time.

"On Friday morning, Nicky will hand deliver copies of lawsuit we intend to file and copies of the film to your employer's CEO and Chief Legal Counsel. I want you to take Friday off, Wanda, don't answer your phone unless you know it is Svet on the line. Svet want them to stew on this over the weekend. On Sunday morning, I will contact them to arrange a meeting for Monday where we will present our list of demands."

Wanda bit her lip. "I'm more than a little nervous, Svet."

"There is nothing to be nervous about, Wanda, this is the part of case that Svet likes best." She crushed an empty soda can in the crook of her arm and pitched it into a wastebasket twenty feet away.

On her way out Wanda bumped into Seth who was patiently waiting in the lawyer's small reception/waiting room. He was eating a pizza slice from the parlor downstairs. She hoped that there wasn't any asbestos on it.

"How's your case going, Wanda?"

"It looks like all hell is going to break loose at my office on Friday, that's when Svet is hitting my company with the legal papers and film."

"That's great, Wanda, that jerk boss of yours won't be hitting on you anymore."

"I'm nervous, but at the same time it's kind of exciting, I've never been involved in a lawsuit before."

"I'm sure everything will work out fine."

"Thank God for Svet; she's the best lawyer, she inspires confidence."

"I hope you're right about that, Wanda, my case is a difficult one. I don't have the leverage that you have, I'm the guilty party."

"Keep the faith, Seth, if anybody can help you, it's Svet Brutalefsky."

<hr>

"Did Lenny tell you that Svet was criminal prosecutor before she became the most successful defense counsel in New York?"

Seth nodded. "Yes, and he told me you won all your cases."

"*Da*, Svet did, Svet get convictions every time. And if Svet was prosecuting you today, Svet would get you sent to prison for fifteen years with no parole."

He slunk down in his chair. "Oh, my God!"

"And Svet would also slap lien on everything you own and earn, now and in future. Svet ask judge to charge you interest on the $22 million while you in prison." She took a calculator from the top drawer of her desk. "At 5.0% interest rate, Seth owe $48 million, give or take a few nickels, when you got out of jail."

"I might as well jump off the Brooklyn Bridge, Svet, my life would be ruined."

She smiled benevolently. "But Svet no longer prosecutor, so Seth not go to jail."

"Are you sure about that?"

Her mood turned aggressive. "If Svet say you get off; you get off! You must believe that; trust is needed between client and lawyer. Otherwise, you must get new lawyer." She arose and turned to punch the wall, however, it already had a hole in it so she sat down again. "But no other lawyer is as good as Svet in these kinds of cases."

"I believe you."

"*Da*, now Svet want Seth to read script; if we forced to go to trial, you must repeat on witness stand, word for word."

"Script?"

"*Da*, like in movie. Svet prepare it for you to memorize."

Seth picked up the sheaf of papers and began reading. "I am the victim in this case?"

"Of course you are victim, you were forced to do those trades because of your love for the bank and its other employees; you wanted to earn lots of money to compensate for large losses in sub-prime loans and credit default swaps your bosses, in their incompetence, so foolishly approved. And you hope your bosses don't lose their cushy jobs after you appear on *Larry King* to explain how easy it was to subvert bank's primitive risk management systems. You will say the same thing to *New York Post* and *New York Times.*"

"Svet, this is wrong, I am not the victim here."

"*Da*, you are victim. Svet wants you to look in the mirror and say 'I am the victim' a thousand times every night before you go to bed until you believe it yourself and are convincing."

He read more of the script. "I am severely depressed?"

"Of course, that is to be expected."

"I'm disappointed in myself, Svet, but I'm not depressed."

"You are depressed, but you don't know that you are depressed."

He read the script. "And I am having a nervous breakdown?"

"That is obvious to anyone who has eyes."

Seth continued reading. "I am delusional?"

"That goes without saying."

"Wait a second, Svet, it says in your script that I am a danger to myself."

"You fit the pattern."

"Oh, Svet, it says that I am under twenty-four hour *suicide* watch?"

"*Da*, Svet must take your belt and shoelaces before you leave so Seth not hang himself."

Seth read the last evaluation entry and threw down the script. "Hold on, now this is too much! You say that I have been diagnosed as a total psychiatric mess?"

The lawyer nodded vigorously. "*Da*, Dr. Boris Vishinsky will testify to that fact as our expert witness on stand if we must go to court."

"Who is this doctor?"

"Boris is ex-KGB chief psychiatrist; he was in charge of terrorizing enemies of the Soviet State. He is expert on creating psychiatric messes, believe you me."

"But I never even met this doctor?"

"No matter, Svet tell him all about your case and he make diagnosis over telephone line from his office in Moscow."

Seth gripped his head. "This is all a charade, Svet, none of it is true and it's not ethical."

"Svet hear about game of charades but Svet never play it."

Seth stood up and threw the script into the wastebasket. "This is all lies, Svet, it is a perversion of the American justice system. There is no honor in this, I should be held accountable for my actions. This is an example of everything that is wrong with the country today, nobody cares, not the politicians, not the business executives, not the generals, not the average guy in the street. It's all about me and what I can scam for myself; never think about the other guy or what's in the best interests of the country. Special-interest groups and lobbyists spend millions and dictate policy; the aim is to get away with as much as you can. I am disgusted by it all! Is there no honor today? What became of the values this great country was founded on? Where are our modern heroes? Who will step into the breach? Are we headed towards oblivion? Will the human race destroy itself? Did God make a terrible mistake in creating us? Is mankind the real problem? Would the Universe be better off if we are extinct as a species?"

Svet twiddled her fingers. "Have you finished your little hissy-fit?"

Seth -- deflated, disillusioned, and discombobulated -- after his tirade, nodded meekly and sat down.

"Svet now ask Seth simple question that require simple answer. Do you, or do you not, want to go to jail for fifteen years?"

Seth lowered his head onto her desk. "No, I'm afraid of going to prison, I watch all those prison shows on TV and they terrify me."

"*Da, is* settled then. Now Seth go home and memorize Svet's script like actor. You need to give Academy Award performance if case goes to court."

"Do you like the Professor, mom?" Allen asked his mother, while playing a Nintendo DS computer game.

Wanda wondered what the real motive for his question was. "Yes, I do."

"I like Georgette a lot. At first, I was a little put-off by her because she is so weird looking, but now that I know her, I think she's great."

"Looks can be deceiving, honey, never judge a person or an animal by the way they look."

"Do you like the Professor as much as you liked dad?"

"I *loved* your father, Allen."

"Do you love the Professor?"

"Allen, I only met him a short time ago."

"My friend Charlie told me that his mother fell in love with his father the first time she saw him; she never even knew anything about him, not even his name."

"That's called 'love at first sight'."

"Did that happen to you when you first saw the Professor?"

"No, although I did think he was very distinguished looking."

"So you like the way the Professor looks?"

"He keeps himself in shape, Allen, he works out regularly at the gym and he's careful about what he eats."

"You work out regularly and you're always on a diet."

"That's true, we have that in common."

"He's an old guy though, mom."

"You know what they say, Allen, today 60 is the new 40."

"The Professor is older than 60, he's 63, going on 64, he told me so at the baseball game he took me to. He said he used to watch Mickey Mantle and Whitey Ford play baseball at the original Yankee Stadium, that's how old he is."

Wanda shrugged. "I'm not a baseball fan; I don't know who those people are. I just played a little ping-pong and volleyball in college."

"Those aren't real sports, mom."

"I beg your pardon, young man; they play them in the Olympics."

"Anyway, mom, Mickey Mantle and Whitey Ford played *ages* ago, long before I was even born."

"Allen, you're only 12 years old, honey, I have shoes older than you."

"You're 44, mom, the Professor is almost 20 years older than you; he'll be 82 when you're his age."

"People are going to be living to 100 soon, thanks to advances in modern medicine. Age is less a factor today than it used to be."

"Mom, 82, is ancient no matter what you say."

Wanda sat down at the kitchen table. "Allen, are you telling me that you don't want me to see the Professor anymore? Is that what this is really all about?"

"No, I think the Professor is cool, he knows stuff you wouldn't believe. And next week he's going to take me up to Westchester to see a PGA event. Tiger Woods is scheduled to play. I hope you marry the guy."

"What!"

"You heard me, mom, I hope you marry the guy. That way I could live in his building on Stone Street and get to play with Leonard, Rocco and Georgette as much as I want. We'd save money on rent, and since the Professor writes his books from his apartment, you wouldn't have to hire a babysitter for me in these tough economic times when everyone is cutting back."

"What do you know about these tough economic times?"

"The Professor and I watch the business news channels on TV. He explains to me what the commentators are saying. I know all about the global economic crisis and the liquidity problems the banks are having."

"Maybe you could explain it to me."

He looked doubtful. "It's kinda complicated, mom."

"Allen, I'm a college graduate!"

"You were a liberal arts major, mom, that's a mickey-mouse degree."

"Wait just a second, young man, I'll have you know that liberal arts graduates are educated people. We're not narrow specialists, we have a foundation in the humanities, in language and philosophy."

He wasn't impressed. "Anyway, you could say that me and the Professor have bonded."

"I see."

"And it's a two-way street. We watch MTV together and I educate him all about the latest bands and rap artists. He really likes *Metallica*, *Coldplay*, and *Young Jeezy*."

"Are you serious?"

"Yes, it's true. I've got his little gray cells working overtime so you won't have to worry about him going senile on you, mom."

Wanda smiled. "Allen, you amaze me, when I was your age I didn't know half the things you know."

"All my friends' parents are in the same boat as you, mom. Kids like myself are the computer generation. We love our parents but we recognize their limitations."

"I think I'm seeing my son clearly for the first time."

"Kids grow up faster today, mom, it's a sign of the times."

She held him close. "Promise me you won't grow up too fast, young man, a normal, happy childhood is important if you're going to be a well-adjusted, caring adult."

"I promise."

"Ok, so, let's get back to the Professor. I take it now that you don't think he's too old for me."

"I only said he was because I wanted to see what your reaction would be. It was a test. His age doesn't bother me; I just wanted to see if it bothered you."

Wanda laughed. "You had me going there, you stinker, you."

"Are you going to marry him, mom? "

"I think it's time for bed, young man, we'll finish this discussion another day."

"Ah, mom, you always pull that bed stuff when it starts to get interesting."

═══════════════

The Professor entered Ulysses and caught Pedro on his dinner break as he had intended to do.

"*Hola, Pedro! Como esta usted?*"

The Mexican smiled. "*Bien gracias, mi amigo.*"

"*Yo vengo a perdite, Pedro.*"

"*Que favor es que, Senor Profesor? Pero, por favor, uso de la palabra en Ingles.*"

"You want to speak in English."

The young man nodded. "*Si,* I am in this country so I must learn to speak in English."

"I notice you get a little better each day."

"Thank you."

"Ok, in English then. Tell me, Pedro, how many years did you go to school in your country?"

He held up five fingers. "*Cinco anos.*"

The Professor nodded. "I would like you to play a little game for me."

"Pedro never play sports," he answered. "Pedro too small, the bigger children knock me down with ease."

"No, Pedro, not that kind of game, I'm talking about a game that tests your mind, how your mind uses logic to figure out the solution to problems."

"Logic?"

"*Logica.* A game that tests your ability to think … to reason things out."

"What kind of strange game is this, Pedro is wondering?"

"It is called Su Doku, a Japanese mind game."

"Mind game?"

"*Si, mente juego.*"

"Hmmm."

"It has become very popular in this country in the last few years. I will show you." The Professor picked up a copy of *The New York Post* and opened it to the page where the crossword and the Su Doku puzzle were displayed. "See, it is a numbers puzzle but requires no knowledge of mathematics to solve."

Pedro studied the puzzle's grid composed of nine columns and nine rows. The grid was further subdivided into nine boxes of 3x3 squares for a total of 81 squares. In some of these boxes numbers from 1-9 had been randomly filled into three or four of the squares; the remainder of the squares were blank.

"The object of the game," the Professor said, "is to fill in the grid so that every row, every column, and every 3x3 box contains the digits one through nine."

Pedro continued to stare bewilderedly at the paper.

"*El objetivo del rompecabezas consiste en llenar en la grilla de m odo que cada fila, columna y caja 3x3 contiene los numeros uno a nueve.*"

"Ah, Pedro understand now," he said, smiling.

"Fine. Would you like to try to solve today's puzzle?" He handed him a pencil.

The busboy wetted the tip of the pencil with his tongue and began to fill in the blank squares with numbers. It took him ninety seconds to complete the puzzle. "Pedro finish, see."

The Professor examined his solution and smiled. "Congratulations."

"Was not so difficult," Pedro replied.

The Professor took a sheaf of papers from his inside pocket and selected one. "I want you to try this one, it is more difficult."

Again Pedro wetted the pencil. This time it took him three minutes to complete it.

After verifying his solution, the Professor handed him a second piece of paper. "Now this game is very, very hard, Pedro, *es muy difícil*. If you are unable to finish it, don't worry, many Su Doku experts were not able to complete it."

Pedro wetted the pencil and stared at the boxes. For two minutes he didn't write any numbers in the blank squares. Just when the Professor thought the puzzle was too difficult for him, the busboy began to fill in the squares. He completed the puzzle in nine minutes.

The Professor vetted his answers and then smiled. "You are an amazing player, Pedro, truly amazing."

The busboy began to clear away his food plate so he could go back to work. "*Gracias a usted, que fue un desafío.*"

"Not challenging enough, Pedro, for someone with your high intelligence. I want you to take another test for me next week. It will be given at New York University and it will take an entire day."

"Pedro no can take off a whole day; Pedro need the money to send back to his family in *Ciudad Juarez*."

"How many days a week do you work?"

"*Siete dias*." He held up seven fingers. "I also have another job besides this one."

"You are a hard worker, Pedro."

"*Si*, like my father was also, before he was killed."

"How did he die?"

The young man's face saddened. "A wild bullet from drug gang war. Is not safe in my town anymore; there is too many killings. I work to send my mother money so she can move with my three brothers and two sisters to where my aunt lives in the desert."

"I think you are a fine son, Pedro, your father would be very proud of you."

"I am the oldest son; I am now the head of the family. It is my responsibility."

The Professor had a bright idea. "What if I pay you a $100 to compensate you for the money you will lose by taking a day off; then will you take the test?"

Pedro shook his head. "That would not be fair to you; Pedro does not make that much money in one day."

"No, I insist, I want to pay you $100 for your time and trouble."

Pedro smiled. "Then I will ask Juan to work for me that day. He will be happy to earn extra money."

"Fantastic, it is agreed."

"*Nos vemos mas tarde, e professor.*"

━━━━━━━━━━━

On his way out of Ulysses the Professor waved to Artie. "How are things?"

The bartender nodded. "I'm making progress on the new book."

"That's excellent."

"It's not exactly a comedy but I think its funny. I'll have some chapters to show you soon."

"I can't wait, Artie, I could use a few laughs."

"Yeah, I know what you mean, Professor, the market's headed into the toilet and God only knows when it'll recover. My customers all got their long faces on."

"You think things are really that bad?"

"Let me put it to you this way, when brokers and traders start coming in here for whiskey shots in the middle of the day in order to keep themselves going, it's time to batten down the hatches."

"Oh, boy."

"And I'm getting 10-15 resumes a week from bartenders looking for jobs. The small bars in Brooklyn and Queens they work at are getting squeezed as their free-spending young customers lose their jobs and go back home to live with their parents."

"Listen to this, Artie, I was talking with a young NYU graduate the other day and he told me that he had been *pre-fired*."

"Pre-fired? What's that mean?"

"He accepted a job offer from a company and then two days before he was supposed to start they called him up and fired him."

"God, that sucks."

"Yeah."

"All I know is that I've been pouring drinks in the Financial District for almost thirty years, Professor, I can see the handwriting on the wall."

"Maybe I should sell my remaining stocks and go to cash. I hate to do it, I'll take a loss, but it could be time to bite the bullet and save what I've got left. At my age, I can't be thinking too long-term."

"It's probably not a bad move."

"Thanks for the tip, Artie."

Upon returning home the Professor found his apartment door slightly ajar. He immediately made himself flat against the wall in the hall and kicked the door all the way open with his foot. "This is the police, you're surrounded, come out with your hands up in the air!"

There was no response from inside the apartment so he peered cautiously through the doorway. "Oh, no, not again." The living room was a mess, tables and lamps were overturned, and books and papers were strewn all over the floor. It was exactly like the previous 17 break-ins -- there was no sign of forced entry and as far as he could tell, nothing was missing and nothing was broken.

"Georgette! Where are you, girl?"

The dog didn't respond so he went into the bedroom; that room was in perfect order and he got down on his knees and peaked under the bed. She was hiding there, looking frightened, whining softly, the same as all the previous times.

"It's ok, girl, the intruder is gone; it's safe for you to come out now."

The Bull Terrier – Chihuahua mix crept out from under the bed and came into his arms for a reassuring hug. "You're safe now, daddy is home."

He picked her up and carried her into the living room. She seemed to enjoy all the attention.

"Things are different this time around, girl, I learned my lesson. Last week I leased the same camera/recorder that Stan did and I hid it in the kitchen where it had a clear view of the living room. This time we'll have the intruder on film; the police will now know what he looks like. He's probably got a long record for burglary so they shouldn't have any trouble picking him up."

The dog yelped guiltily.

Stan went into the open kitchen and removed the camera/recorder from where he'd hidden it behind a stack of plates. Returning to the living room he plugged it into the TV and hit the PLAY button.

An overturned table falling to the floor had activated the camera/recorder and the toppling of other items of furniture had kept it rolling. The intruder wasted no time in creating a mess of the living room. He could see the culprit very clearly; it was Georgette. After the last book hit the floor she went over to the door, got up on her hind legs, and turned the doorknob with her teeth until the door was ajar.

"It was all an act, Georgette, it was you all along. Now I know what that cop meant when he said my break-ins were an inside job."

The dog had her back to the TV and her head was hung low.

"How could you do this to us?"

She made a high-pitched whining noise.

"Well, what have you got to say for yourself, why are you trashing your own apartment?"

Georgette barked once

"Why are you so upset, girl?"

The dog barked several more times.

"What has all this got to do with Rocco?"

More barks.

"Georgette, we discussed this many times before, you can't marry Rocco and have babies. Rocco is a rodent and you are a dog; it is physically impossible for you two to mate. I'm afraid that your love for Rocco will have to remain platonic."

More barks.

"Don't get upset with me, I don't make the rules. You'll have to go and complain to Mother Nature about it."

More barks.

"Mother Nature doesn't have an address, Georgette, she is a personification, an imaginary being representing an abstraction."

More barks.

"Yes, I agree, it is a sad situation, but I wouldn't feel too badly about it if I were you. There is another reason why you and Rocco can't have babies together. I never mentioned it to you before because, well, I saw no harm in you and Rocco being friends. But now that your relationship has blossomed into something beyond mere friendship, I have no choice; I'm going to have to give you the bad news. You better brace yourself."

The dog emitted another high pitch whine and sat down.

"You see, Georgette, Rocco isn't Rocco; Rocco is really a female."

An ear-splitting howl shook the room.

"It's not a lie, Georgette, it's the truth. Merle's vet told her when she took Rocco in for a checkup; it came as a surprise to her too. She never changed his name because, by then, everyone knew the squirrel as Rocco."

There was a knock at the door and it opened. Merle stuck her head in. "What's going on in here? Are you beating poor Georgette, Professor?"

"No, of course not, I was just explaining the facts of life to her and why she and Rocco can't have babies together."

"Now that's a lecture I'd like to hear." She saw all the overturned living room furniture. "My God, you've had another break-in!"

"No, there weren't any break-ins, Georgette was behind them all. She took out her frustration over Rocco on the furniture and then made it appear to be a break-in so she wouldn't get in trouble."

"I can't believe that sweet Georgette could do something sneaky like that."

"She's a Bull Terrier – Chihuahua mix, Merle, that's a volatile combination of English bullheadedness and Mexican *machismo*. I should have figured this out much sooner."

The dog barked at Merle.

"Yes, honey, I'm afraid it is true, Rocco is a she, although I don't think he knows that he's a she."

Georgette slumped dejectedly to the floor.

The Professor rubbed her head. "It's ok, girl, I forgive you."

Merle sighed. "It never ceases to amaze me, the crazy things that we females do for love."

━━━━━━━━━━━

The man in the immaculate white suit entered Ulysses and surveyed the large Friday night crowd. Standing there by the door, he appeared to be a mystifying figure from another time and place.

Jill came out from her station behind the bar as soon as she saw him. "Al asked me to keep an eye out for you. He has a table in the other room, I'll take you back."

"Thank you, young lady."

As Death passed along the busy bar the seeing-eye-dog, a black Lab, of a patron let out a squeal and scurried for cover under its owner's legs.

Death bent over to pet the dog but it pulled frantically away from his outstretched hand.

Jill shot him a calibrating look.

"Alas, I was never very good with animals."

"Yes, I can see that."

"What spooked you?" the blind man inquired as he reached down to quiet the dog.

"Frank, it's ok," Jill assured him, "Brownie is fine now."

"He's never done that before, I can't think what got into him."

"There are too many loud people in here, Frank, that's all it was," she said, at the same time wondering to herself if there was more to it than that.

"The dog is definitely black, "Death remarked, "not brown," after they had left the blind man at the bar.

Jill nodded. "True, but nobody had the heart to tell Frank that when he first got Brownie and picked the name."

As they continued towards the rear of Ulysses the patrons at that side of the long bar experienced a deep chill up and down their spines. Most attributed it to a momentary quirk in the air-conditioning system.

Al was sitting by himself at a small table near a window that looked out onto Stone Street. Despite his firm resolve to remain stone, cold sober, his face was slightly pink from drinking three brandies to steady his nerves.

"Your guest has arrived," Jill said.

Al rose to his feet. "Thank you, Jill, for escorting him to me."

Death smiled at Al as if he were a long-lost friend. "Greetings and salutations, Mr. Hanratty, it is a glorious evening; is it not?"

Al was torn between being terrified and trying to recall where he'd seen him before. "Uh, it is, yes, please have a seat."

The two men sat down.

"This seems to be a convivial tavern," Death said, glancing around at the boisterous, but well-behaved crowd.

"Yes, Ulysses is that; would you care for a drink? I take it you *do* drink."

"That would be wonderful, Mr. Hanratty, I have come a long distance to see you tonight."

"Jill, a drink for my friend here," Al said, "he'll have a … a …"

"A *Maker's Mark* whisky on the rocks," Death said, "and please make it a double."

"You got it." Jill moved away from their table faster than Al had ever seen her move before.

"I am curious, Mr. Hanratty, what did the ORACLE tell you about me?"

"All he said was that I shouldn't get you mad."

Death laughed. "The ORACLE is a class act, however, he has a strange sense of humor, don't you think?"

"I couldn't say, I really don't know him that well."

"I know him very well, that's why I'm here tonight."

"I … I never expected to meet you."

Death raised an amused eyebrow. "Everyone gets to meet me, Mr. Hanratty, *sooner or later.*"

"I meant like this, in person, over a drink in a bar; it's surreal, a scene straight out of *The Twilight Zone.*"

"The world is a more mysterious place than you know, Mr. Hanratty."

"Yes, it appears to be."

Jill returned with the whisky and Death tasted it. "Ah, that's delicious. Thank you so much, young lady."

Death watched her disappear into the crowd. "Women are much more perceptive and intuitive than men, don't you think so?"

"I'm no authority on women; I've been a bachelor all my life so my knowledge of women is limited."

"Take that bartender, for instance, she may not know *who* I am, but she senses *what* I am."

"Jill is adept at sizing people up."

"That young woman is definitely frightened of me. "

"Everybody is frightened of you."

Death took another sip. "Not true, but that's a discussion for another day. We are here to talk about you tonight."

"Yes, we are."

"The ORACLE believes that the world would be a better place if you could live in it for a while longer, Mr.Hanratty. You are an artist with tremendous potential, so I am told."

"I think I can do some fine work if I had a little more time."

"Why is that important to you?"

Al had anticipated the question. "I want to leave something beautiful behind me after I depart this life, a kind of legacy so that future generations will know that Al Hanratty once lived and that his life amounted to something. So far, to be totally candid, my life hasn't amounted to much of anything. I have no children, no family, and I haven't done anything in my life to make the world a better place. The paintings could atone for all that, I wouldn't be a failure any more."

"I see."

"I could show you samples of my art if that would help persuade you."

"That won't be necessary, I accept the ORACLE's judgment of your talent." He finished his drink and held up the empty glass. "Would you mind ordering me another whisky?"

Al signaled across the room to Jill for a re-fill.

"Did the ORACLE explain to you how the system works, Mr. Hanratty?"

"No, he didn't."

"Then permit me to elaborate. In certain circumstances, if I feel that a person who is about to die has something important to contribute to mankind, I have the discretion to postpone that person's death for a limited period of time."

"Hmmm."

"However, the system must always be kept in a state of equilibrium; if one person's life is extended, then another person's life must be shortened."

"Oh."

"Yes, it is a zero-sum game, so to speak, Mr. Hanratty. By that I mean, if you were to receive an extra year to live, for example, then someone else must die a year before their allotted time."

Al's face seemed to drain of all hope. "I'd like to paint a few pictures before I kick the bucket but I wouldn't want to deprive another person of any of the precious time they have left on Earth."

"That is very decent of you." Death smiled at a server who was carrying a tray of drinks to the next table. "For some people, however, time is not precious, it means added pain and suffering. Dying would actually be a release for them, a solution to a problem. In their eyes it would mean the difference between coming to a peaceful end and a horrible end."

Jill brought the fresh drink and Death handed her a crisp $50 bill. "You may keep the change, young lady."

She hesitated and eyed the money as though it might be contaminated. Finally she reached out and took it from him. "Thank you, sir."

Death took a mouthful of the whisky. "There is a woman living in Hermosa Beach, California, who has terminal cancer and is in great pain despite all the morphine she is receiving from her doctors. Her religious convictions rule out suicide as an option. Unfortunately, her scheduled time to depart this life will not come for another seven months."

"That's too bad."

"As you might expect, she has prayed for an earlier demise."

"I see."

"I could arrange a swap; Aloysius Hanratty in New York gets an additional seven months to live and Marcia Howell in California gets to mercifully die tomorrow night in his place. How does that sound to you?"

Al swallowed deeply and tried not to appear too eager. "If she is agreeable to the swap, I am also agreeable."

"Fine, then consider it done, Mr. Hanratty, you have been officially granted a temporary reprieve of seven months."

The tension left Al's body and he felt like running back to his apartment so he could begin painting immediately.

Death drank the last of the whisky. "Do you have any questions of me before I leave?"

"I have about a thousand questions but I'm afraid to ask any of them because you might get mad at me."

Death smiled. "A deal is a deal, Mr. Hanratty, you needn't fear that I will renege on our arrangement. I always keep my word, the ORACLE will attest to that."

Al nodded. "Ok, then tell me this, why was I scheduled to die just when my life had finally turned around for the better?"

Death sighed as if he'd been asked the same question a few hundred thousand times over the millennia.

"It doesn't seem fair."

"Look around at what's going on in the world, Mr. Hanratty, think about all the young innocents who I take with me every day of the week, simply because they were born in the wrong place at the wrong time, through no fault of their own, their pathetic, unlived lives claimed by disease, starvation, war's collateral damage, or simply by cruel parents who didn't want them. Is that fair, I ask you?"

Al bowed his head. "No, it certainly is not."

"You have lived for 76 years, Mr. Hanratty, which is more time than most people have been given. And you've been one of the lucky ones, you weren't born retarded or deformed, you got to enjoy all those years in a democratic, prosperous country with a stable government and the freedom to practice, or not practice, any religion you chose to. You've had access to clean drinking water, wholesome foods, sanitation, healthcare and higher education. What reason do you have to complain?"

Al nodded again. "You're absolutely right, I have nothing to gripe about."

"That's better."

"But it's still not fair to my way of thinking."

Death raised his voice. "Who told you that life is supposed to be fair, Mr. Hanratty? Or did you read that in a book somewhere?"

"Ok, ok, you're telling me that life isn't fair, I get it."

"I am."

"So why isn't life fair?"

Death shrugged. "I don't know."

Al was taken back. "What do you mean you don't know? You're Death, for Pete's sake, you're supposed to know everything; aren't you?"

"People have a basic misconception about me and my role in the order of things."

"Then let me ask you another question," Al said, "how is the length of time each person gets to live on this Earth determined? Why do some people like me get a long time while others get barely a few years or even die stillborn?"

Death shrugged again. "I don't know that either."

"Really?"

"I do not determine who lives and who dies, Mr. Hanratty, I merely take people to the other side when their allotted time is up."

"I see."

"I do, however, know *when* and *how* people are going to die." Death glanced over at a group of young men and women happily conversing in a corner. "Two people here tonight will die before you, Mr. Hanratty, one in a car accident and the other in a fall. Would you like me to point them out to you?"

Al closed his eyes. "No, please don't do that, I couldn't bear to look at them."

"Very well, then I won't."

Al opened his eyes. "Who does determine life spans? Is it God?"

"Some questions can only be answered after you have passed; that is one of them."

"What lies on the other side?"

"That, too, Mr. Hanratty, is another one of those questions."

Totally exasperated, Al gazed across the barroom and noticed that Amelia was talking to an exotic redhead he had never seen before in Ulysses. Whatever the woman was saying seemed to be greatly upsetting her.

"Your friend, Amelia, is pregnant," Death said, "soon she will begin to show."

"Oh, is she now?"

"Yes, and she is trying to decide whether or not to have the baby or to go for an abortion."

Al grimaced. "I didn't want to know that particular piece of information."

"All knowledge is a useful thing, Mr. Hanratty, the ORACLE will tell you the same thing."

"Who is the woman that Amelia is speaking to?"

Death frowned. "She is the original 'Welcome Wagon Lady'. Just as I am present at the end of life, she is present when life begins."

"Hmmm."

"Think of me and her as the *Yin* and *Yang*."

"I get it."

"As you can see for yourself, Mr. Hanratty, she has no sense of fashion or style and dresses like a $40 whore."

Al smiled. "She looks like she'd be fun at a party though."

Death stood up. "I must be leaving, Mr. Hanratty, our business is concluded and I have several other appointments."

Al rose to his feet. "Thank you for the extra time that you have given me."

"Don't thank me; Marcia Howell gave you the seven months, not I."

"Yes, I understand, please thank her for me."

"I will."

"One last question," Al said, "do you remember the faces of all those you have taken to the other side?"

"I remember some better than others, Mr. Hanratty, however the answer is yes, I remember them all -- the young and the old, the good and the evil, the penitent and the unrepentant."

"That's interesting."

"And I will certainly remember you."

Al went to shake hands with him but thought better of it.

"Until next time then, Mr. Hanratty, until ..." Death consulted his watch calendar, "... until seven months hence, the early evening of December 12. I will come for you then, wherever in the world you may be, whatever you may be doing. Please see to it that you are ready, there can be no further reprieves."

"I will be ready."

Death left the bar the same way that he had come in and its patrons breathed a collective, subliminal, sigh of relief as the door closed behind him.

Al sat back down and held the empty whisky glass up to the light; there were no fingerprints on it that he could see.

Jill approached the table. "Are you all right, Al?"

He dabbed at his temple with a napkin. "Yes, I'm tip-top now."

"Your friend is a big tipper."

"He's not exactly a friend."

"The guy gives me the willies."

Al nodded. "Yes, he has that effect on most people."

"Another brandy, Al?"

"No, Jill, I need a clear head and a steady hand tonight, I have some paintings to complete and there's no time to waste."

━━━━━━━━━━━━━━━━━

Amelia noticed that Al was engaged in rapt conversation with a man wearing an expensive white suit on the other side of the barroom. The overhead lights played tricks with their table; Al was brightly illuminated in a cone of light whereas his companion seemed to cloak his face in the shadowy areas between tables. The man was very good-looking in an unsettling kind of way; so she averted her head whenever he glanced in her direction. Amelia was certain that she had never seen him before and instinctively knew that she never wanted to see him again.

A woman with flowing red hair and wearing a very low cut green satin dress and over-the-knee black boots sat down beside her. She had a heart-shaped face, brown eyes, thick lips, and an infectious smile. Though not classically beautiful, she was comely in a flamboyant sort of way.

"Bartender, I'll have a double bourbon with a slice of orange and a half-clove of chopped garlic."

Noel, an attractive brunette, scratched her head. "I've served a lot of drinks in my time but that's a new one on me."

"I invented the drink," the woman said, "I call it the Elixir of Life."

"That's a catchy name; I'll have to try it myself."

The redhead and the man in the white suit nodded to each other ever so slightly as if they had been acquaintances for a very long time but had never become fast friends.

"Here you are," Noel said, "enjoy."

"Thank you." The woman turned to Amelia. "Would you like to try it, sugar, I'm buying?"

Amelia begged off. "No thanks, maybe some other time."

She smiled at her. "You're pregnant, sugar, aren't you?"

Amelia moved closer to her. "I'm not showing, am I?"

"No, your secret is safe for another six weeks."

"How do you know my name?"

"It is my business to know young women who are with child."

"Who are you?"

The redhead's eyes went across the barroom to the man in the immaculate white suit. "Amelia, do you see who your friend, Al, is speaking to?"

"Yes, I see him."

"Most people meet him only once in their lives and that's at the very end of their lives."

"I don't follow."

"The man in the white suit is Death."

"What?"

"Yes, and he's telling Al that his allotted time on Earth is almost up. You see; Al is scheduled to die tomorrow night."

"Oh, my God!"

"It is a rare occurrence that he and I are in the same location at the same time; and it is rarer still for Death to appear in physical form to someone who is not on their deathbed. Your friend, Al, must be a very special case."

Amelia recognized the expression of repressed anguish on Al's face and realized that the woman was speaking the truth.

The redhead made a sour face. "I don't understand how he can wear that same dreadful white suit day in and day out, it is such a *passé* look."

Amelia turned to her. "If he is Death, then you must be … Life."

"You are very insightful, sugar, most people don't think I even exist.

That's because no movies have ever been made about me. Now Death, on the other, is depicted in lots of movies. Brad Pitt played him a few years ago opposite Anthony Hopkins in *Meet Joe Black*. I get so angry that I don't get the notoriety I deserve."

"My head is suddenly spinning," Amelia said, touching her forehead.

"Then maybe we should find a table, sugar, we don't want you falling down and having a miscarriage. That would defeat the purpose of my visit here tonight."

"No, let's stay where we are, I'll be ok in a minute."

"As you wish."

"You sitting down on the stool next to me today is no accident, is it?"

"No, sugar, I came here solely to see you."

"Why?"

The redhead took a drink of the bourbon concoction and licked her rosy red lips. "I always show up when a pregnant woman is about to make a life or death decision affecting her unborn child."

"Let me ask you a question," Amelia said, "do you know how my baby will turn out, what kind of a person he or she will be, if I decide to have it?"

"No, sugar, I cannot see into the future."

"Yet you have come to try and persuade me to have it?"

"Yes, that is my role in the order of things. I am your unborn child's advocate, I am here to see to it that your fetus gets the chance to experience all the joys and wonders that life has to offer."

"What about life's sorrows, hardships and disappointments?"

"Yes; those too."

Amelia watched the man in the white suit get up from Al's table and exit the bar. She felt a greater sense of well being as the door closed behind him. "For as much as you know, my child's life could be *all* sorrow, hardship and disappointment."

"Yes, sugar, it could, that's true."

"Then why should I risk it? This world we live in is getting worse, not better, why should I bring a child into it, especially a child with no father? The odds are stacked against it."

"*It* happens to be a boy, Amelia, you are going to have a son."

"You know that for a fact?"

"Yes, some things I do know. And I also know that you are thinking of naming him Arthur, after your paternal grandfather. Aren't you?"

Amelia rested her forehead on her arm. "That makes it harder, knowing the sex, I mean. Now he has an identity, a personality of his own."

"I am here today to make it *harder* for you; it was equally hard for your mother as well."

Amelia lifted her head. "What do you mean by that remark?"

"When your mother was pregnant with you, sugar, your father lost his job."

"I wasn't aware of that."

"Your parents were worried about money and didn't think they could afford to have you." She held her thumb and index finger a fraction of an inch apart. "They were that close to aborting you when I showed up and convinced them to do the right thing and go through with your birth."

Amelia's face hardened into disbelief and her voice grew strained. "That's a lie; my mother would never have considered abortion. She's a very religious person; abortion is against everything she holds sacred."

"I do not lie."

"And my mother loved me too much to have an abortion."

The redhead took a long drink of bourbon. "Do you think she loved you more than you love Arthur?"

"It's not true, I tell you, you're mistaken."

The redhead picked up Amelia's cell phone off the bar and offered it to her. "Telephone her if you don't believe me. After all these years, your mother should be able to talk about it openly with you now."

"I just might call your bluff."

"Do it, by all means get her on the line."

"I will!" Amelia grabbed the instrument and stormed outside onto Stone Street where she would have some privacy.

"What got into Amelia?" Noel came over and asked.

"She's got a bee in her bonnet."

"Huh?"

"It's an expression that was popular about forty years ago; in today's lingo it means she's got a bug up her ass."

"You don't look that old to me."

The redhead took out a compact and checked her face. "I've been around for eons and eons."

"How do you manage to stay so young looking?"

"I don't exercise and I drink plenty of bourbon, which reminds me, please bring me another drink."

"You got it. By the way, I'm Noel, what's your name?"

She pursed her lips. "Today my name is Juanita."

"Today?"

"Yes, I change my name every day, I find it keeps me fresh."

"That's awesome!"

"What do you do to stay fresh, Noel?"

"I'm constantly updating my info on Facebook, I practically live on that site. Do you have a page?"

"No, I don't."

"It's a great way to stay in touch with your friends."

"I don't have any friends."

"That's not possible, Juanita, a friendly, outgoing person like you has got to have lots of friends."

"You would think so, wouldn't you?"

"Click on my page on Facebook, Juanita, and I'll make you my friend."

"That's very sweet of you, Noel, but I'm off to Madrid in a few hours and then I have to be in Berlin early tomorrow morning. I'm never in one place for very long."

"You're so lucky, Juanita, I wish I could travel around the world like that to glamorous places."

"You are well-liked, Noel, that's one of the reasons this place is so popular. And you're surrounded by friends here, that's always a good place to be."

"I suppose."

A group of people came in the Pearl Street entrance and walked up to the bar, asking for menus.

"I gotta go."

"See you, Noel."

The redhead sipped her new drink very slowly, as if it had to last a lifetime, yet her glass was half-empty by the time Amelia returned.

Amelia slammed her cell phone down on the bar and looked angrily around to see if someone was spoiling for a fight. "I'm so upset I could drink a whole bottle of *Wild Turkey*, pregnancy or no pregnancy. Then I want to go to *Bloomingdales* and spend every last cent I have on clothes I'll never wear."

"Let's see," the redhead said, "then you would be either an alcoholic shopaholic or a shopaholic alcoholic, I'm not sure which. English is not my strongest language."

"She never told me!" Amelia said, "even after all this time I had to practically drag it out of her."

The redhead nodded. "It is not something that you casually tell a child over the breakfast table, Amelia. *Oh, by the way, dear, I almost had you killed when I found out I was pregnant with you. Enjoy school today.*"

Amelia's eyes became teary and she searched for a tissue in her purse.

"It doesn't mean your mother didn't love you, sugar, it's more complicated. You should know that since you find yourself in the same situation today as your mother did almost three decades ago."

She found a rumpled tissue.

"I mean, you do love Arthur, sugar, don't you?"

Amelia was forced to nod because she couldn't find her voice.

―――――――――――――

The Professor walked into Ulysses and went up to the bar. "Hey, Artie, I want you to know I sold my stock. Thanks to you, I got out almost in one piece, the market's down a thousand points since then, you saved me some bucks."

"Yeah, I've been watching the slide. Business at the bar has picked up but the kitchen is slow. People have cut back on eating lunch and dinner out."

"It's belt-tightening time."

"It is. Me and the missus used to eat out a couple of times a week, now it's going to be twice a month."

"Frugality is back in vogue."

"It's about time, Artie, things were getting out of control."

"I know, my wife's brother took out a home equity loan on his house in Rockville Center a few years ago and he's sorry he did. He figured his place would continue to go up in value so he used it like an ATM; bought a new BMW, took expensive vacations, paid college tuition for his three kids. Now he lost his job and his house is worth a lot less than he thought it was. He can't sell it and is facing foreclosure if he doesn't catch a break soon."

"I'm sorry to hear that."

Artie shrugged. "We all have our problems these days."

"So what else is new?"

The bartender's smile brightened. "Well, I'm a hundred pages into the new novel now."

"You don't say?"

"It's true."

"I know you said it was funny but what's the plot about?"

"I took your advice and decided to write what I know about. It takes place mostly in a bar very much like this one."

"So you're writing about all the oddball characters that you've come into contact with over the years while tending bar."

"Not exactly."

"Oh?"

"It's about a group of magical animals who hang around a bar and help the customers there to realize their dreams."

"That sounds intriguing."

"The leader of the animals is a cat who can read minds."

"Really."

"The cat also drinks a lot of beer."

The Professor laughed. "You mean like Stan's cat?"

"Yeah, that's where I got the idea. And I also have a dog in it like your Georgette."

"I'll have to tell her when I go upstairs, she'll be thrilled."

Artie looked around the cavernous space. "You know, it's amazing what you can learn about people as a bartender if you keep your eyes and ears open. People let their hair down when they step into places like this; they say what they really think about themselves, about their families and friends, their jobs, their lives."

"I don't doubt it, Artie, I do it myself. Bars are like sanctuaries in a storm where people can safely let off a little steam so they can remain sane the rest of the time. They can be honest and be themselves for a while. And there'll be no repercussions afterwards as along as they don't drink too much and lose control."

"I'm not a gossip, Professor, and I would never repeat anything that I overheard in here, but, as a writer, there isn't a better place to be. You wouldn't believe the crazy situations that ordinary folks get embroiled in."

"I bet I'd be flabbergasted."

"I swear; life *is* stranger than fiction. And the dialogue you hear is so heartfelt and genuine, I couldn't make up better lines in a million years."

"I wish I could go back in time to a tavern in the 17th. Century Caribbean, Artie, where pirates hung out and simply listen to their conversations. My own books would be much the better for it, I can tell you that."

"Anyway, I showed my wife the first six chapters and she laughed her head off. I even find myself smiling as I'm writing it."

"When you've got a few more chapters, Artie, maybe I could take a peek."

"Absolutely, Professor, I'd appreciate getting your critical comments. I'm sure they'd help me a lot."

"Have you decided on a title yet?"

"No. I might wait until I finish it before deciding."

"Give it some serious thought. A catchy title can help sell books."

"I'm very excited about the book, Professor, I think this could be the one, my break-out novel. I have a confident feeling about it."

"If anybody deserves success, Artie, it's you, no writer I know has worked any harder for so long."

"Thanks, it's kind of you to say that."

"That's the God's honest truth."

"It's also the easiest book I've ever written. You know, the words just seem to pour out of me, I can write pages and pages without stopping, I lose all track of time; last night I had to force myself to turn off the computer because it was 3:00 A.M. and I had to get up for work in a few hours. I've never had that experience before. All the other books were so difficult to write."

"That's because you're finally in your element, Artie, you're at home with the material. You have found your niche, as they say."

"And I never realized before that I could write humor well."

"I'm not surprised at all, Artie, I've always known that you were a very funny guy."

Artie laughed. "And here all my life I thought I was the serious type."

The Professor nodded. "All the best humor is very serious."

━━━━━━━━━━━━━━━━━

Seth sat glumly on the sofa in Lenny's apartment facing Lenny and Leonard but not daring to look at them squarely in their five eyes.

"So how'd it go when you told the family that you wanted to chuck Wall Street and become a chef?" Lenny asked.

"My father thinks I'm crazy and went ballistic; my mother cried a lot; my brother found the whole situation terribly funny."

"Well, I guess it could've gone worse." The iguana made a clacking sound with his tongue to signify that he agreed with Lenny.

"The bottom line is that I'm a disgrace to the family, a black mark on the record of the Wharton Business School, and a traitor to my class."

"Hmmm."

"And I'm also a profound disappointment, a total loser, a moron, a quitter, a misfit, a laughing-stock, and an ungrateful, spoiled brat."

"Is that all?"

"Oh, I almost forgot, my ancestors are turning over in their graves back in Germany and I'll regret this stupid decision for the rest of my miserable, mediocre life."

Lenny spun the wheelchair in a tight circle. "I think I might be lucky not to have a family."

"Believe me, you are."

"Well, look at it this way, kid, the worst is over, you've exploded the bombshell. I mean, what else can your parents do to you?"

"I'm also being written out of the will."

"Cripes, that's bad, real bad."

"I don't care, Lenny, I told them that my life isn't all about making a lot of money, it's about acknowledging my passion, smelling the roses, satisfying my inner child, going with my gut, following my bliss; so that I am a happy and contented person."

"I'm guessing that didn't go over big either."

"My father slammed the door in my face."

"It sounds like you've burned your bridges."

"I have; there's no going back now."

"Blood is thicker than water, kid, your family will come around eventually, it may take a while, but it will happen. In the meantime, go out and become the best damn chef that you can be."

"You really think they will forgive me?"

"Yeah, I'm certain of it," Lenny lied.

"Marko is letting me cook the entrees tonight at the restaurant for the first time."

"That's great, I'll alert the gang; we'll all show up for dinner."

The Professor had taken Wanda and Allen to the circus that day so Stan volunteered to walk Georgette for him. He allowed the dog to pull him haphazardly without paying attention to which direction she was taking him while his thoughts centered on Amelia and her unborn son. By the time he ceased daydreaming he found himself in front of Al's walk-up on Ann Street. Stan decided to ring Al's buzzer; the elderly man was home and invited them up.

"Hey, Al," Stan said, wheezing for breath after climbing to the fourth floor, "I hope we're not interrupting a master at work. We found ourselves in the neighborhood and I had an urge to come up and see how you were progressing."

"Come in, Stan, and no, you're not interrupting me." An easel was standing by the window where the light was better. Paints and brushes were in readiness. "The fact of the matter is that I've been staring at this empty canvas for the better part of a week and I haven't so much as painted a brush stroke. I'm stuck, I have no idea how to begin."

"Maybe you have 'painter's block'."

"Is there such a thing?"

Stan shrugged. "I don't know, writers get blocked; why not painters too?"

"I think the creative side of my brain must have atrophied over the years from non-use."

"You're probably just trying too hard."

Al rubbed his hands together for warmth as the landlord was skimping on the heat. "I'm don't mind admitting that I'm starting to panic."

"You need a jolt of inspiration, that's all, then your creative juices will start to flow."

"That's what I thought too, Stan, so I went up to the Met and the MOMA a few days ago to see if I could find some inspiration there. No dice, I stared at all the great paintings for hours and came away empty."

Georgette jumped up on the window seat and began to whine at a black squirrel sitting on a branch in a nearby tree.

"Easy, girl," Stan called to her, "that's not Rocco out there, it's only a distant relative of his."

The squirrel suddenly leaped from the tree branch to the window ledge of the apartment and Georgette jumped backwards knocking over the easel and a tube of blue pigment. When she landed on the floor her feet stepped on the tube, squeezing the paint onto the floorboards. She made a series of tracks across the empty canvas with her nails in her rush to the door.

Stan pulled on her leash. "I'm terribly sorry, Al, it's all my fault, I should've kept a closer eye on her."

Al didn't respond, instead he seemed mesmerized by the erratic marks the dog had made on the canvas.

"Al?"

"That's the impetus I've been looking for, Stan, and thanks to Georgette I now know what I have to do."

"You do?"

"Yes, and please don't take offense, Stan, but I'm going to ask you both to leave now, I have a great deal of work to do."

Stan went to the door. "I'll let myself out. See you later."

Al never heard him; instead, he had picked up a brush and began to paint furiously."

―――――――――――――

"Stan, I told my parents about the baby," Amelia said. She had come to his building to visit Merle and knocked on his door on the way out.

He nodded. "I'm sure that took courage."

"It wasn't easy."

"No, I can imagine. Please, come in."

She sat on the sofa. "I told them that I had decided to give birth to the baby, that I wasn't going to have an abortion."

"I'm glad to hear that, Amelia, really glad."

"I also told them that I was still undecided about *keeping* the baby, that I might very well put it up for adoption."

"His name is Arthur, remember?"

" … that I might very well put *Arthur* up for adoption."

"I see."

"My mom was fine with that, she thinks it's for the best. She said that I'm young, that I have my whole life ahead of me, that the last thing I need at this point is a kid to tie me down."

"What did your dad say?"

Amelia looked away. "He wants a grandchild by hook or by crook, especially a boy that he can take to Giants football games and spoil a hundred different other ways."

"I like the way your dad thinks, Amelia, only I'd take Arthur to Mets games. Who knows, maybe the three of us guys could go together. I'd spring for the hot dogs."

"Oh, Stan, you don't make this any easier."

"My marriage proposal still stands, Amelia, you know where I come out on this matter."

"You can't want to marry me, you don't really know me!"

"I know all I need to know about you, it's that simple."

"Put yourself in my position, Stan, and tell me what you honestly would do."

"That's easy, I'd have the baby and marry me so we could live happily ever after together."

"That's absolutely no help at all, Stan, I'm asking you to be rational."

"Ok, Amelia, let me try and answer you in a more rational manner." He thought for a long moment. "If I had a son and I put him up for adoption, I know that I would think about him every day for the rest of my life. I'd wonder where he was during the day and what he was up to; I'd wonder if he looked like me; if he was safe and happy, if he had my personality, if he was a dancer. Most of all, though, I think that I'd miss seeing him grow up, going to all those hokey grammar school plays and lopsided Little League baseball games, the teacher conferences, the summer camps, the onset of angst and acne in high school, his first girlfriend, his first car, the prom, the SATs, college, his first job, marriage, and my first grandchild. Speaking for me, Amelia, and for me alone, if I gave Arthur up for adoption, I'd end up living a life of eternal regret."

At that point the ORACLE strolled into the room from a bedroom where he had been meditating. He sat down by the window and yawned.

"Does that help you any, Amelia?"

She arose abruptly and left the apartment without replying.

Stan looked at the cat. "Women, you can't live with them, and you can't live without them."

The ORACLE blinked three times.

"Thanks, O, but no thanks, I don't want to take a magic potion that will cure me of my attraction to the opposite sex."

=====================

Bobby sat down on the bar stool next to Stan and ordered a Diet Coke from Artie. "Hi, guy."

"Hey, Bobby, I was about to report you to the police as a missing person."

"Sorry about lying low, Stan, I was building up my nerve."

Artie brought the soft drink and busied himself nearby filling a fruit tray with olives, maraschino cherries, orange slices and limes.

"What news do you have to tell me, Bobby?"

"I have good news and I have not-so-good news, Stan, which do you want to hear first?"

"Right now I could use some good news, so let's hear that first."

"I told my dad about the scholarship to Juilliard and that I had decided to go."

"You didn't!"

"I did!"

"How did he take it?"

"I was surprised, Stan, he took it very calmly."

"Hmmm."

"It was like he had been expecting it."

"Maybe he knows more about you than you think."

Bobby shrugged like he didn't buy that.

"Your dad didn't try to change your mind?"

"No, and that's the strange part. I was prepared for an argument; I had all my reasons lined up. But I didn't have to go into any of them."

"Great, ok, so now give me the not-so-good news?"

"You're going to kill me, Stan, when you hear what I've done."

"It can't be *that* bad, can it?"

"Before I tell you, all I want to say in my own defense is that I didn't know about you and Amelia at the time."

"What about me and Amelia?"

"I wasn't aware of the fact that you had asked her to marry you."

Stan's face became suddenly mottled with splotches. "You know about that?"

"Everybody in the building knows about that; and so do a few thousand other people who frequent Ulysses."

"What!"

"Yeah, I'm afraid the word spread as fast as those wildfires in California."

"But I never told a single, solitary soul?"

Bobby glanced at Rocco who was hanging by his tail from the fire escape outside on Stone Street while peering into the bar and reading their lips. "I guess the windows have ears."

The squirrel ran up the fire escape just as Stan turned towards the window to see what Bobby was looking at.

"Anyway, Stan, the cat is definitely out of the bag."

Stan took a drink of ginger ale and winced as though it was 100 - proof alcohol. "Ok, so what's the rest of the not-so-good news?"

"I'm afraid it's a double whammy, Stan."

"I suspected as much."

"Well, when I spoke to my dad I was very nervous about him suspecting that I might be gay. So I told him I had a girlfriend. It just slipped out of my mouth. Once I said it, of course, it was too late to take it back."

"I see."

"My dad got all excited and pressed me for details about her. I became flustered and … well … I told him that her name was Amelia and that she worked for a non-profit foundation that helped underprivileged kids."

"What!"

"That's not the worst part though, Stan."

"What can be worse than that?"

"My dad is coming here to have brunch at Ulysses on Sunday to meet her. I couldn't say no when he asked to see her."

"Oh, boy!"

"Yeah, I know, what am I going to do?"

Stan pinched his lip. "You are going to have to tell Amelia what you've done."

"She's probably going to be really ticked off."

"I would think so, I know I would be if I was her."

"Daniel got very pissed off when I told him what I'd done."

Stan looked at him curiously. "Who is Daniel?"

Bobby folded his arms defensively. "Um, my boyfriend."

"You're chock full of surprises today, Bobby, aren't you?"

He nodded guiltily. "I guess I am."

"All this comes from living a lie, Bobby, you know that; don't you?"

"Daniel said that a lie always catches up to you in the end."

━━━━━━━━━━━━━━━━

Stan, Amelia and Bobby got together in Ulysses on Saturday afternoon to discuss the brunch date with Bobby's dad the following day.

Bobby had apologized profusely to Amelia for putting her on the spot. She groaned a bit at first, however, she agreed to play along and pose as his girlfriend on a one-time basis provided he and she 'broke-up' immediately thereafter.

"Thanks, Amelia," Bobby said, "I really appreciate your doing this favor for me."

"I'll do my best to be convincing, Bobby, but I'm not sure that I can pull this off. For one thing, I'm older than you."

"I could say that I like older women."

"And with high heels on, I'm taller than you."

"Don't wear high heels, go barefoot," Stan suggested, "and stoop like a sad sack when you're standing up. Most young women today have bad posture; they think it makes them look sulky and sexy."

"Another crack like that out of you, Stan, and I'm out the door."

"Stan, be serious!" Bobby implored him.

"Sorry, just adding a little levity to a ticklish situation."

"I'll wear torn jeans and a tank top, Bobby, and I'll put my hair in a ponytail and wear more bling-bling, flashy bracelets and rings. Maybe that will help me look younger."

"And show more cleavage," Stan said, "all the younger women do these days."

"I warned you."

"I'm not being facetious, Amelia, it's true, younger women like to flaunt their racks."

"Why are men so obsessed with breasts?"

"It's a male genetic thing and one of the reasons I think that God is probably a woman."

"Why would you think that?"

"Only a female God could think up something irresistible like breasts so that the female of the species would completely enthrall the male of the species."

"I'm not obsessed with breasts," Bobby said.

At that moment a young man with green eyes and long chestnut hair that nearly reached his shoulders approached the table. He suffered from a bad case of five-o'clock-shadow and was dressed in a blue cardigan sweater and jeans. A pipe stem jutted from his shirt pocket. "Aren't you going to introduce me to your friends, Bobby?"

"What the blazes are *you* doing here?"

"I guess you're not, so I'll do my own introductions then. Hello, folks, I'm Daniel Hoffman, Bobby's lover and significant other."

Stan stood up. "Stan Kane; pleased to meet you." He extended a hand and the two men shook.

Amelia remained seated. "Amelia Mancuso, I am Bobby's new girlfriend. Take a seat and join us, Daniel, you and I can compare notes."

"Thank you, Amelia, I'd be delighted to share."

Bobby buried his face in his hands. "This is my worst nightmare come true."

Stan caught the attention of Michael, the youngest bartender in Ulysses and the definite favorite of all the young women who waited tables there.

"What are we drinking today?" Michael asked.

"Daniel?"

"Scotch and water, please, easy on the water."

"Two strong scotch and waters, Michael. Thanks."

"Ok."

"Stan, you told me you don't drink, " Amelia said.

"I do now, woman, you've driven me to it."

"I'll have one too," Bobby said, "I'm going to need it."

"Three, Michael, if you will."

"You got it."

"Well, Daniel," Stan said, "to what do we owe the pleasure of your unexpected company on this fine day?"

"I know what you're cooking up and I'm here to say that what you're doing is dishonest. Bobby's dad deserves better and I deserve better."

"Daniel, I just told my dad that I'm quitting the family business," Bobby said, "that's a *huge* deal to him, I can't say or do anything to complicate matters right now. If it pleases him to think that Amelia is my girlfriend, so be it for a while."

"How long is a while?"

"Until I feel the time is right."

"Knowing you, Bobby, that could be years."

"Don't be a wuss, Daniel, you're so damn needy. Just go along with me on this."

"I think it's reprehensible of you."

"It's a little white lie, Daniel, don't make a mountain out of a mole hill."

The conversation halted momentarily as their drinks were brought to the table.

"Thanks, Michael, you better stand by for re-fills."

"Will do."

"Our entire relationship is built on a lie," Daniel continued, "that's what this is really all about."

"Don't be so dramatic," Bobby said, "you're behaving like an old queen."

"You always have to have things your way. You deserve a thrashing, Bobby, maybe then you'd realize all the harm you're causing."

"Easy, guys," Stan intervened, "let's all calm down."

Daniel glared at him. "That's easy for you to say."

"Look, Daniel, this is as uncomfortable for me as it is for you. The fact of the matter is that I have asked Amelia to marry me, so I don't like this situation any more than you do."

"Oh, I'm sorry, I didn't know that."

Amelia was mortified. "Stan, you had no right to divulge that information, that's our personal, confidential business."

"I'm afraid that everybody knows, Amelia, don't ask me how, but the whole building knows that I proposed to you."

"Everybody knows?" Her mouth hung open.

"Yes, isn't that the truth, Bobby?"

"It's true, Amelia, in fact, all of Stone Street knows, probably all Wall Street too by now."

She crumpled a napkin. "This is so embarrassing."

Stan cleared his throat and attempted to change the subject. "So, Daniel, tell us about yourself. What do you do for a living?"

"I'm an NYPD detective assigned to the Two-Four."

"The Two-Four?"

"The 24th. Precinct on the Upper Westside."

"Are you putting me on?"

"No." He pushed back his sweater to reveal a .9 mm Glock automatic resting in a holster on his belt.

"I had you pegged for a teacher or a writer, something cerebral like that."

"You figured wrong, Stan, it's my long, hippie hair that throws people off."

"Yeah, I seem to be doing a lot of bad figuring these days."

Bobby put his elbows on the table and rubbed his face with both hands. "Help me out here, people, just for tomorrow. Then I'll find a way to break the news of my being gay to my dad, I promise. What do you say?"

Three heads eventually nodded reluctantly.

Amelia stood up. "I need to go home and start ripping up a pair of old jeans so I'll look hip and with it tomorrow."

Bobby also got up. "And I'm meeting my dad for dinner."

Stan turned to Daniel. "Are you going on duty anytime soon, officer?"

"No, I'm off till Tuesday."

"Excellent, then let's leave these two lovebirds to their little tasks. Down the hatch, Daniel, there is a cat and a parrot upstairs that I want you to meet."

―――――――――――

"Svet, you're my lawyer now, right?" Lenny asked.

"*Da*, Svet officially represent you."

"So that means that everything I tell you then is covered by lawyer-client privilege?"

"That is so, Lenny, Svet's lips are sealed tight even if the police use electrodes on Svet's private parts to get information on you; even if they drill holes in my teeth; even if they put hood over my head and use waterboarding in their interrogation."

"They may do that in Russia but the police can't do that in this country."

"The time is coming, Lenny, Svet can see the signs."

"Oh, God, that's something else to worry about." He spun his wheelchair fast in a circle.

"Why you do that all the time with wheelchair?"

"It relaxes me. Before the accident, when I could still walk, I raced cars to unwind."

"Svet thinks you need to go into business with less stress."

"Yeah, I've been thinking the same thing; Leonard is worried about me getting caught and going to jail. And the truth is that I think I've developed a conscience for the first time in my life. That's a real handicap in my racket."

"Svet also worry about Lenny very much."

"You do?"

The attorney blushed. "*Da*, Svet not get her beauty sleep, she stay awake at night worrying about Lenny."

"Gee, Svet, that's so nice of you. Except for Leonard, I don't think anybody ever cared enough about me to worry."

"Svet not all rough and tough, you know, Svet have tender side too."

Lenny suddenly became awkward and didn't seem to know what to do with his hands. "Eh, I was wondering, Svet, would you like to go out to dinner with me one night?"

"You mean, we have date?"

He spun the wheelchair again. "Yeah, sure, that's exactly what I mean, a date."

"Svet knows great Russian restaurant, Lenny."

"I've never been to a Russian restaurant."

"You will like; cold borscht, shish kebab, pierogi, blini, sturgeon, red cabbage and, of course, lots of Russian vodka to wash caviar down."

"If I get loaded, Svet, you'll have to push me home, otherwise I'll get a DUI ticket."

"No problem, Svet drive better when drunk, all Russians do."

Lenny laughed. "I'm looking forward to it."

She batted her fake eyelashes at him. "Restaurant is one block from Svet's apartment, you can stay with me if you drink too much vodka."

"Really?"

"Да, тогда мы могли бы пойти купаться в сено."

"Huh?"

" Maybe we go for roll in the straw."

"You mean, a roll in the hay."

"Same difference."

Lenny looked apprehensively down at his useless legs. "I ... I gotta warn you, Svet, that I can't feel anything below the waist. Sometimes I think I feel a tingling sensation, but it could only be wishful thinking on my part."

She winked saucily at him. "No worry, Lenny, leave everything to Svet. You will feel much more than tingling below waist, Svet guaranty it."

===

The next afternoon at 1:00 P.M. Amelia waited for Bobby and his dad at Ulysses. Her torn jeans, silver bracelets, multiple rings, a tight fitting blouse that revealed an impressive cleavage, and a ponytail made her look several years younger than she was.

Stan and Daniel strolled through the door together and ambled over to where she was standing.

"What are you two jokers doing here?"

Stan flashed her a grin. "It's a free country, Amelia, we have as much right to be here as you do."

"What'll it be, gents?" Artie asked.

"Two scotch and waters." He nodded at Amelia. "And I'd card this young woman if I were you, Artie, she looks like jail bait to me."

Artie laughed and left to mix the drinks.

"Bobby is going to be very upset when he sees you guys here."

"Tough!" Daniel said testily.

Amelia snatched up her purse in a huff. "If you'll excuse me, I'm going to wait outside." She exited the bar onto Stone Street.

Daniel admired her retreating back. "Amelia is definitely more attractive when she's angry."

"Yes, I've noticed the same thing about her."

"You know, Stan, women like Amelia sometimes make me wish that I was straight."

Artie brought their drinks and then proceeded to use a damp cloth to wipe the dust off the rows of liquor bottles behind the bar.

Stan laughed. "So how's the crime business, Daniel?"

"It's been booming for the last six months. The crime rate always jumps before the economy heads south."

"I didn't know that."

"Yep, it's a little known fact but a very reliable leading stock market indicator, crooks seem to know the economy is circling the drain long before economists ever do."

"I believe it, I never heard an economist say anything that I could understand, even when they're speaking English. They seem to talk out of both sides of their mouth at the same time; you never get a plain yes or no answer to a question, everything is hedged or qualified so they can't be accused later of being wrong in their forecasts."

"Until oil prices dropped so much recently, the crime *de jour* was hijacking oil trucks that deliver gasoline to service stations."

"Is that so?"

"You bet; gasoline was Black Gold. And the trucks were easy targets; we're not talking Brink's armored vehicles here with armed guards. There was an average of two hijackings a week in my precinct alone. Fortunately, none of the drivers were hurt."

"How come I never read about that in the newspapers?"

"The NYPD kept it quiet, Stan, they were afraid of encouraging copycats."

"I wonder about what other bad news never makes it into the papers."

"Plenty. The crime of the moment is arson; people torching their small businesses and homes to get out from under debt."

"Yeah, you'd expect that."

"Insurance company investigators usually take the lead on those cases, not the NYPD."

Stan finished his drink. "I guess I'm not the first person to ask you this question, Daniel, but did you ever shoot anyone while on the job?"

"Once. A couple of years ago my partner and I rolled on an armed robbery in progress and we confronted the two perps as they were coming out of the liquor store. They fired on us and I returned fire and killed one of them. My partner collared the other one."

"Wow."

"Better him than me."

"It never bothered you?"

"A little, right after it happened I had some sleepless nights in the hospital, but eventually I got over it."

"Why were you in the hospital, Daniel?"

"I caught two bullets in my shoulder from the second perp before he was apprehended by my partner."

"My God! Bobby must have been apoplectic."

"I didn't know Bobby at that time. We didn't meet until nine months later."

"What about your parents?"

"They live in Tucson, that's where I'm from. I didn't tell them about it until I was all healed."

"Did they want you to quit the police force and leave New York when they found out?"

"No, my dad is a deputy sheriff back home. He and my mom

understand the risks in law enforcement. They were concerned about me but they never pressured me to leave the job."

"I'd like to buy you a drink, officer."

"Thanks, Stan, but I haven't finished this one."

"Well, I need one. Artie, another round; if you please."

Daniel smiled and emptied his glass. "It's a little early in the day for me, but what the hell, I'm an adult and I'm off-duty."

Artie delivered the drinks and went back to polishing bottles nearby.

"I was born here in New York," Stan said, "and except for my travels as a dancer, I've always lived here. That's *my* excuse. What brings a cowboy from Tucson to the Big Apple?"

"My parents took the family here once for the Christmas holidays when I was a kid. There was snow on the ground and it was freezing. Nevertheless, we walked everywhere, checking out all the window displays at Lord & Taylor, Bloomingdales, Saks; the ice rink at Rock Center; the tree at the Met. We also went to Chinatown, Greenwich Village, Little Italy and Times Square. I had never seen anything like it before, the city made a deep impression on me."

"In other words, you got hooked."

"Yes. I remember looking out the window of the plane as we passed over Manhattan on the way back home to Arizona and telling myself that this is where I wanted to be."

Stan nodded. "New York has its share of problems – too many people, it's too expensive, too fast-paced, too competitive – but it's an addictive city. Once it hooks you, that's it, nowhere else will do."

"That's what happened to me."

"Do you have any brothers or sisters, Daniel?"

"I have a brother back in Tucson, we are identical twins and share all the same genes. Peter is married and has four kids."

Stan looked surprised.

"Yeah, I know, go figure."

At that moment Amelia entered Ulysses followed by Bobby and a well dressed, older man with wavy gray hair and tortoise shell glasses. They were seated at a table by the Carvery where kitchen personnel were busy slicing ham, turkey, and roast beef. If Bobby knew they were present, he gave no indication of it.

While Stan and Daniel sulked at the bar, a high time seemed to be had by all at the table, judged by the loud laughter and smiles that lit up that part of the room during brunch. Bobby held Amelia's hand through most of the meal and he even pecked her on the mouth several times.

"Aw, that's so cute," Stan observed, "an affectionate kiss, but not too steamy so as to give dear old dad heart palpitations."

"Bobby is a great kisser, no question about it."

"He looks like he enjoys kissing Amelia."

"Do you, Stan?"

He frowned. "I've never kissed her."

Daniel did a double take. "You asked her to marry you and you've never even kissed the girl?"

Stan nodded. "Ours is a complicated relationship."

"I'm in a complicated relationship myself."

"Is there any other kind?"

"Well, I must say that I heartily approve of Amelia's cleavage," Daniel continued, "very sexy, but not so in-your-face raunchy that the old guy's eyes are popping out of his skull. That was an astute recommendation on your part, Stan."

"Thanks, I rather like Amelia's cleavage myself."

"You know, dressed like she is, Amelia does look much younger."

"Too young for me, you mean?"

"I didn't say that, Stan."

"You didn't have to, Daniel, the thought has crossed my mind several thousand times."

"I'm almost eight years older than Bobby."

"The gap is double that for Amelia and me."

"You make it sound like you're robbing the cradle, Stan."

"Maybe I am."

"Does the age difference bother her?"

"It bothers me."

The two men did not speak for several minutes.

"You know, Stan, this is getting boring and I feel like a Peeping Tom being in here."

"I agree."

"Can you think of a good reason to hang around here any longer?"

"Let me think." A second passed. "No, I can't even think of a bad reason to be here."

"Let's drink up and vacate this establishment."

"I'm with you. There are some movies playing at *Angelika* that we might check out."

Stan paid the tab and the two men left the bar, an action that did not go unnoticed by Amelia and Bobby.

━━━━━━━━━━━━━━━━━━━━

That same day Svet sent text messages to the CEO and CLO of Global Insurance alerting them to the fact that she and Wanda would be arriving at 9:30 A.M. at their offices on Monday morning to discuss the lawsuit they planned to file against the company, against the members of the Board of Directors, and against Vice President Rodney Herkimer and his wife.

Svet wore a dress the color of homemade vodka and shoes with steel stiletto heels that were so sharp they left impressions on the concrete pavement when she walked. She also had a formidable zircon diamond ring on her right hand that could tear flesh and bone should the negotiations go badly and she found herself in a hand-to-hand combat situation.

A coterie of company officials met them in the lobby and escorted them up in the private elevator to the executive floor. There, the CEO, Edwin Huffington, IV, a patrician looking man with silver-gray hair and wearing a three-piece chalk stripped suit and yellow tie, led them to the Board Room. A dozen other company officials were waiting for them around a magnificent, oval Chippendale table made from cherry wood that extended the length of the large room.

After introductions, they were seated and offered coffee. Then Huffington took the floor and launched into a long, well-rehearsed, discourse on how deeply the Board of Directors regretted the deplorable actions of Rodney Herkimer; how he had been immediately terminated for cause; how they in no way condoned or could be held morally or legally accountable for his deplorable sexual harassment of Wanda Pearlmutter; and how this very sordid incident must be hushed up for the sake of the company and also so as not to tarnish Wanda's own reputation which would surely be trashed in the tabloids should this lurid sex scandal become public knowledge. She must also consider the welfare of her young son in this matter as he would suffer, undeservedly of course, from the snickers of gossipmongers in school that might well cause him emotional distress and stunt his development into manhood.

Huffington concluded his remarks by stating how much the company valued Wanda's ten years of loyal service and hoped that she would continue in her present position as an AVP in the Underwriting Department for the remainder of her working life, secure in the knowledge that the company would always look out for her best interest in these dangerous economic times where people who were fired from jobs often ended up losing their homes and living on welfare. Then he took his seat and surrendered the floor to Svet.

Svet stood and spread her papers in neat piles in front of her. Then she raised her hand high into the air and drove her fist down with all her might into the cherry table. The zircon ring smashed into the antique tabletop and gouged a hole in it, destroying the elegant patina it had acquired over the past century and causing the papers to scatter around the room. Then she took off a shoe and pounded the hole with its steel stiletto heel until a large chunk of the table fell away so that the carpeted floor was visible through it.

"My God, woman," the CEO cried aloud, "have you lost your mind?"

"Svet not insane, Mister CEO, but you insane if you think you can bamboozle my client." She picked up papers and waved them in the air. "You know what Svet have here? I tell you, invitations for Wanda to go on *Montel Williams Show,* on *Howard Stern Show,* on *Tyra Banks Show,* to play tapes and tell her shameful story. The producers go into frenzy after Svet showed them the tapes. They see their ratings go sky high through the roof."

"They … the producers saw the tapes?" the CEO asked worriedly.

"*Da,* and Svet also show them to the people at *You Tube* and *Facebook.* They also go wild; they say they will put Rodney Herkimer and Global Insurance all over the Internet. Everybody in the world will know about Wanda and how badly she suffered working here. The name of Global Insurance will be infamous like the name of Enron, it will be turned into shit; your reputation will stink like yesterday's vomit; your female shareholders will scream bloody murder; women's civil rights groups will picket this building; customers will drop you like hot potato; the hedge funds will short your stock and price will fall like a cursed stone; your blood will be in the water and the sharks will take this corporation apart piece by piece. "

The CEO stood up on rubbery legs. "Eh …perhaps I was a trifle hasty in my comments earlier. Global Insurance will, of course, wish to compensate Miss Pearlmutter for any pain and suffering that she experienced." He picked up her personnel file and checked it. "How does $200,000 sound? That's more than two years salary. I think it's a very generous offer on our part."

Svet shook her head. "Is too late for offers, I am thinking."

"What do you mean?"

"Svet is thinking it better that Wanda go to court and sue; she become instant celebrity; she write tell-all book and give lots of speeches for much money. Maybe she even gets her own TV show on cable. Women on jury be plenty mad at Global Insurance, be very sorry for Wanda, will award her very big punitive damages. Wanda be set for rest of her life." Svet nodded. "*Da*, that is what we do, we leaving now, we see you in court."

The Chief Legal Officer, a thin man with wire-rim glasses, whispered into the CEO's ear and then stood up. "Hold on, Miss Brutalefsky, I'm sure that we can work out a more satisfactory settlement here for your client. Please give me a few minutes to talk to the Board of Directors. If you will kindly wait outside, I'll call you back into the room shortly."

The two women left the Board Room and were taken to an adjacent conference room. "Is it going well?" Wanda whispered as soon as the door closed.

Svet closed her hand tightly into a fist. "Svet got CEO by the *cojones* and is squeezing hard as she can. Does Wanda hear him screaming in agony in the other room? Walls are thick but Svet can hear him squeal."

Ten minutes later they were admitted back into the Board Room and took their original seats. The CLO became the spokesman. "Global Insurance is anxious to make this noxious problem go away and put it behind us once and for all. So we are substantially upping our offer to seven figures. The Board has empowered me to offer Miss Pearlmutter the sum of $1.0 million in settlement of all damages and claims she has against Global Insurance. In consideration for that payment, she must turn over all films in her possession to the company and she must also sign a confidentiality agreement vowing to keep this entire matter a secret forever."

Wanda was tempted to jump up and down at the news; however, she kept a stern expression on her face just as Svet had warned her to do. Svet leaned over and whispered into her ear, "Shake head like you insulted and want to leave immediately."

Wanda did as she was instructed and whispered back, "This is so exciting."

Svet turned to the Chief Legal Officer. "My client reject offer; we sue." She started to get up.

"Wait." The CLO wiped his sweaty brow with a handkerchief. "I will raise the offer to $1.5 million, the same terms and conditions apply. That's our *final* offer."

Svet leaned again to Wanda and whispered, "Shake head like you doubly insulted and pound the table like you mad as hell."

Wanda hit the table so hard that it groaned.

"My client say she will drop sex harassment suit against Global Insurance for payment of $5.0 million in cash. She also must have promotion to Vice President and head of Underwriting Department with salary of $300,000 a year. She also must have iron-clad ten-year contract stipulating guaranteed raises and bonuses each year."

"That is an outrageous, over-the-top demand, Miss Brutalefsky!"

Svet leaned over to Wanda and whispered, "Pound the table harder."

Wanda whispered back, "I'm loving this," and pounded the table so hard that her hand hurt.

"We done talking, Mister Chief Legal Officer, it is take-it-or-leave-it time. We strike deal now or we see you in court; in meantime, you see my client all over the TV and the Internet showing films of officer of company assaulting her. Is for you to decide, decision must be made now or we sue you for $25.0 million."

The Professor took Pedro for a hearty breakfast of bacon, eggs, and pancakes at a diner near Washington Square Park so he would have the stamina for the all-day testing session at NYU. After escorting him to the assigned classroom, he headed to the *Bobst Library* to do historical research on Caribbean pirates for his newest romance novel. From time to time his thoughts drifted to Wanda and Svet who were negotiating with the insurance company. He didn't see Pedro again until 4:00 P.M. when all of the test results were in and he had the opportunity to confer with his former colleagues at the university.

"*Pedro, tengo una gran noticia, tengo las puntuaciones de sus pruebas.*"

"Professor, please to speak in English to Pedro."

"I have received your test scores, Pedro."

"Did Pedro do well?"

The Professor gave him the thumbs-up sign. "Yes, very well, you are what is known as a 'gifted individual'. Your scores were so high, in fact, that the university wants you to become a student here."

The busboy shook his head. "Pedro no can be student; have no money; need to work."

"Listen, the university has a special program for people like you. They will arrange for you to have a paying job here at NYU while you attend classes so you can continue to send money home. And you will receive a scholarship so your tuition, books, and room and board will be free. You can move from Queens to a campus dormitory in Greenwich Village."

"But I only go to school for five years in Mexico?"

"That makes no difference, Pedro, you will be admitted as a disadvantaged student with great potential, the normal admittance requirements will be waived in your case."

"Waived?"

"*Renunciar.*"

"I no *comprende*; why does large university do this for Pedro?"

The Professor's crows-feet wrinkles on his face deepened as he considered how best to explain. "The university invests in intelligent people like Pedro so that some day, after they graduate and go out into the world, they will become important teachers, doctors, lawyers, writers, businessmen, scientists; they will make big contributions to society; they will become leaders in their own countries. And this will bring high honor to the university, the university will be known far and wide in the world as a center of great learning."

Pedro stared out the window as the words percolated in his superior brain.

"Also, some of these gifted students will become very wealthy individuals after they graduate. One day they may even decide to donate money to the university to build new buildings, or to pay the tuition of other gifted students like Pedro."

The busboy smiled. "Ah, *si*, Pedro now understand."

"I thought you would."

"You think that Pedro might be rich man some day?"

"Yes, I think that is very possible."

"Pedro never dream he be rich; Pedro always too tired to dream."

The Professor put his arm around the busboy. "Then it is high time that you have some happy dreams of your own."

The party celebrating Wanda's legal victory was impromptu and people began showing up at the Oracle's apartment as soon as they heard the news.

The Professor had been over at NYU with Pedro so he was late arriving. "You're a rich woman now, Wanda, you can afford to move to Manhattan."

"That's true. Thanks to Svet, my schlepping days back and forth to Brooklyn are over."

"Any idea where you'll look for a place?"

She smiled at him like she had a secret. "I want to be able to walk to work so I'm hoping I can find something down here."

"In the Financial District?"

"Yes. I spoke to a realtor the other day and he has some condominiums on John Street he wants me to look at."

"That's wonderful, Wanda, we'll only be a few blocks apart then."

She moved closer to him. "Actually, I told the realtor that I really wanted to live on Stone Street but he said there weren't any vacancies at present."

"Oh, that's too bad."

She put her arm through his and they went to get him a glass of wine. "My first choice would be to live here in this building; Allen is so fond of all the animals."

"The animals are fond of him too; all of us living in the building are."

"Is that so?"

"Yes, I'm particularly fond of him; to be honest, Wanda, he's like the son I never had."

Her lips almost touched his ear. "And are *you* fond of me as well, Professor?"

"I … I'm more than fond of you, Wanda, I think I *love* you."

"You think?"

"I mean, yes, I *do* love you, there's no question about it."

She kissed him. "I have an idea, why don't Allen and I move in with you?"

"With me?"

"Yes, Allen could use the second bedroom as his room."

"But what will Allen say about that? "

"Oh, it's fine with him, he's already told me that he wants me to marry you."

"The dear boy said that?"

"Yes, it seems that he's fond of you too. So what do you say, Professor, are you ready to give marriage a second try?"

"Wanda, you make me so happy."

―――――――――――――

Amelia was sitting at the bar in Ulysses sipping an orange juice and flipping through a fashion magazine full of designer clothes that she couldn't afford on her salary.

A well-dressed man with wavy gray hair and tortoise shell glasses walked up to her. "I was hoping that I would find you here, Amelia."

"Mr. Rankle, this is a surprise."

He glanced at her juice. "Can I get you something with a little more kick?"

"No, thanks, I'm fine with this."

Artie came over to take his order.

"A *Jameson* neat, please."

Amelia's eyes went to the Stone Street entrance of the bar.

"Bobby won't be joining us, Amelia, he's working late tonight."

"Oh."

"The fact is, Amelia, I wanted to speak to you privately." His drink arrived and he tasted it. "I need this badly."

"What's the matter?"

He nervously adjusted his glasses and then fidgeted with a napkin. "Amelia, do you like Bobby?"

"That's a strange question to be asking me, Mr. Rankle."

"Do you?"

"Of course, I do."

"Do you *love* Bobby, Amelia, like in true love?"

She hesitated. "Bobby and I are dating because we enjoy each other's company. We'll have to see where it goes from there."

"Have you two had sex yet?"

"Mr. Rankle, that is a very inappropriate question, and it's also none of your business."

"I can tell from your reaction that you haven't."

She said nothing.

He examined the whisky glass that was now almost empty. "Forgive me, Amelia, it's not that I have a prurient interest, far from it. I was just hoping that you could assure me that my son isn't gay."

She sighed and remained silent.

"Do you know what a *beard* is, Amelia?"

"I ... I..."

"It is a person who is used to mask the true character of another person. Half-way through brunch last Sunday, I suddenly came to realize that's what you were."

"Mr. Rankle, I think ..."

"It's not your fault, Amelia, you played your part beautifully. After all, you really are the lovely, sweet, charming girlfriend that every parent would like his son to bring home to meet the family one day."

"I don't think you should be having this conversation with me, Mr. Rankle."

He nodded and beckoned Artie for the check. "That's true, Amelia, I should be talking to Bobby."

"Why don't you?"

"Because I'm afraid."

"Afraid of what, Mr. Rankle?"

"I'm afraid that he'll tell me the truth."

Amelia sighed. "Whatever Bobby is … or is not, Mr. Rankle, he is still your son."

"That's true."

"And you love Bobby, don't you?"

He removed his glasses to clean them with a napkin but mostly used the napkin to dab his eyes. "Yes, with all my heart, he's all I have in the world."

"Then I'd go back to the office this minute and tell him that if I were you."

Mr. Rankle put his glasses back on, cleared his throat, and placed a hand on her arm. "Amelia, I'm going to sorely miss not having you in the family, my dear, I surely am."

"Good luck, kid," Lenny said, "and watch out for the kidney punches."

Seth tried to smile. "Thanks, I'm going to need it."

"Svet is on your side, you'll do fine."

"The bank CEO is a demagogue and he's also got a Napoleon complex."

"Is he a midget?"

"Taller than a midget but shorter than Svet."

Lenny frowned. "Small guys like that often get inferiority complexes about their height. They can be a pain in the ass to deal with."

"You got that part correct, he likes to pick fights with people."

"This time he picked a fight with the wrong person."

"I hope you're right, Lenny, I hope he doesn't eat her lunch."

"Don't worry, kid, Svet will be the last-man-standing."

The downstairs doorbell buzzed. "That'll be Svet now."

"See you later, Lenny, say a prayer for me."

"I would if I knew any, kid, but God and me don't talk."

Seth emerged from the building and found Svet and a tall, ox-like man with a full beard waiting for him on Stone Street.

"Seth, please to meet Svet's investigator and friend, Nicky Gordunov."

"Hello." The two men shook hands and the trio walked up William Street towards Wall Street where Seth's bank had its offices and where he was now *persona non grata*. Seth stared mostly at the sidewalk and recalled an old admonition from his childhood -- *step on a crack and break your mother's back* -- so he was careful not to.

"Nicky is great help to Svet with your case."

"Really?"

"Yes, Nicky have many friends in Russia, he able to find out many things."

Seth furrowed his brow. "What has Russia got to do with my case?"

"All business is global today, what happen in one part of world affect what happen in other parts of world."

"I don't understand."

"Not to worry, Svet is fully prepared."

They were shown into a large, ornate conference room with an exquisite antique table and chairs just off the trading floor where Seth had previously worked until being summarily dismissed after confessing to the $22 million currency loss. Howard Korcher, CEO of the bank, was waiting for them. A garishly dressed man with high levels of testosterone for someone who was only 4'10" in stature, he had slicked back black hair and hooded brown eyes that seemed to be constantly probing for your weaknesses when he looked at you. A diamond pinky ring glistened on his left hand that also held a massive, smoldering cigar.

"Is smart of you to meet with us," Svet said, "is in both our interests to settle this matter quietly and without publicity."

"As I told you on the phone, Miss Brutalefsky," Korcher said, "this is a privately owned bank and we are not afraid of bad publicity. If you are counting on that to help your client avoid prosecution, you are sadly mistaken. As far as we are concerned, your client is no better than a common thief. He willfully subverted the bank's control systems and engaged in unauthorized trades that resulted in many millions of dollars of losses for our shareholders. And he filed fraudulent reports and deceived senior management in an effort to hide these losses. We intend to inform the District Attorney of his actions and see to it that your client is punished to the full extent of the law."

Svet smiled. "My client not seek personal gain, he try to earn money for bank that lost many hundreds of millions of dollars this year because senior management make bad loans for sub-prime mortgages and because bank have to buy back auction-rate securities it misrepresented when sell to its customers. If my client must go to jail, then you as Chief Executive Officer of bank must go to jail for longer time since you lose bank more money than he did."

"That's ridiculous. Your client is a rogue trader, plain and simple. What he did is in no way comparable to the losses that a bank takes in the ordinary course of business."

"Ordinary course of business," Svet said, slowly repeating the phrase aloud, "what means that exactly?"

Korcher rolled his eyes as though he was conversing with an idiot. "This bank is in the business of making loans, it stands to reason that, from time to time, a portion of these loans will go into default."

"Bank also in business of taking deposits?"

"Of course."

"Bank also in business of moving funds around the world for its customers?"

"Yes, that too." The CEO looked impatiently at his Rolex. "I have another appointment and there's really not much to discuss. As I told you earlier, we are going to turn this matter over to the D.A. and prosecute your client for grand theft. My lawyers tell me that he should get a sentence of 15 or 20 years to think about what he did." He arose from his seat to indicate that the meeting was over.

The lawyer remained seated as did Seth and Gordunov. "Did you know that Svet was prosecutor before she become defense counsel?"

"No, and I couldn't care less."

"Svet prosecute Russian Mafia cases, get to know them very well. You know Russian Mafia, Mr. Korcher?"

The CEO's eyes narrowed. "No, certainly not."

"That very strange because Russian Mafia knows you."

His demeanor turned hostile. "You are a shyster, Miss Brutalefsky, and you will leave these offices immediately or I will have Security forcibly remove you."

"A minute ago you kindly tell me that penalty for theft in New York will get my client 15 to 20 years in prison."

"That is correct."

"Svet now ask you question; do you know what the penalty for money laundering in Russia is today?"

Silence.

"Svet enlighten you: the penalty is death by firing squad."

Silence.

"In Azerbaijan, former Soviet Republic where your bank also have office, penalty is even worse -- punishment there is death by decapitation and the wild dogs get to play soccer with your head until they get tired; then they eat it."

The CEO sat uneasily back down in his chair. "What has all this got to do with me?"

"Svet wish to introduce her friend and investigator, Nikita Gordunov." She turned and put her hand on his shoulder.

Gordunov nodded at the banker. *"Prijatno poznakomitsa."*

"Mr. Gordunov is former KGB officer; he also work for it under its new, more friendly sounding name, the FSB." Svet winked at the little man. "Name is changed but security service is still up to same old dirty tricks."

"This is all very interesting," the CEO said, "but I have another appointment."

"While in KGB, Mr. Gordunov work under the covers in Russian Mafia."

"I worked *undercover*," Gordunov said, correcting her phrasing.

"Yes, thank you, Nicky, he work undercover in Russian Mafia for years. He meets many gangsters; makes many friends. You see, in old days it was hard to tell the difference between KGB and Mafia, both steal billions of rubles."

Gordunov laughed.

Svet opened her briefcase and removed several papers. "Thanks to Mafia friends of Mr. Gordunov, Svet have here names of dummy corporations, account numbers, dates, and dollar amounts your branches in Russia and Azerbaijan make illegal money transfers to for organized crime mobsters in violation of government currency controls. Amounts total $15.0 billion dollars; in return your bank receives large fees for transfers and for investing money in American stock market. Money transferred by your bank is profits from drug trafficking, prostitution, and white slavery; is *blood* money. Very bad business, many peoples murdered and many more lives ruined."

"Banks can't be expected to know how their customers earn their money; that's not our concern."

"So your hands clean; what about your conscience?"

"As I said, Miss Brutalefsky, we are in the banking business, we're not out to save the world. Don't confuse us with a church."

"Bank also help gangsters to evade paying lawful income taxes on this money. Svet ask another question: Do you know what penalty for tax evasion in Russia and Azerbaijan is today?"

Silence.

"In Russia, you get minimum of ten years at hard labor in Siberia."

Gordunov nodded vigorously.

"In Azerbaijan, they are Muslims there and have no money for prisons, so they just chop off your hands."

The CEO tugged on his shirt's monogrammed French cuffs and looked around with pride at the expensive furnishings in the room. "Don't let the fancy suit and the $200 haircut fool you, counselor, I wasn't born with a silver spoon in my mouth. And I didn't go to no ivy-league university like your thieving client did. No, I came up the hard way and I fought for everything I have. I'm no soft touch, and I know a bullshitter when I see one; I'm looking at one now. You're a third-rate lawyer arguing a losing case."

"Svet have proof," she said, shuffling the papers in front of her.

"You don't scare me, shyster, I have influential friends in high places. And I am a large contributor to both the Democratic and Republican parties. Even if you think you have proof of what you say, I will never be convicted. The statutes covering money laundering and tax evasion are very complex; no simple-minded, blue-collar American jury could understand them."

"Svet no shyster," she said, balling her fists.

"And these alleged offenses you speak of took place abroad, outside the jurisdiction of U.S. courts. My lawyers tell me that the U.S. does not have extradition treaties with Russia and Azerbaijan so there's no way I can be extradited for these charges."

Svet raised a warning finger. "The trouble with corporate lawyers is that they look at things only from legal point of view; that can be fatal mistake for their clients."

"I am legally untouchable, you're wasting my valuable time."

Svet chuckled. "FSB not care about American legal niceties like extradition and jury trials; if they decide you guilty, you have big problem. *Da*, you may be legally untouchable as you say, but are you bullet-proof if get shot between your eyes in elevator? If you standing on crowded subway platform during rush hour and someone standing behind you push you into path of incoming train, will you not be crushed to death? If you walking across street at night and hit-and-run driver run over you with five ton SUV, will not every bone in your body be broken?"

"Are you threatening me?"

"Svet not threaten; Svet merely educate. Did you read story of Alexander Litvinenko, ex-KGB officer, who was poisoned in London three years ago?"

"Yes, I read about it."

"Radioactive polonium was slipped into his tea in fancy hotel restaurant because he speak out too loudly against the security service."

"What's your point?"

"Point is that long arm of FSB reach out from Moscow to London where Litvinenko think he safe. Point is that no one is safe from long arm of FSB; one minute you are smiling and admiring beautiful Christmas decorations on Fifth Avenue, next minute you are laying dead on Park Avenue with maggots eating your eyes from inside out."

"They wouldn't dare attack a prominent American citizen in New York."

"We will see." She put the papers back in her briefcase. "Svet leave now and take taxi to Russian Embassy. Give proof papers of your guilt to Second Consul for Agricultural Affairs, who is really FSB station chief in New York." She stood up and Seth and Gordunov did so as well. "Have best day of your life."

The CEO smiled defiantly. "You talk a good game, counselor, but I don't think you have the brass balls to go to the Russians. As a lawyer you are an officer of the court and have to abide by strict ethical rules of behavior or you could lose your license to practice and end up in jail yourself."

"*Da*, but you know how lawyers are, they have very bad reputation, are sneaky and not trustworthy. Svet learn that on her first day in class when she go to law school in Moscow."

"It would take a cold-hearted bitch to rat me out. No, counselor, you won't put my life in danger because you have scruples; for law-abiding citizens like yourself the end never justifies the means."

Svet leaned across the table. "Make no mistake, Mister Banker, Svet will go get her hair done at expensive beauty salon and wear her best clothes to cemetery on the day of your funeral. There, she will give sad condolences to your widow and then she spit on your coffin." The lawyer raised her hand high in the air and drove it down into the antique table, splitting it in two with a karate chop.

An hour later the three of them were back out on Wall Street and heading to Stone Street.

Seth looked cautiously over at his lawyer. "That *was* a ballsy move you made."

"*Da*, situation call for it."

"Would you really have gone to the Russian Embassy if Korcher hadn't signed the settlement agreement?"

She smiled. "Svet must politely decline to answer question on grounds that answer might incriminate her."

"Korcher is a despicable human being, Svet, I'm glad to be off the hook but it's a shame that he gets to skate on all this."

"Skate? What means that?"

"It's an American colloquialism, it means he gets off scot-free, without being punished for his crimes. He gets no comeuppance."

"No, Seth mistaken; banker not get to go skating."

"I don't understand, Svet, you agreed not to go to the FSB with your evidence."

"*Da*, Svet not go, but this morning, before our meeting start, Nicky went to FSB with copy of papers proving banker guilty as hell."

Gordunov laughed heartily.

Seth took a deep breath. "What do you think the Russians will do to him?"

Gordunov was still smiling as he slowly drew a long index finger across his throat.

"You signed his death warrant, Svet."

"Svet do no such thing, banker play dangerous game with dangerous people. He cooked his own duck."

"You mean he cooked his own goose."

"*Da.*"

"I ... I don't know how I feel about that. I mean, I was never a party to a man's murder before."

Svet put her arm through Seth's. "Think like this. Banker is very bad man; he hurt many peoples. Seth is good man, deserve chance to be chef and have new life. Svet kill two birds with one rock; that is all she do."

"Kill two birds with one stone."

"*Da;* that is what I do. World is better place with banker gone from it."

Merle was coming out of her building on Stone Street as they approached the entrance.

"Svet, how did everything turn out?" Merle asked.

"Meeting end happily; bank kindly decide not to prosecute Seth."

"Svet was terrific," Seth said, "you should have seen her in action. I owe her my freedom."

"I'm so happy for you."

Svet put her hand on Nicky's shoulder. "Merle, please to meet my friend, Nikita Ilyich Gordunov. I tell him all about you and what a wonderful girlfriend you would make for him. Maybe you both have drink later, fall in love, and make many babies together."

Everyone laughed.

Merle smiled enticingly at the Russian. "Svet, you are terrible, I'm sure that a strong, handsome man like Mr. Gordunov has many girlfriends."

"Please to call me, Nicky, lovely lady. And no, Nicky have no girlfriend for a long, long time."

"I'm Merle."

He had a puzzled look on his face. "Merle? That is not Russian name."

"No, it isn't. I took Merle as a stage name some years ago. My real name is Mariska Tatiana."

"Now *that* is real Russian name to be proud of."

"Yes, actually I've been thinking of changing back to it."

"Wonderful. To me you will only be Mariska Tatiana."

Svet whispered something into Nicky's ear and his eyes widened in surprise. "Lovely lady is related to Vladimir Vladimirovich?"

"Yes, we are cousins."

"It is truly a small world, Mariska Tatiana, Vladimir Vladimirovich was my superior in KGB for many years."

"Really."

"But yes, and the war stories I could tell you would curl the lovely hair on your lovely head."

"Seth," Svet said, "me and you go tell Lenny you not going to jail. We leave these two wonderful people alone to get better acquainted. Come!"

—————————————

Bobby came into Ulysses and went immediately to Amelia who had just finished Twittering her girlfriends and was drinking green tea because the OJ gave her an upset stomach.

"I want to thank you."

"For what, Bobby?"

"My dad told me about your conversation the other night, Amelia, you broke the ice. We ended up having that heart-to-heart talk that you told him we needed to have."

"All is well, I hope."

"It was touchy at times but it's a start; it's going to take a while for him to get used to who I really am."

"So you're finally out of the closet, Bobby, congratulations."

"Yes, I am, and it's a huge relief. No more sneaking around and always looking over my shoulder."

"How's Daniel?"

"He's ecstatic, we're renting an apartment in Chelsea together."

"Great."

"And we plan to get married."

"I didn't think that gay marriage was legal in New York."

"It's not, at least not yet, so we plan to tie the knot in Massachusetts."

"I see."

"Then we intend to adopt."

"Is that legal here?"

"We can petition to adopt in New York provided we were married in a state where same-sex couples are eligible to wed."

"Then we'll be parents together, Bobby, our children can play together."

"Won't that be great, Amelia."

"I'm so thrilled, and your dad will get to be a grandfather after all."

"Yes, he will. However, I'm jumping the gun a bit, the next step is for me to introduce Daniel to my dad. Frankly, Amelia, I'm dreading that."

"I understand; the first meeting could be a little awkward."

Bobby spread the palms of his hands on the bar. "I hate to ask you this, Amelia, but would you do me another huge favor and be there when they meet?"

"I'm not family, Bobby, I don't know if that's appropriate."

"My dad really likes you, Amelia, I know it would make things easier for him."

"Are you really sure about this?"

"I am."

"All right, Bobby, just tell me when and where to show up."

"Thank you so much."

"I'm very happy for you."

"But enough about me, how are things going with you?"

She shrugged. "Not much to report."

"If you don't mind my asking, how are you and Stan doing?"

"Stan's got blinders on when it comes to me. He thinks I'm some kind of living saint, that I can do no wrong."

"I'm trying to remember my Sunday school classes; was there a real St. Amelia in history?"

"Yes, there was, St. Amelia of Lobbes, she lived in the 7th. Century in Belgium and her kids turned out to be saints too."

"I owe Stan big-time, Amelia, as far as I'm concerned, you couldn't do better in a man. And he'll make a great dad."

"Is that an impartial, unbiased, totally objective appraisal, sir?"

Bobby chuckled. "Did you see Stan's muscular Abs and thighs after he danced that night in the apartment? For an older dancer, he's got a freaking hot body."

"I noticed."

"I thought I saw you giving him the eye."

"So, Bobby, it seems that no matter how hard I try, I can't get you to say anything derogatory about the guy?"

"No way, Amelia, not even if you offered to have sex with me."

"In your dreams, buster."

He laughed. "Seriously, Amelia, if I was a woman, I'd marry Stan in a heartbeat."

═══════════════

As they were leaving the bar they bumped into John 'Jacko' Darcy, who was practically a fixture in the place. Tall, barrel-stomached and 58, he was a man of few words except to say hello, so long, and I'll have another 7 & 7.

"Bobby, I don't mean to bother you but I'm getting scared about the market. My 401-K is down more than 50%. It's my retirement nest egg and I can't afford to lose it. What do you think is going to happen?"

"I wish I could tell you, Jacko, but I honestly don't know. I asked my dad that same question the other day and he just shrugged. He's been in the brokerage business for thirty-two years and he said he's never seen such panic on a global scale."

"I've been listening to the so called experts on TV but they don't seem to have a handle on the situation either."

"They don't, Jacko, we're sailing in unchartered waters, there's no road map to look at. What's going on now is unprecedented, it's never happened before, not even in the Great Depression."

"I'm always hearing people talk about what the 'smart money' is doing," Amelia said, "what *is* the smart money doing, Bobby?"

"For many years money managers preached diversification as the smartest way to invest. And they practiced what they preached, they spread their money over a bunch of different asset classes like stocks, bonds, hedge funds, commodities, private equity, real estate, foreign currencies, energy, oil, emerging markets, gold, and so on. In the past, this proved effective; while some asset classes declined in value, others always rose in value. This time around, however, it didn't work out that way, *everything* declined sharply in price and people lost money across the board."

"So where is the smart money putting their cash now?"

"Some are buying distressed mortgage loans from banks at steep discounts; some are buying corporate debt at steep discounts; some are buying Asian stocks that have dropped 70% or so in value in anticipation of an early rebound in that part of the world; many are parked in Treasury Bills and gold waiting until the smoke clears."

"I'm in the not-for-profit area," Amelia said, "and we've seen charitable donations from corporations and wealthy individuals drop way off. A lot of poor people are going to suffer terribly next year."

Jacko's hand trembled as he ran it through his thinning gray hair. "Should I hang in or should I sell my stocks, Bobby? Or should I dollar-cost-average and use my remaining cash to buy more stocks now that they've fallen so much in price?"

"It's a bad time to sell, Jacko, and it's not a good time to buy either."

"That doesn't help me much."

Bobby knew that Jacko had spent his entire career with AIG and probably had already lost a bundle when the Government took them over. "Are you sleeping at night, Jacko?"

"A few hours, but mostly the wife and I stay awake and worry."

"Then my advice to you is to sell down to the sleeping point, Jacko, to a cash level where you can sleep through the night."

"Thanks, Bobby, I'll talk to Betty about that."

Outside on Stone Street it was overcast and looked like rain was on the way.

Amelia sneezed.

"*Gesundheit.*"

"Excuse me."

"I've has some sniffles myself. There is a chill in the air, winter is on the way."

"I always catch a cold when the weather changes."

"Me, too."

Amelia pulled her collar up. "Jacko's not the only one having trouble sleeping, everybody is frightened, including yours truly."

Bobby nodded. "We are being tested as a nation."

"What if the Federal Government can't fix things? Who's going to bail out the U.S. Government if it goes bankrupt?"

"Only the Chinese have enough money."

"God help us, Bobby, to think it might come to that."

"Sweet dreams, Amelia."

"I'll try; you try too."

━━━━━━━━━━

A middle-aged, dowdy looking woman in an expensive wool suit and wearing thick glasses came into Ulysses. She paused to ask Artie Finch a question. He directed her to a table where Wanda was sipping a white wine and scanning a newspaper while she waited for the Professor and her son to return from a game at Yankee Stadium.

"Miss Pearlmutter?"

Wanda looked up. "Yes."

"I'm sorry to bother you like this but I was hoping we could talk for a few minutes. My name is Doris Chandler."

"Do I know you?"

"My maiden name is Chandler, my married name is Herkimer."

Wanda's face became taut. "Herkimer, you say."

"Yes, Rodney Herkimer is … eh …will soon be my ex-husband."

"I see."

"My attorney told me I might find you here. May I sit down for a minute?"

Wanda hesitated. "Of course, please do."

"Thank you." She deposited a large *Coach* purse on the table and pulled in her chair. "I'll be brief and not take up much of your time."

Michael approached the table. "What can I get for you, madam?"

"Eh, no, thank you, I won't be having anything."

"Are you sure?" Wanda asked. "You look to me like you could use a stiff drink."

"Maybe you're right. On second thought, I'll have a dirty gin martini."

"Coming up."

She put her elbows on the table and interlaced her fingers. "I came here today to apologize for what Rodney did to you. It was disgraceful and inexcusable. I am truly sorry for all that you suffered."

"That's very kind of you, Mrs. ... Miss Chandler."

"Please call me Doris."

"That's very kind of you, Doris, but you have nothing to apologize for. What happened to me wasn't your fault."

"In looking back I think maybe the signs were there with Rodney, but I chose not to recognize them. I don't know; I'm not sure."

"Hmmm."

"I'm not a pretty woman, Miss Pearlmutter, as you can see. I was so pleased when Rodney asked me to marry him. Now, of course, I know that he was interested only in my money."

"You can't be certain of that."

"I am, and I've come to terms with it."

"I'm sorry."

"I first began to have my suspicions about Rodney being unfaithful several years ago; at least I found out about a few of his dalliances. But I had no idea that he engaged in sexual harassment or the other things he got into. Please believe that."

"I do."

Her drink was placed on the table. She stirred it and took a mouthful. "My father was a womanizer and so were my uncles and my grandfather. It seems to have been a defective gene passed down in the family, like autism or cancer. I remember how my mother kept silent and put up with the philandering while it tore her apart on the inside. All the women in my family did; it was never discussed; a dirty family secret that everybody knew about."

"My family had their own secrets, Doris, all families do."

"When I received that film from your lawyer, I was so shocked and embarrassed."

"Listen, Doris, I want to apologize for that; it was a mistake in judgment on my part. I should never have allowed my lawyer to send you that. My only excuse is that I was so angry at the time that I wanted to lash out. I deeply regret what I did. Please forgive me."

"I understand, I probably would have done the same were I in your shoes."

"You said earlier that you're getting a divorce."

"Yes, my lawyer tells me it will be finalized in a few months. I'll get full custody of the children."

"That's great."

"I am more fortunate than most women in my situation, I have money of my own. I'm not financially dependent on a man."

"I'm a widow and I have a twelve year old son. With the money I received from the settlement with Global Insurance, I am also financially independent now."

"I'm glad that some good has come out of all this."

"I have also met a wonderful man, we're going to get married."

"Oh, I'm so happy for you."

"Thanks, I've been a widow so long that I never expected to meet anyone."

"Does your son like him?"

"They've become best buddies. In fact, they're on their way back from a ballgame at Yankee stadium as we speak. They should be here soon."

Doris finished her drink. "All the more reason that I should be going." She opened her purse. "Let me pay for my martini."

"No, Doris, consider it my treat."

"Thanks, it's very gracious of you."

"Please call me Wanda."

"Thanks, Wanda, it was nice meeting you."

"Likewise. Do you get into the city often, Doris?"

"I haven't in the past, I'm afraid that I was a typical suburban housewife and soccer mom. But I think I'm going to start coming in more often in the future; it can be boring out there, once the kids get to be a certain age they only want to be with their friends."

Wanda wrote her number on a napkin and handed it to her. "Give me a call, Doris, we'll talk and have lunch."

"Thank you, Wanda, I intend to take you up on that."

The apartment phone rang and the parrot flew from his stand to press the speakerphone button with his claw. "Hello, this is the Kane residence," the bird said in his best Cary Grant imitation voice.

"Hello, this is Doug Fowler, I'd like to speak to Stan."

"One moment, old chap, I'll go fetch the bloke."

The bird flew into the bedroom where Stan was folding laundry. "You have a call, it's Fowler from Juilliard."

"Thanks." Stan went to the phone. "Hey, Doug, what's up?"

"Stan, who was that man who just answered the phone?"

"Eh, a neighbor."

"The guy sounded exactly like Cary Grant, it's uncanny."

"Yeah, he does stand-up comedy, he's always practicing his imitations. I'll tell him you liked it."

"Amazing, absolutely amazing. Anyway, the reason I'm calling is about that dance routine you choreographed for Bobby Rankle. It has generated a lot of buzz here at Juilliard and, long story short, the producer of a new variety show on NBC would like to talk with you about becoming their choreographer."

"Are you kidding me?"

"No, I'm serious, he's going to call you in the morning."

"I'm shocked."

"It couldn't happen to a nicer guy, Stan."

"Thank you for saying that."

"Let me know how it all works out."

"I will. Bye."

The parrot shrieked.

"Yeah, isn't that wonderful? I've always wanted to work in TV ever since I was a young student at NYU."

The parrot shrieked again.

"It's funny how things can happen just out of the blue, isn't it?"

The ORACLE strolled into the room, sat down, and yawned.

Stan stared at the cat and then the realization gradually dawned on him. "You got me this TV gig, O, didn't you?"

The ORACLE yawned again.

It was a Wednesday evening and the popular West Village bistro was jammed with people. The place didn't take reservations and the average wait for a table was two hours. A three-deep crowd at the bar was blissfully passing the time consuming cosmos and Bellini cocktails. Marko circulated amongst the tables, chatting cheerfully with the customers, inquiring how they liked the food.

The older couple waited outside on a bench rather than at the bar and ended up getting seated in ninety minutes. They ordered a bottle of Pinot Grigio and decided to share a Caesar's Salad as an appetizer. She selected poached salmon for an entrée and he went for the veal scallopini. Because the tables were set up close to each other they had no trouble eavesdropping on those diners around them.

"The chef here is the hottest in New York now," a portly man to their left told his companion, "on the weekends you can't get near the place."

"I heard that Robert de Niro wants to hire him for *Nobu*," another commented.

"The review in *The New York Times* was spectacular," her friend crowed, "this place will be a gold mine."

"They should franchise it," a young woman said, "that's what I would do."

After a delicious dinner the couple paid their bill and left the bistro. A long line of people was still waiting to be seated. The woman began to cry as soon as they turned the corner.

"What's the matter, Rachel, you didn't like the food?"

"I loved the food."

"Then what's with the tears?"

"I'm so sorry for the things I said to Seth; I am going to call him the first thing tomorrow morning and beg him to forgive me."

The man was silent.

"Did you hear what I said?"

"I heard; I heard."

"And?"

"And what?"

"What are *you* going to do, Mister Big Mouth Know-It-All?"

The man sighed. "Do we have any humble pie in the fridge at home?"

Amelia arrived at Ulysses early for her dinner with Bobby, his father, and Daniel so she could make sure that everything was perfect. The dining area was beginning to get crowded. She had reserved the table farthest from the bar so the chatter there wouldn't make hearing difficult. Artie came over to her for his last-minute instructions.

"Artie, now it's important to keep Mr. Rankle's whisky glass full, keep the *Jameson* flowing freely; don't wait for him to ask for a re-fill."

"Will do."

"And fill his glass higher than usual. I don't want him to get drunk but I want him to experience a warm, friendly buzz as quickly as possible."

"Got you, my friendly buzz special, it is."

"Now that I think of it, Artie, give him a larger glass than you normally use."

"Ok, a bigger glass filled to the brim with Irish whisky."

She rapped her knuckles on the tabletop. "I guess that's all, Artie, we'll just have to wing it and hope for the best."

Artie leaned closer and whispered. "You may not have noticed, Amelia, given all the stress you're under, but they're all here."

"What do you mean?"

"The Professor told me that they have decided to call themselves the *Stone Street Irregulars*, you know, after the band of street urchins that worked for Sherlock Holmes in Victorian London." Artie's eyes moved upwards to the ceiling.

High in the rafters Amelia spotted the parrot and the black squirrel staring down on her. Rocco had been allowed back into Ulysses on a trial basis on the proviso that he stay clear of the electrical wires. Merle had warned her that Rocco could read lips so she surmised that he would be passing on whatever was said at their table to the others via mental telepathy. "Oh, that's just peachy."

Next Artie peered through the window to a table out on the street where Wanda, the Professor, and Allen were eating hamburgers. They smiled and waved to her. Georgette interrupted her eating of a potato chip and barked.

Amelia waved back, forcing herself to smile.

Artie glanced over his shoulder to a table where Stan, Al, Lenny,

Svet, and Seth were about to order drinks. Leonard opened his mouth and made a loud clicking sound when she turned in their direction.

"Oh, Lord, save me from my friends."

Artie stepped aside so she could see that Merle and a brawny man with a full beard occupied the closest table to the bar.

Merle called to her. "Amelia, I like you to meet my new boyfriend, Nicky Gordunov. He is the love of my life, I swear it."

"It is nice to meet you, Mr. Gordunov."

"Please to call me, Nicky, pretty lady. And not to worry, Nicky is on the job and prepared for all emergencies." He tapped a bulge in his suit jacket.

Artie whispered again into Amelia's ear. "I understand that the gentleman is ex-KGB and that he is armed in case there is any trouble later."

"Don't be ridiculous, Artie, there's not going to be any trouble."

"You did say that Mr. Rankle has a large gun collection."

She felt a migraine coming on. "This is unbelievable."

"You never know with people, Amelia, why I remember a time once in a bar when …"

"Artie, get out of here and go about your business!"

Artie returned to his station at the bar where he commanded a view of her table. Pedro stood in readiness near the Men's Room.

Amelia thought about the information that Stan had provided her with on Daniel. She intended to put it to good use tonight; it might just do the trick. Then she remembered the ORACLE; where the dickens was he?

"HARRUMPH!" Artie coughed to catch her attention.

The ORACLE was slinking down the bar towards Artie. The cat sat down next to him, looked at her, and yawned.

I'm glad you're so calm.

Three men came in and approached her table. "Amelia, it's great to see you," Mr. Rankle said, giving her a strained close-mouthed smile.

She stood up. "Mr. Rankle, hello."

"And I'm told that you already know Bobby's friend, Daniel Hoffman."

"Yes, we've met. Hello, Daniel."

The cop had gotten himself a short haircut and a close shave since she last saw him so he no longer had a five-o'clock-shadow.

"Hi, Amelia," Bobby said, bringing up the rear.

"Hey, Bobby."

She sat down and the men selected chairs and did the same, Mr. Rankle sitting between his son and Daniel.

Michael appeared immediately to take their drink orders and to deliver menus.

"I must say, the service in this place is excellent," Mr. Rankle said, "usually in New York you have to wait fifteen minutes in restaurants before a waiter will deign to acknowledge that there is a customer at one of his tables."

"Yes, it's first-rate," his son agreed, "especially when you're with Amelia. All the male servers and bartenders in here have a crush on her."

"Oh, Bobby, you're such a liar."

Everyone laughed.

Their drinks were delivered to the table.

"Wow, that was fast," Mr. Rankle said, "and will you look at my whiskey glass, it's absolutely humongous."

"To peace and prosperity!" Amelia said, holding high her iced tea in the air.

"To peace and prosperity!"

They chitchatted about the tough economy, the falling stock market, the Presidential election campaign and the near-zero interest rates, skillfully skirting the subject of Bobby and Daniel's relationship. Without anyone having to ask, fresh drinks automatically showed up at their table whenever a glass became half empty. An hour and several rounds later they perused the menu and finally ordered food."

"Mr. Rankle, I understand that you were in the marines," Amelia said.

"That's right, I volunteered for Advanced Force Recon after college. We were trained to operate far out in front of a main body of troops to reconnoiter the territory and report back on the disposition of enemy forces. It was a tough job and we were an elite outfit. I tell you, I came out of the service a much better man than I went in. The marines taught me discipline, self-reliance and how to survive off the land in a hostile environment."

"It sounds like you were a commando."

"No, nothing like that," he replied, his eyes more than a bit glassy now.

"Did you fight in combat, Mr. Rankle?"

He shook his head ruefully. "No, Amelia, unfortunately, I was too late for Vietnam and too early for Operation Desert Storm."

"It sounds like you would have enjoyed being in combat."

"No, but I'd liked to have been able to test myself in a combat situation, to see if I had what it takes to perform under fire. That's what I mean."

"I see."

"And it would have been exciting to be in combat. Vets I talked to say there's no other experience quite like it."

"It's also dangerous, Mr. Rankle, you run the risk of being killed or seriously wounded."

"That's true enough, Amelia, but it would have been worth it to me." He put down his drink and slowly checked out the room. "You know, I feel like there are a hundred pairs of eyes watching us now."

"Really?" Amelia casually glanced around. "Ulysses is crowded but I don't notice anyone paying us special attention."

"Neither do I," Bobby said, ignoring the surreptitious glances from his animal and human friends, especially the two high up in the rafters.

"Are you sure, son?"

"Positive, dad."

"That's strange, I'm usually right about these things. I developed a kind of sixth-sense while in the marines, Amelia. During field maneuvers I saved my unit from walking into ambushes a few times. My CO was so impressed that he made me the point man for the entire brigade."

"That must have been exciting."

"I actually thought about offering my services to the CIA when I was discharged. I would have been a natural at all that cloak and dagger stuff."

"I don't doubt it, Mr. Rankle."

"Yes, Amelia, one of my biggest regrets in life is that I missed not getting into combat."

"Speaking of combat," she said, "how's the shoulder, Daniel?"

The cop rolled his left shoulder and rubbed it with his hand. "It's ok, it only hurts when the weather turns damp."

"What's all this about his shoulder?" Mr. Rankle asked.

"Oh, I thought you knew, Daniel took a couple of bullets in the shoulder in a shoot-out with two heavily armed robbers. He killed one of them and his partner arrested the other."

Mr. Rankle looked incredulously at his son. "Bobby, why didn't you tell me about this before?"

Bobby shrugged. "I don't know, dad, I didn't think it was important."

"Well, *I* think it's important," Amelia said, "after all, Daniel was awarded the Police Combat Cross for bravery under fire. It's the second highest award that the NYPD can bestow for valor. In my book, that makes him a genuine hero."

The parrot shrieked his agreement high above their heads, however, nobody paid him any attention.

"Bobby's right, Mr. Rankle," Daniel said, "I merely did what I was trained to do in a violent confrontation."

Mr. Rankle eagerly moved his chair closer to Daniel's. "I want to hear all about it, my boy, every last detail, don't leave anything out."

Michael arrived with their dinners. For the remainder of the meal Mr. Rankle and Daniel were locked in a deep, exclusive conversation about the merits of different handguns, muzzle velocities, and SWAT tactics.

Amelia and Bobby were left to their own devices. She smiled at him and winked slyly.

After dinner, on their way out of the restaurant, Mr. Rankle took her aside as his son and Daniel paid the bill. "I want you to know, Amelia, that I'm not as drunk as I look ... and I'm not as dumb as I look either."

"I don't understand."

"You're a smooth operator, my dear, there's no question about that."

She laughed. "There are no flies on you, Mr. Rankle."

════════════════════════

Al sat on the bed and emptied his pockets of all the money he had left. It amounted to $22.61. The balance in his checking account was $12.02. All told then his estate, excluding his paintings and the rickety furniture, totaled almost a whopping $35.00. It looked like he was going to be dying just in the nick of time. He recalled one of those financial planners on CNN saying that you should spend all your money before you died and not leave behind a single cent to anyone. Maybe he should drop that guy a note and tell him that he had followed his advice. Who knows, the guy might even give him a plug on the air.

With the assistance of the ORACLE he had managed to scrape up enough money to pay his rent for the full month of December. The landlord would have almost three weeks to find another tenant for his apartment; it shouldn't be difficult now that real estate prices were declining and buyers were waiting on the sidelines for the market to bottom out. Stan would try and get his security deposit back. He told Stan that he wanted him to use the money to buy drinks for the regulars at Ulysses. His modest American Express credit card balance had been paid down to zero. All his other small bills had also been taken care of. He would die with his pristine credit rating still intact; nobody would be able to say that Aloysius Hanratty stiffed his creditors when he passed.

He took note of the fact that he had been born in 1933 during the depths of the Great Depression and would be leaving the world at the onset of what many pundits thought might be the Second Great Depression. There was no question that these were historic times. Barack Obama, the first African-American President certainly had his work cut out for him. He wished that he could be around to see how things turned out.

In a way it was very disturbing to know beforehand precisely when you were going to die; on the other hand, it gave you sufficient time to do all the little things that needed to be done before departing on a long trip you would never return from. Two days before he had carried four shopping bags full of clothes to Goodwill after throwing out his underwear and socks. His most prized personal possession, a Donald Duck watch that his father had given him on his 10th. Birthday, he sealed in a padded envelope and mailed to Stan along with a note suggesting that he give it to his child.

Then he purchased a pack of cigarettes for the first time since he had quit smoking thirty years ago and enjoyed a satisfying double jolt of nicotine and caffeine with a hearty breakfast of bacon & eggs from the local greasy spoon. Afterwards he rode the subway uptown and went to visit all his favorite places for the last time -- Central Park, the Metropolitan Museum, the MOMA, the Chrysler building, Times Square, Grand Central, and the main reading room of the library at 42nd. Street. He stopped into St. Patrick's Cathedral and lit a candle for all the people he had ever met in his life. Standing there in the great church he started to try and figure out how many people that might have been, however, he soon gave up the task as hopeless.

Next he splurged for a late lunch at Peacock Alley in the Waldorf Astoria, a hotel he had always wanted to stay at but never did. Then he went to the Peninsula Spa on Fifth Avenue and had his nails manicured for the first time in his life. At dusk he mingled with the hip after-work crowd in the posh King Cole Bar at the St. Regis Hotel on East 55th. Street and slowly sipped a three-olive vodka martini under the famous Maxfield Parish mural. He hadn't been inside the place in more than ten years, not since his former boss had taken him there for drinks after his company had forcibly retired him at the age of 65.

For dinner he went to a lively karaoke bar in Chinatown, something he'd never had the nerve to do before. When his turn came he sang the Frank Sinatra hit, *Send in the Clowns*. He was sure that his voice sounded terrible, however, the people there had been drinking heavily and kindly clapped for him anyway.

On his walk home he thought about what he would like for his epitaph if he were to have a gravestone, which he wasn't, since he had decided on cremation. Several possibilities came to mind, none of which was very pithy or complimentary. As he was crossing Canal Street it suddenly came to him : *Here lies Aloysius Hanratty, a late bloomer if there ever was one.*

In the morning he woke up refreshed and decided to visit his old neighborhood in the Bronx where he grew up. It had been a tough area in the 1940's and it looked to be even tougher today. A cadaverous figure now as he walked the same streets he had played stickball and roller-skated on as a child, memories he didn't know he had filled his mind. All his familiar haunts -- Manny's comic book store, Clem's soda fountain, the Loew's Olympia movie theater, Sammy's cobbler shop, Fell's Bar -- had disappeared; replaced by bodegas, fortune tellers, and storefront evangelical churches. The grammar school he had attended looked smaller than he remembered and the student body exhibited considerably darker complexions than in his day. He noted that the church where he had been an altar boy had more Masses now in Spanish than in English.

Everything had changed. He glimpsed his reflection in a shop window as he went by; he didn't look like himself anymore either.

Before heading back to the subway he paused for a long time in front of the old tenement building he had once lived in and stared at its crumbling façade and rusted fire escapes. The structure, much like himself, had not aged gracefully. He checked the name on the bell of the apartment he used to occupy with his parents and brother all those many years ago. The Hispanic name meant nothing to him. For a split second he was tempted to ring the bell and ask to see the place, but he didn't.

═══════════════

Arriving at Stone Street later that evening, Al could see the Christmas lights blinking on and off up in the window of Stan's apartment. It was 8:30 P.M. on December 11 and he was certain to be amongst the last of the guests to arrive as he had decided, on the spur of the moment, to take a stroll along the Hudson River promenade at Battery Park City. He'd always loved the river; the flowing, churning water seemed to have a calming effect on him. The harsh wind sweeping off the harbor had penetrated his clothes and chilled him to the bone. Ordinarily he would have worried about catching a bad cold, however, tonight he had other things on his mind.

When the elevator doors opened on the top floor Al cracked a large smile; he intended to have a great time during his last twenty-four hours on Earth. The Christmas party was in full swing. Seth cooked in the open kitchen preparing a leg of lamb and pork loin. Merle, Nicky and Svet were teaching Amelia and Daniel to sing *Silent Night* in Russian. Rocco was atop the Christmas tree chewing on a mozzarella stick and threatening to topple the star while Georgette growled worriedly up at him. The Christmas Yule Time log burned silently on two TV screens; the *Nutcracker* played on the third set. The Professor doled out eggnog from a big punch bowl to Lenny, Stan and Pedro. At the request of the

ORACLE, Artie was mixing Singapore Slings according to the original recipe invented by Ngiam Tong Boon for The Long Bar at the Raffles Hotel in Singapore in 1910. Wanda, Allen and Bobby were setting the dining room table. Leonard munched happily on a poisonous poinsettia plant. The parrot and the ORACLE, being the gracious hosts they were, did nothing but keep out of everybody's way.

Dinner was served at 10:00 P.M. and everyone complimented Seth on the delicious food. Red wine flowed like water and holiday cheer filled the apartment. The last of the desserts was consumed just before midnight. It was at that point that the parrot asked Amelia to tap on her glass with a spoon to call for order.

"The Oracle wants to wish everyone a Merry Christmas," the parrot said, "and he also wants to announce that he has special presents for Stan, Merle, the Professor, and Lenny." Amelia went to a sideboard and returned with four envelopes that she placed before each of the four people mentioned.

"Go ahead," the parrot said, "please open them."

They did so and stared at the document inside.

Stan was the first to speak. "This is a new apartment lease from the Singapore Overseas Investment Corporation reducing the rent on this apartment to $1.00 a year. I ... I don't understand."

"It's simple," the parrot said, "the Oracle is your landlord and he is giving each of you a free rental apartment for as long as you want it."

Lenny swiveled his wheelchair in a circle. "Thanks, O, I'll be the first to say that I don't deserve your generosity."

"I'll be the second to say that," Al said, laughing.

"I am touched," the Professor said, "and I want you to know that I will never vacate my apartment, they'll have to carry me out feet first."

"That goes for me, too," Wanda said.

Merle brushed back a tear. "I want us to be one big happy family here together."

"A toast," Stan said, lifting his glass, "To the ORACLE."

"To the ORACLE!"

The cat yawned.

People began leaving during the next hour as the dinner winded down. Stan hugged Al before departing to escort Amelia home. Wanda and Allen would spend the night in the Professor's spare bedroom. Pedro returned to Ulysses to finish the night shift. Svet was staying with Lenny. Nicky was staying with Merle. Bobby and Daniel took a cab to their new place in Chelsea. Al dawdled until almost 2:00 A.M. and became the last remaining guest.

"Did you have an enjoyable time?" the parrot asked him.

Al nodded. "I can't recall when I had a better time, which probably means that I never had a better time in all my entire life."

"We are glad."

"It was kind of you to hold the Christmas party early so that I could attend."

"Stan insisted upon it."

"He will come to my apartment the first thing?"

"Yes, he and Amelia will be there."

"Does she know?"

"We haven't told her, however, she did see you and Death talking in Ulysses that day."

Al nodded, reached into his pocket and took out an envelope that he placed on a table. "This is my last Will and Testament. As I discussed with you both, I leave my paintings to the Singapore Overseas Investment Corporation. They are to be put on public exhibition and lent to galleries of your choosing around the world during the next fifty years. At the end of that time you are to dispose of them as you see fit. If any are sold, half the proceeds are to be donated to Manhattan College's General Scholarship Fund; the other half is to go to Doctors Without Borders."

"We will see to it that your wishes are carried out."

Al looked at the cat. "I want to thank you for everything that you've done for me. My only regret is that I leave behind some true friends I haven't had the chance to get to know as well as I would have liked to; friends that I never would've had unless I met you."

The ORACLE blinked three times.

"That's so great to hear, O, I hope they will remember me, I know I will remember them." Al stood up a bit unsteadily on his feet as the wine had yet to burn up in his system, struggled into his overcoat and moved towards the door. "One last question before I go; will we ever meet again?"

The ORACLE blinked three times.

Al smiled. "You could knock me down with a feather."

════════════════════════════

When Al returned to his apartment it was very late and he felt tired after an active day, however, he was ambivalent about going to bed. How could he go to sleep when this is to be his last night on Earth? Shouldn't he stay up all night and do something special? Like what? Read a book? Watch TV? Drink too much brandy? Go for a walk on the freezing streets? In the end, the issue resolved itself as he nodded off in his favorite chair and slept like a log until almost noon.

Al painted all that afternoon and it was 7:00 P.M. that evening when he finally put down the easel, wiped his hands clean, and covered the canvas with cheesecloth. He was finished; the last of his five paintings had been completed. He felt a sense of accomplishment; at the same time he was upset with himself for not painting for all those years. Why hadn't he? He had no answer; it wasn't because he was lazy; he just hadn't had the self-confidence to paint. With luck he might be able to accomplish more in death than he had in life.

He decided to fix himself a cup of coffee because his head still throbbed a bit from drinking so much red wine at the Christmas party. A grin crossed his face. It had been his first Christmas party in fifteen years and he was surprised that he had still remembered most of the words to the Christmas Carols that they had sung. He looked at the clock and realized that the final finality was at hand.

When he finished the coffee he washed the cup and spoon, put the sugar and milk away so no roaches would be attracted, and wiped the counter dry. Then he brushed his teeth and went to the bathroom even though he hadn't felt the urge to go. It was a ritual his mother had ingrained in him long ago as a child. Before he was allowed to leave their apartment every morning he was required to use the toilet. Public bathrooms were hard to find in New York and every trip, long or short, posed the risk of an embarrassing bladder accident in her eyes.

A few minutes later there came the soft knock on the door that he had been expecting. "Come in, it's unlocked."

Death entered the drafty studio apartment still smartly dressed in his immaculate white suit as if it was still a balmy Spring evening like the last time they met. "I trust I am expected, Mr. Hanratty."

"Yes."

"Are you ready to come with me?"

"I am."

"That's a relief, you would be surprised at how many people try to wheedle more time from me. Believe me, I've heard all the excuses."

"I'm sure you have."

"You'd also be surprised at how many people are very eager to go with me. They're not ill or in pain, mind you, it seems they are just weary of life."

"Now that *doesn't* surprise me, I used to be one of them."

Death noticed the five paintings under cheesecloth. "May I see what you have been up to during the past seven months?"

"Of course."

Death uncovered each painting in turn, carefully dissecting them with his dispassionate eyes. "Yes, you have used the time well, very well."

"I think so too."

He lingered the longest over the last picture; a portrait of himself seated alone at a table in Ulysses with a partial view of Stone Street in the background. "I wonder what people in the years to come will think when they see this."

"I don't identify you."

"Then I'll remain a figure of mystery forever."

Al stood beside him and studied the likeness. "You have an actor's face."

"No one has ever told me that before."

"If you should decide to change careers, you might do well to consider the stage."

Death smiled. "I will remember your advice."

Al moved the paintings closer to the wall where they would be more out of the way.

"I can understand now, Mr. Hanratty, why the ORACLE was so insistent that you be granted the additional time. The paintings are all masterpieces."

"Thank you."

Death glanced at his watch. "Do you have any last words?"

"As a native New Yorker, I'm sorry my obituary won't be appearing in *The New York Times.* I know I don't deserve a mention, but that would have been grand."

Death dismissed the self-belittling comment with a wave of his hand. "You will become very famous, Mr. Hanratty, rest assured about that."

Al chuckled. "Maybe one day in the future a struggling artist will forge a painting in my style and try to pass it off as an original Hanratty."

Death nodded. "Yes, I would not be at all surprised."

"So, I guess that brings us to the reason for your visit. Tell me, how do we do this dying thing?"

"Would you like to lie down on the bed, Mr. Hanratty?"

"Please call me Al."

"Al."

"No, I'd prefer to sit in my favorite chair. I bought it with my first paycheck after college and the service. It's old but it's comfortable."

"That will be fine."

Al sat down and ran his hand over his hair, straightening a few loose ends. He fussed briefly with his shirt collar and the buttons of his jacket so that everything would be neat and tidy when his body was discovered. "Am I going to feel any pain?"

"No."

"What do you want me to do?"

"All you have to do is put your head back and close your eyes."

"That doesn't sound so hard."

Death frowned. "People make such a fuss about dying. Take it from me, Al, it's no big deal."

"Are the scenes of my life going to flash before me?"

"No, I don't do melodrama."

"I'm relieved, I'd really hate that." Al glanced around his tiny apartment knowing that the next time he woke up he would be dead. There wasn't much to look at; he was sitting in the only decent piece of furniture in the place. The streetlamp outside illuminated the cold December night and he could see that it was beginning to snow. He'd always disliked the winters in New York and wondered if it was going to be cold and snowy where he was going. Then he realized how silly it was of him to think that as his final thought on the planet.

"Al, it is getting late."

"One more second." He took out his wallet and removed a ragged photo of himself and Maureen Ryan holding hands at Coney Island by the Ferris wheel. Staring at it, he gently touched her youthful face with the tip of his index finger and held the photo against his chest. Then he rested his head on the chair and closed his eyes. "Ok, you can punch my ticket now, I'm ready for my big trip."

━━━━━━━━━━━━━━

Amelia left her apartment at 7:30 A.M. and walked towards Ann Street where she was to meet Stan. As she crossed Broadway near Trinity Church she spotted Death on the far side of the street dressed in his white suit and carrying a briefcase. He looked like a securities salesman making his early morning rounds of calls on clients. He didn't see her, or maybe he did and pretended not to. She was tempted to call out to him and inquire about Al -- Did he die well? Was he in peace wherever he went? -- but she restrained herself. What would be the point? Al departed this life when his time was up, just like billions of people before him had done, and just like billions of people after him would do, herself included.

Stan was waiting for her in front of Al's building when she arrived. He was drinking from a container of coffee and had brought one for her. "I thought you could use some java."

She took the steaming coffee. "Thanks, I can, it's cold out."

"Are you up for this, Amelia?"

"I'm as up as I'll ever be."

"Are you sure, Amelia, wouldn't you rather wait down here while I go upstairs alone?"

"I'm no shrinking violet, Stan, I've seen dead people before. My aunt, Emily, died in my arms when I was sixteen years old."

"Sorry, I just didn't want you to get upset."

"I appreciate your concern but let's get on with it."

"Very well." He used the spare keys Al had given him and unlocked the building's front door.

Al still had the same serene smile on his face when they let themselves into his apartment.

"He looks at peace," Amelia said, "we should all be so fortunate when the Grim Reaper comes for us."

"Yeah, it sure beats checking out in a hospital bed at Sloan-Kettering hooked up to all sorts of tubes and machines."

"What's that photograph he's got clutched in his hand?"

Stan took it. "I think it's a picture of Al and a girl he almost married a long time ago. Her name was Maureen. Al told me once that not marrying her was the biggest mistake of his life."

"That's so sad."

"Yeah, he found himself on a road he never meant to travel."

"That happens to many people."

Stan slipped the photo into his pocket. "I guess he always loved her."

"It looks that way."

"That just goes to show you, Amelia, when the right person comes along, you shouldn't hesitate, you have to take a chance and go for it, otherwise, you could end up like Al."

She sighed. "You're beginning to sound like a broken record."

"Yes, I guess I'm repeating myself. That happens when you're getting old and on the verge of dementia."

Amelia started to say something but changed her mind and instead took out her cell phone. "I'll call 911."

Twenty minutes later a burly police sergeant examined the corpse and confirmed the absence of a pulse. "What was the decedent's full name?"

"Aloysius Hanratty," Amelia answered.

The cop wrote the name down on a death form. "Do you know his age?"

"76."

"What was his occupation?"

She was going to say 'retired accountant' but she changed her mind. "Al was an artist, a painter."

"Oh, yeah, was he any good?"

"Judge for yourself." She removed the cheesecloth covering from the fifth painting of the portrait of Death.

The sergeant nodded. "I'm no art connoisseur but I'd say he was damn good."

"Yes, I think so too."

"You know, miss, I'm almost certain that I've seen this guy in the painting walking around the neighborhood."

Amelia studied the face that she had last seen only minutes earlier. "I have the same feeling."

"Are you a relative of Mr. Hanratty's?"

"No; I'm just a friend."

The policeman looked at Stan. "And you, sir, are you a relative?"

"No; I'm a friend too. As far as I know, he had no relatives, they were all deceased."

"You have a key to his apartment; you must have been a close friend."

Stan nodded. "Yes, I'd like to think so."

"When did you see the deceased last?"

"The other night, at a friend's Christmas party."

"How is it that you decided to stop by his place so early this morning?"

"We had a date with Al to meet for breakfast this morning," Amelia interjected, "he was going to take Stan and me out to celebrate."

Stan gave her a surprised look.

"Oh, if I may ask, what was the celebration all about, miss?"

Amelia hesitated for a few seconds as though she was still making up her mind about something. "We just became engaged, we're going to be married soon."

Stan almost tripped over his own feet. "Eh, sorry, I should watch where I'm going."

"Are you feeling all right?" the sergeant asked.

"I ... it felt like someone hit me with a crow bar."

"That's shock setting in, sir, you'll be fine once your friend's body is taken away."

"I see."

The policeman beamed at Amelia. "That's great news, miss, you two make such a romantic couple; marriage is a great institution."

She noticed his wedding ring. "Have you been married a long time, sergeant?"

He laughed; it was a smoker's laugh, more like a dry cough, hoarse and worrisome, six months away from turning into full-fledged emphysema.

"No, not for long, miss, but *often*. I'm just after marrying my fifth wife."

════════════════════════════

Per Al's wishes, no formal wake or religious service was held for him and his body was cremated shortly after the coroner released it. Instead, everyone gathered in the ORACLE's apartment a few days later for memorial drinks. The group included about forty or so of the regulars at Ulysses who were mostly sitting and chatting on the three flights of stairs leading down to the street, drinking free booze supplied by the bar.

Al's five paintings were resting on easels along a wall in the living room. On the day after Christmas the ORACLE had arranged for four of them to be shipped to four different cities -- Los Angeles, London, Tokyo, Moscow -- where private dealers were going to put them on long-term display in their galleries. The portrait of Death would remain in New York to be exhibited at a Madison Avenue gallery selected by the ORACLE.

"I wish I had an amazing talent like Al's," Amelia said, after inspecting the paintings again for the umpteenth time.

Stan nodded. "I remember you said the same thing after seeing Bobby dance."

"Well, it's true, they both had that in common."

Artie raised his glass. "A toast, to Al, may he earn a lot more dough after his death than he ever made while alive."

Merle drained the vodka in her tall glass. "I hope Al is in a better place."

Lenny looked around the warm, cozy apartment, a hot toddy in his hand, the fireplace blazing, Christmas tree lights dazzling, brightly wrapped presents neatly stacked under it. "If you ask me, folks, there's no better place to be today than right here."

"It's too bad that Al's artistry wasn't discovered much earlier in his life," Daniel mused, "then the world might have had a hundred paintings to remember him by, not just these five."

The Professor shrugged. "I guess that's one way to look at it."

"Is there another?"

"I think that for every artist like Picasso and Michelangelo who managed to live long, creative, productive lives, that there were many other equally gifted people born over the centuries who never had the opportunity to express their talent. They died in childbirth or of some common malady before vaccines were discovered; they were killed in some long-forgotten senseless conflict; or they were worked to death as slaves to some pharaoh or king. So to my way of thinking, Al received a better shake than most, at least he left something wonderful to be remembered for."

"That's a point well taken," Daniel said.

Wanda nodded. "I feel a little better about Al's death now."

"*Budem zdorovy!*" Svet finished her drink and hurled her glass into the fireplace, smashing it to bits against the bricks.

"Why did you do that?" Bobby asked.

"In Russia when we finish toasting a friend who die, we always do that so glass cannot be ever used again. It is sign of respect."

"I like that." He finished his drink and hurled the glass into the fireplace.

Soon the sound of exploding glasses filled the room.

"Somebody is going to have to clean up that mess," the parrot shouted in his best Clark Gable accent.

"I'll take care of it later," Stan promised.

Seth smiled at the Professor and Wanda who were holding hands. "So when's the wedding day?"

Wanda glowed. "We're going to have a small ceremony on New Year's Day in our apartment as a fitting way to start off the coming year. Of course, you're all invited. Later in the afternoon, we thought we'd do a Buffet downstairs in a private room at Ulysses where friends can graze as they please."

"That sounds great."

Merle put her arm around Amelia's enlarged stomach. "What are your wedding plans, dear?"

"I'd also like to have a small ceremony but the family is insisting on a full blown church affair since I'm an only child. I'll let you all know when and where as soon as the details are worked out. All I know is that I won't be wearing a white gown since my belly will be huge by that time."

"I told her that a simple purple dress would be cool," Stan said.

Daniel made a pained face. "Straight guys have no taste; that color would be so tacky."

"I agree," Merle said, "maybe a soft lime green."

"Nyet," Svet shouted, "orange is good luck color in Ukraine."

Daniel threw up his hands in disgust. "No, a citrine is what I was thinking!"

Amelia laughed. "We haven't decided on the dress color, however, we have decided on a name for the baby. He's going to be called Arthur Aloysius Kane."

The parrot shrieked and everybody else clapped, whistled, or kissed her.

A short time later as coffee was being served Amelia looked up at Stan and whispered, "They say that next year is going to be very tough economically, if you believe the doomsayers, it could be Armageddon time. "

Stan slipped an arm tightly around her waist and rubbed her big stomach with his other hand. "The three of us will get through whatever comes our way, honey, the three of us can survive anything as long as we're together."

She grasped his hand. "I think so too."

He kissed her.

"Speaking of next year," Stan said, "are you going to be making any New Year's Resolutions?"

"Hmmm. I haven't given it much thought but I guess I should."

"I bumped into Faith the other day and I asked her the same question. She told me that she was going to resolve to try and be a better person."

Amelia was surprised. "But Faith is already one of the best people we know?"

"That's what I told her. She just laughed me off."

A spark glistened in Amelia's eye. "I have the perfect New Year's Resolution for us."

"What is it?"

"Let's resolve that I get pregnant again next year."

Stan smiled. "I agree; it is perfect.

The black Lincoln town car pulled up in front of India House on Hanover Square at precisely 9:00 PM on Christmas Eve and the chauffeur got out and held the rear door open so the Oracle, the parrot, the dog, the squirrel, and the iguana could climb into the backseat. The streets were deserted by that hour so the sight of five animals piling into a limo raised no eyebrows. In 1908 when they had first begun taking these tours of the city's Christmas decorations, they had ridden in a Ford Model T automobile that had no windows or heat. It had been an unusually cold evening that night and they almost froze to death. Today they were much more comfortable as they sped up the FDR to Midtown Manhattan.

Their first stop was the traditionally decorated window display at Lord & Taylor's on 38th. Street. Next they hit the always-great Saks Fifth Avenue windows across from St. Patrick's Cathedral and then drove down 48th. Street in order to get a sideways view of the huge Christmas tree at Rockefeller Center. They turned uptown on Sixth Avenue to Columbus Circle where they left the car and boarded a waiting hansom cab for a horse-drawn ride through Central Park. It had started to snow lightly and a white blanket covered the grass and trees as they began to sing Christmas carols. The car picked them up again on East 60th. Street about forty-five minutes later when they emerged from the park near the Pierre Hotel.

Then they drove very slowly down Fifth Avenue to view the lights and window decorations at Bergdorf's, Harry Winston's, Cartier, Escada, Dunhill, Gucci, Prada, Trump Tower, Tiffany, Ferragamo, Louis Vuitton, Fendi, Bottega Veneta, Van Cleef & Arpels, Bulgari, Henri Bendel, and Takashimaya. They stopped in front of the Public Library at 42nd. Street to see the two stone lions, Patience and Prudence, proudly wearing their Christmas wreaths and then followed Broadway all the way downtown through Greenwich Village, SOHO, and past the Christmas tree at City Hall. When they finally arrived back at Hanover Square it was almost midnight.

The ORACLE perched at the highest point on the roof and blinked three times at the Andromeda Galaxy in the cold night sky. A responding flicker of light danced briefly on the dark horizon and ricocheted far into deep space.

The parrot flew up from the apartment below and settled atop a ventilating shaft. Rocco scooted up the fire escape, closely followed by Georgette and Leonard. Their eyes flashed in the weak light generated by the nearby Goldman Sachs office building where a few weary investment bankers apparently still burned the midnight oil working on the next M&A deal.

They had the house to themselves. Stan and Amelia were at her parents' home in Connecticut and he was scheduled to begin his new job at NBC on Monday. The Professor, Wanda, and Allen were at Disney in Orlando. Merle and Nicky had left town for a romantic weekend in the Poconos at a hotel that advertised a heart-shaped jacuzzi in every suite. Lenny had retired from the 'rumor mongering' business and he and Svet were snuggled comfortably in at her apartment where she was cooking Russian delights for him. Seth had reconciled with his family and his restaurant was going gangbusters. Bobby was fast making a name for himself at Juilliard and his father had become his biggest fan. Pedro would be starting NYU next month. Artie had finished his new book and had sold it for a six figure advance to a major publisher and was anxiously awaiting the first galleys.

Together the five of them did *tai chi* in the moonlight, meditating as their shadows silently glided from pose to pose in the ancient Chinese exercise discipline, their minds and bodies gradually fusing as one. After an hour they rested and inhaled deep breaths of the crisp night air, purging their bodies of all vestiges of negative thoughts and influences. Then, refreshed and in sync with Nature's rhythm, their inner selves and surroundings, they formed a loose semi-circle around the ORACLE.

The ORACLE looked up at the Andromeda Galaxy and blinked three times. A beam of light suddenly illuminated the rooftop and then shot far out into deep space where it imploded in on itself and formed a new twinkling star. The cat, parrot, dog, iguana and squirrel smiled at each other. Yes, it was true, congratulations were definitely in order; they had done an excellent job and deserved the high praise they had received.

The rejoicing was short-lived, however, as each of them already had been given the name and personal history of the individual who was to be their next assignment. On Monday the never-ending struggle to help a new, lucky group of Ulysses patrons to become stars and realize their dreams would begin anew.

FIFTY YEARS LATER

The ORACLE looked out the window at the cobblestone street below and noticed that a large crowd of young Wall Street types was beginning to occupy the rows of outdoor tables. Soon they would be hitting on each other when they weren't scanning their microchip implanted retinal databases for messages and market updates. This section of the Stone Street Historical District of Lower Manhattan was lined on both sides with bars, cafes and restaurants and it was closed off to vehicular traffic. Servers scurried about carrying trays of beer, burgers with fries, and deep-fried Buffalo wings in hot sauce with chunky blue cheese dressing, his all-time favorite finger-lickin'-good snack.

The cat glanced at the grandfather's clock in the living room and saw that it was 6:00 P.M. The stock and commodities markets in Singapore, the financial capital of the word ever since the year 2030 when it had eclipsed the New York and London Stock Exchanges, wouldn't commence trading for another two hours. It was time for him to go to work and make some money.

He squeezed under the slightly opened window and tiptoed across the narrow ledge that led to the building's fire escape. After descending three floors he leapt to the top of a lamppost near the open front door of the Ulysses Bar and then shimmied down a rope that was holding aloft a banner advertising Budweiser Beer, another favorite of his. Once on the ground he quickly darted into the bar.

Two older regulars, Larry and Bert, were seated at the rear of the bar drinking beers and scanning sections of the newspaper on their hand-held supercomputers. "Listen to this, Bert, it says here that a painting was sold at a Sotheby's auction yesterday for $182 million. The artist, Aloysius Hanratty, didn't begin painting until he was in his mid-seventies."

"Holy smoke, Larry, I guess an old dog can learn new tricks after all."

"It would seem so."

"That means there's hope for you yet, Larry, you still have time to write that great American novel you've been talking about starting for the past five years."

"Hmmm, I just can't seem to get a handle on what it is I want to say."

"I'm sure if you wrote the first chapter, the rest of the book would write itself."

"It says here that at his death in New York City fifty years ago that Hanratty was virtually penniless."

"It was around the time we had the Second Great Depression, wasn't it?"

"Yes, Bert, the bankers started jumping out of windows a few months later just like they had done in 1929. Wall Street was a dangerous place to be walking then, what with all the falling bodies."

"My father told me about it. A buddy of his took the long dive from an office on his floor. One minute the guy was telling everybody jokes, the next minute he was a red stain on the sidewalk twenty stories below."

"God rest his soul."

"I bet Hanratty would be pissed off if he knew about the auction money, Larry, I know I would be. I mean, what's the sense of being rich and famous if you're dead as a doornail and can't enjoy it; know what I'm saying?"

"That's the way it is with most artists, Bert, they don't make any money until after they die. Andy Warhol was one of the few artists I can think of who made it big while he was still alive. Most everybody else sucked it up for their art."

"I saw some of Warhol's stuff in a museum once, soup cans and Marilyn Monroe silk screens, very weird if you ask me."

"It's called Pop Art."

"Like I said, the guy was a real weirdo."

"Hanratty's painting is untitled but over the years art critics have dubbed it, *Man in a White Suit*. Here, take a look at the photo of it. The guy could really paint."

Bert leaned over the computer screen. "You know, Larry, I could swear I saw that dude in the painting walking near the stock exchange last week. The only reason I remember is that he was wearing the same old-fashioned white suit."

"Nah, it couldn't be him, this was painted too long ago."

"Yeah, you're probably right, besides that guy doesn't look very healthy. Does he? "

"No, he looks like death warmed over."

"He sure does, I wouldn't be surprised if he croaked right after sitting for his portrait."

Larry scrutinized the background in the painting. "You know, that street in the window behind the guy could be Stone Street."

"You think?"

"I do, the buildings are the same. And the article says the artist lived downtown near here on Ann Street, that's only a few blocks away."

"Maybe this Hanratty guy came into Ulysses for a drink when he was alive. The bar opened in 2003 so it's possible."

"That could very well be, Bert, he might have been a regular just like us."

"I wonder if anyone who drank in here then is still alive today; maybe they knew Hanratty and spoke to him."

"That's highly doubtful, they'd have to be ancient and I don't remember seeing any old geezers in this place."

"Yeah, I suppose so, Larry, everybody in here is fairly young except for you and me."

"The article says that Hanratty has four other paintings scheduled to be auctioned later this year."

"If they all sell for as much as this one, you're talking almost a billion dollars in sales."

"That's right, Bert, not bad for a guy who didn't have a pot to piss in when he died."

"Who gets all the money, Larry?"

"The paintings are owned by an outfit called The Singapore Overseas Investment Corporation."

"That figures, the Asians own everything these days."

"It says that the company in Singapore is donating the sale proceeds to Doctors Without Borders and to Manhattan College, the school up in Riverdale. It seems that Hanratty graduated from there back in 1953."

"Now that's very decent of them."

The ORACLE strutted down the bar past the parrot sitting on the shoulder of a middle-aged man who didn't realize that he would become a great sculptor in a few years if only he didn't give up on himself. High overhead, to the delight of a young man who might be elected Governor of New York one day if only he could conquer his fear of public speaking, the black squirrel was running along the rafters where the music speakers were hung. A beautiful woman afflicted with schizophrenia, and destined to be an award-winning actress if she stayed on her meds, walked to a table leading the large iguana on a leash. The Bull Terrier - Chihuahua mix licked the hand of a broker who had just lost his job and was wondering if the trophy wife was going to dump him now that the well had run dry.

Bert looked around disapprovingly. "They shouldn't allow animals into Ulysses, this place is like a freaking zoo. Next thing you know there will be chickens and snakes under your feet like you'd find in a Third World country."

"A long time ago there was a guy who wrote a very funny book about animals in a bar very much like this one."

"Yeah, Larry, I remember, it was on the Best Seller Lists when I was a kid. But I never read it, the plot sounded too preposterous to me."

"It was one of the best novels I ever read. Every few years I pick it up and read it again. It's an American classic. Artie Finch was the author's name."

"Yeah, that's the guy. He was a one-book-wonder, wasn't he?"

"Finch wrote a bunch of books but that was his best known one. It sold millions and millions of copies over the years. Unlike poor Hanratty, Finch died a wealthy man."

Bert watched the dog slobber all over the broker; the squirrel was biting on a live wire in the rafters; the parrot shrieked at God only knows what; the iguana was loudly banging a table leg with its tail. "Nobody can make me believe that animals can talk and read minds. They can't even help themselves, never mind helping people solve serious problems in their lives."

"I think in literature they call it Magic Realism."

"Like I said before, Larry, the whole premise is totally preposterous."

"It's an Urban Fantasy."

"It's ridiculous if you ask me."

The ORACLE leapt up onto the surface of the bar and sidled up to the two men.

"Don't look now, Larry, but that cat's back again and he's looking to score a free brew."

Larry signaled the bartender to bring a Bud Light and a bowl.

"I wonder what the little knucklehead would do if I slipped a Yuengling into his bowl instead of a Bud Light. Do you think he'd notice the difference?"

"Yes, he would definitely know you were pulling a fast one." Larry rubbed the star on the cat's chest and the cat blinked at him three times. Suddenly the clouds parted in his mind and he had a clear vision of the statement he wanted to make in his novel.

"Are you ok, Larry, you look like somebody just whacked you hard across the face."

"I ... I think the cat just gave me the outline for my novel."

"Ah, that's insane, you're hallucinating."

"You're wrong, Bert, I think there is more here than meets the eye."

"He seems like just another dumb alley cat to me."

"The Earth could stand still and you wouldn't notice."

Bert looked closer at the cat's face. "His eyes got a slight slant to them, he's definitely Asian, if you ask me."

His friend sighed. "I often stop and ask myself why I bother to hang around with you. A lot of other people have asked me the same question."

"You know, Larry, when I first started coming into Ulysses about fifteen years ago, this cat was hustling free beers even back then. And he's still going strong at it, can you believe it after all this time?"

"Some things never change, Bert, and it's a good thing they don't."

THE END